SINISTER
CARGO

SINISTER CARGO

Stanley Hart Page

COACHWHIP PUBLICATIONS
GREENVILLE, OHIO

To my wife, but for whom this little tale might never have been written, I affectionately dedicate this book.

S. H. P.

Sinister Cargo, by Stanley H. Page
© 2025 Coachwhip Publications edition
Introduction © 2025 Curtis Evans

First published 1932
Stanley Hart Page, 1902-1979
CoachwhipBooks.com

ISBN 1-61646-621-9
ISBN-13 978-1-61646-621-3

ANOTHER ONE FOR THE PHILO BRIGADE

STANLEY HART PAGE AND THE CHRISTOPHER HAND MYSTERIES

CURTIS EVANS

In 1929 the prestigious firm of Alfred A. Knopf published Dashiell Hammett's tough and violent crime novels *Red Harvest* and *The Dain Curse* (*The Maltese Falcon* would follow the next year), forever altering the face of crime fiction with what reviewers dubbed the "hard-boiled" style. Yet at the very same time that Hammett commenced his great crime sweep, traditionalist American mystery writer S. S. Van Dine (Willard Huntington Wright), whose best-selling Philo Vance detective novels were published by Knopf's rival Scribner's, stood resplendent at the height of his popularity, having also in 1929 produced *The Bishop Murder Case*, the book which proved the most popular and enduring of his mysteries. Although the future of American crime writing might lie with the tough guys, what Hammett's Sam Spade or the Continental Op might have termed the "pantywaist" genteel amateur detectives were hardly down for the count. Indeed, that very same year Frederic Dannay and Manfred Lee, the two New York cousins who wrote as Ellery Queen, introduced, in *The Roman Hat Mystery,* a monocled amateur detective named, appropriately enough, Ellery Queen, a gentleman who in his studied affectations shared considerable affinity with Philo Vance, particularly in his early years in print. Five years later, Rex Stout's obese, orchid-loving eccentric genius,

Nero Wolfe, would make his first of many fictional appearances in the detective novel *Fer de Lance*. In between those epochal events in American mystery genre history, myriad Philo Vance wannabes made brief their own brief struts on the crime fiction stage. One member of this troop of toff tecs was Christopher Hand, who between 1932 and 1935 appeared in a quintet of novels by forgotten American mystery writer Stanley Hart Page.

Stanley Hart Page, who, ironically enough likely was distantly related to native Marylander Samuel Dashiell Hammett through mutual Dashiell ancestors of French Huguenot lineage, was born in prosperous circumstances in Chatham, New Jersey, on March 10, 1902, to Laurence Stanley Page and his wife Emma F. Jowett. Stanley's colorful entrepreneurial paternal grandfather was self-made millionaire coal tar king George Shephard Page (1838-1892), originally of Reading, Maine, and Chelsea, Massachusetts. Upon his death at the age of fifty-four George Page, the renowned "millionaire chemist" who was then an inmate of the New Jersey State Insane Asylum ("his mind was broken down by the worry introduced by a severe attack of the grippe" according to the newspapers), bequeathed to his four sons and one daughter the substantial fortune (about thirty-five million dollars in modern worth) which he had accumulated through his various business ventures, the best known of which today is the Vapo-Cresolene Company. This profitable enterprise with great success marketed Vapo-Cresolene, a therapeutic vaporizer used in the United States during the late nineteenth and early twentieth centuries in the hope of providing lasting relief to sufferers from such ailments as asthma, bronchitis, croup, whooping cough and diphtheria, despite the fact that the American Medical Association reported with dry derision in 1908 that "Vapo-Cresolene is a member of that

Stanley Hart Page

class of proprietaries in which an ordinary product is endowed, by the manufacturer, with extraordinary virtues."

Perhaps to salve his moral conscience George before his breakdown became a great advocate of both alcohol temperance, founding the New Jersey Temperance Association, and of universal free public-school education. He also founded Chatham's Stanley Congregational Church. After his death, Page's own rather more fortunate offspring inherited from the family patriarch his highly profitable, if arguably somewhat dubious, patent medicine business, over which they maintained firm control, with Stanley's uncle Albion Lambert Page serving as president, his uncle Henry de Bacon Page serving as vice president, and his own father, the aforementioned Laurence Stanley Page, serving as secretary. All three men additionally served as directors of the company, the remaining two of whom were Stanley's youngest uncle, Raymond Page, and his aunt, Florence Page.[1]

With a family fortune behind him, Stanley Hart Page might simply have lived a dilettante life, like the fictional Philo Vance, Albert Campion and Lord Peter Wimsey, taking a sinecure job from the firm; yet he went to work, rather, as the manager of the Montclair bureau of the *Newark Evening News* (then New Jersey's newspaper of record), after attending the Pawling and Peddie prep schools and Brown University and taking a token vagabond year out west employed as a cowboy and farm-hand. Yet in 1930, as he approached the age of thirty, he was still single and living under his parents' spacious roof in Chatham, New Jersey, the 64th wealthiest inhabitation in the United States in 2018, according to *Bloomberg News*. However, the next year he got himself an apartment in nearby Short Hills, where he found time—having been "[s]ince his boyhood . . . absorbed with mysteries and fictional detectives"—to write a pair of detective novels, *Sinister Cargo* and *The*

Resurrection Murder Case, which he successfully placed with none other than Alfred A. Knopf's Borzoi Books imprint.

Knopf evidently was on the hunt for another Philo Vance, judging from the back flap blurb description of Page's book, which boldly, if perhaps a bit precipitately, proclaimed that the author's sophisticated dilettante sculptor and amateur criminologist, Christopher Hand, already belonged in the pantheon of Great Detectives:

> We nominate Mr. Christopher Hand for a place in that distinguished company of detectives whose work has thrilled so many readers of crime fiction in both England and America. His ability as a forger, his utter disregard of such ordinary necessities as food and sleep, the fact that he is a dilettante of the arts and sciences, and his uncompromising persistence, make him worthy in every way to stand behind those masters—Sherlock Holmes, Philo Vance, Lord Peter Wimsey, Father Brown, Hanaud, Poirot, Dr. Thorndyke, Charlie Chan, Reggie Fortune and [Knopf's own] Sam Spade.

Certainly Knopf was no wallflower when it came to boosting its detective fiction to the American mystery-reading public. Beginning in 1919, the publishing firm had launched a hugely successful effort to boost the middling mainstream English novelist J. S. Fletcher as the greatest British mystery writer since Arthur Conan Doyle. In this aggressive commercial campaign Knopf made great use of the fact that President Woodrow Wilson had read Fletcher's detective novel *The Middle Temple Murder* (1919) and expressed his enjoyment of the tale.

"PRESIDENT WILSON HAS BEEN READING THE MIDDLE TEMPLE MURDER A Fine Detective Story by J. S. Fletcher," boasted Knopf's advertising in the November 22, 1919, issue of *The Publishers' Weekly*. Knopf made a similar effort with Stanley Page's Christopher Hand mysteries, though nothing was said on their part about the admitted detective fiction predilections of President Herbert Hoover, who was highly unpopular as the nation staggered through its third year of crushing economic depression.

Knopf, which published Page's first three Christopher Hand mysteries (*Sinister Cargo,* 1932, *The Resurrection Murder Case,* 1932, and *Fool's Gold,* 1933), excelled itself in the production design of the books, with each volume in the series having a striking dust jacket and an appealing uniform board design of serpentine lines. *Cargo* had dark green lines on a lighter green background, *Resurrection* blue lines on an orange-brown background and *Gold,* the fanciest of all, red lines on a faux gold leaf background. The jacket to *The Resurrection Murder Case* in particular is memorably ghoulish, but all three jackets are fine indeed.

Sinister Cargo, about endangered New York financier Robert Garrison and his retired stage musical actress spouse, begins with a miraculous country house murder and goes to some very queer corners indeed, was praised by Isaac Anderson in the *New York Times Book Review,* who in his notice avowed: "This story offers a continuous succession of thrills . . . . Christopher Hand has methods of his own. Sometimes they are more than a bit high-handed, and sometimes they are without the law, but they get results. This is Mr. Page's first detective story, but we gather that he intends to give us more stories of the exploits of Christopher Hand. We'll be waiting." In the *Saturday Review* William C. Weber was equally enthusiastic, writing, in a notice which made the book sound more like a Doyle

Sherlock Holmes or Hammett Continental Op novel: ". . . the story does stand up. . . . There are two picturesque villains named Spitz and Spawn, a variety of successful and unsuccessful attempts to kill a wealthy New Yorker and his friends, and a pitched battle finale on a little island off the Maine coast. . . ."

Sinister Cargo's weird and colorful climax on a "haunted" Maine island at times seems like an anticipation of John Carpenter's classic ghostly fright film *The Fog* (1980). For this final section of the tale the author drew on the "many summers he had spent with his family on the coast of Maine." The narrative is punctuated by a series of wild criminal episodes which sometimes savor of pulp fiction, with Christopher Hand's slavishly loyal chronicler, Ralph Clark, getting more pieces of the action, as it were, than Philo Vance's poor pale shadow Van ever did. As in Doyle's *The Hound of the Baskervilles,* Hand is absent from a substantial chunk of the narrative but returns to the scene to elucidate all of the remaining mysteries. Despite their social standing Christopher Hand and Clark prove something more of men of action than the cerebral Philo

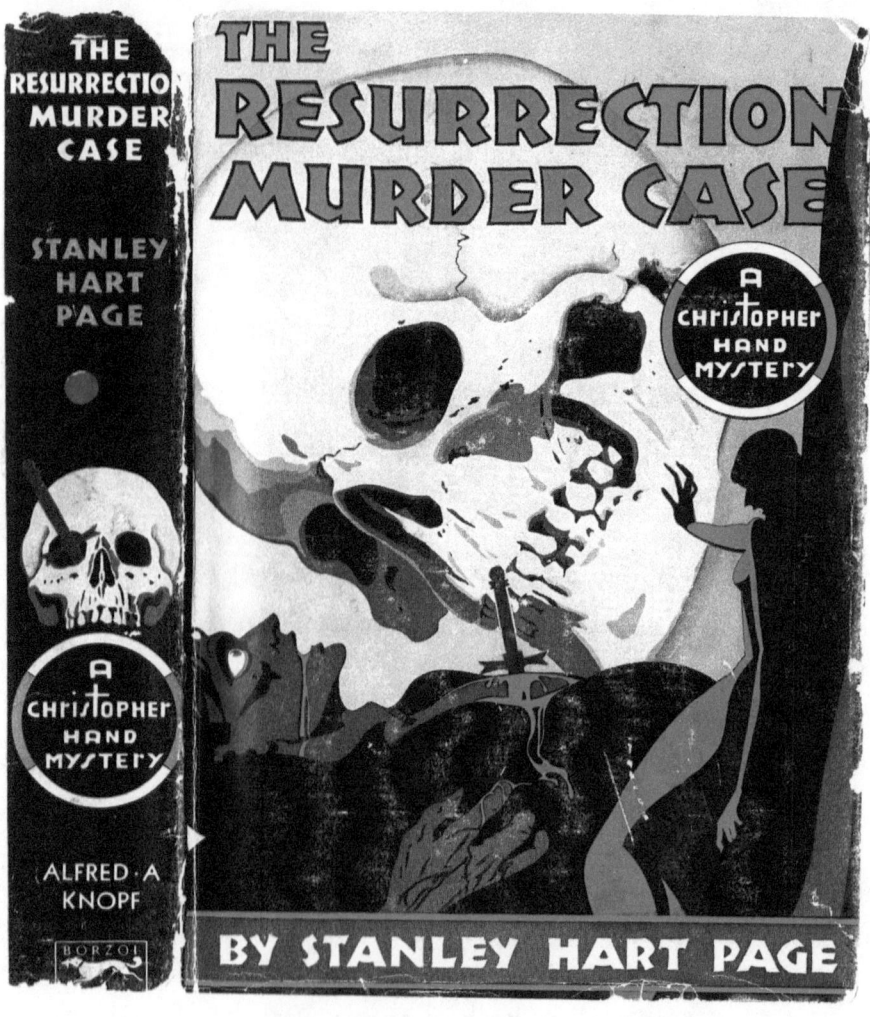

Cover courtesy Curtis Evans

Vance and Van, at least until the late Van Dine's late Vance detective tale *The Kidnap Murder Case* (1936). The body count in the novel ends up rather high indeed.

Upon the appearance of Page's follow-up, *The Resurrection Murder Case*, the reviewer in the *Boston Transcript* huzzahed: "The many friends of Christopher Hand will rejoice to meet him again . . .The devious paths followed until the crime is brought home are sufficiently interesting to hold the attention and to make it difficult to lay down the book. . . . One reads many pages half expecting the crack of a bludgeon on one's own head." For his part A. P. Bryan in the *Lexington Herald-Leader* wrote: "Mr. Page takes the most complicated plot that has come to the attention of this reviewer in many months and weaves it into a logical and interesting, yet baffling story of mystery and adventure. . . . [Christoper Hand] eventually solves the entire mystery by one of the most ingenious devices yet introduced to detective fiction." In the *Philadelphia Inquirer*, E. W. P. raved of the novel: "Hand the investigator is brilliant, and the dénouement is breath-taking."

Page dedicated *The Resurrection Murder Case* to retired New York police captain Grant Williams, a pioneering specialist in reconstructing faces from the skulls of murder victims (Dominick La Rosa and Lillian White were two of his most noted cases) whom the press in the Twenties dubbed a "modern Sherlock Holmes."[2] The so-called "sculptor-sleuth" headed New York City's Bureau of Missing Persons, between its organization in 1914 and his retirement in 1928. Read the novel to see wherefore the dedication. It is set in and around Mill Ridge, New Jersey, "a fashionable community of larges estates" located on a ridge above the Great Swamp, which sounds a lot like places where the author himself had lived, like Chatham and Millburn.

Page's third mystery, *Fool's Gold,* which he penned in 1932 and published with Knopf in the Spring of 1933, reads rather like a Sherlock Holmes pastiche, allowing for the fact that it is set in Depression-era America rather than Victorian/Edwardian England. In the novel it appears that some criminal fiend has murdered a pair of grizzled gold prospectors, who had traveled to New York to find investors in their Alaska mining concern, and purloined from them the bills and gold they had kept stashed in their money belts. Unhappily involved in the problem are the congregants of the Hendley Congregational Church, who contributed to the ill-fated venture the sum of $50,000 (over a million dollars today), constituting their life savings.

The presence of the Hendley Congregational Church recalls the real-life Stanley Congregational Church, which Stanley Hart Page's grandfather as mentioned had founded and which Stanley would attend all of his life. Along the way to the solution of the various crimes Hand confronts a locked room murder problem as well. The notice in the *Los Angeles Times* declared of the inventive novel: "[T]he reader will be caught and will hold on until the [culprits] are discovered. . . . [T]here is a trick in this tale that will almost fool an experienced student of mystery yarns." Almost! The reviewer for Kentucky's *Lexington Herald-Leader,* on the other hand, avowed that "there's no chance of [readers] beating the author to the solution," adding: "You'll be flabbergasted by the number of clues that appear and the amount of action that is jammed into a 24-hour period." On May 7, 1933, the *San Francisco Chronicle* listed the novel as the Bay Region's #6 fiction bestseller of the week.

Page's mysteries won praise as well in the United Kingdom, where the author did not even have a really prestigious publisher behind him. When the second Hand opus, *The Resurrection Murder Case,* was published by Stanley

Paul in England in 1933 (the author's name was abbreviated there, for some reason, to S. Hart Page) an anonymous reviewer for the *Manchester Evening News* roundly praised the mystery as "[a]n American thriller of the most intense kind." In the *Leicester Mercury,* the writer of the column "From My Library Table" reflected that "with the thousands of 'thrillers' that are turned out every year it is amazing that we can still be mystified over any plot. But

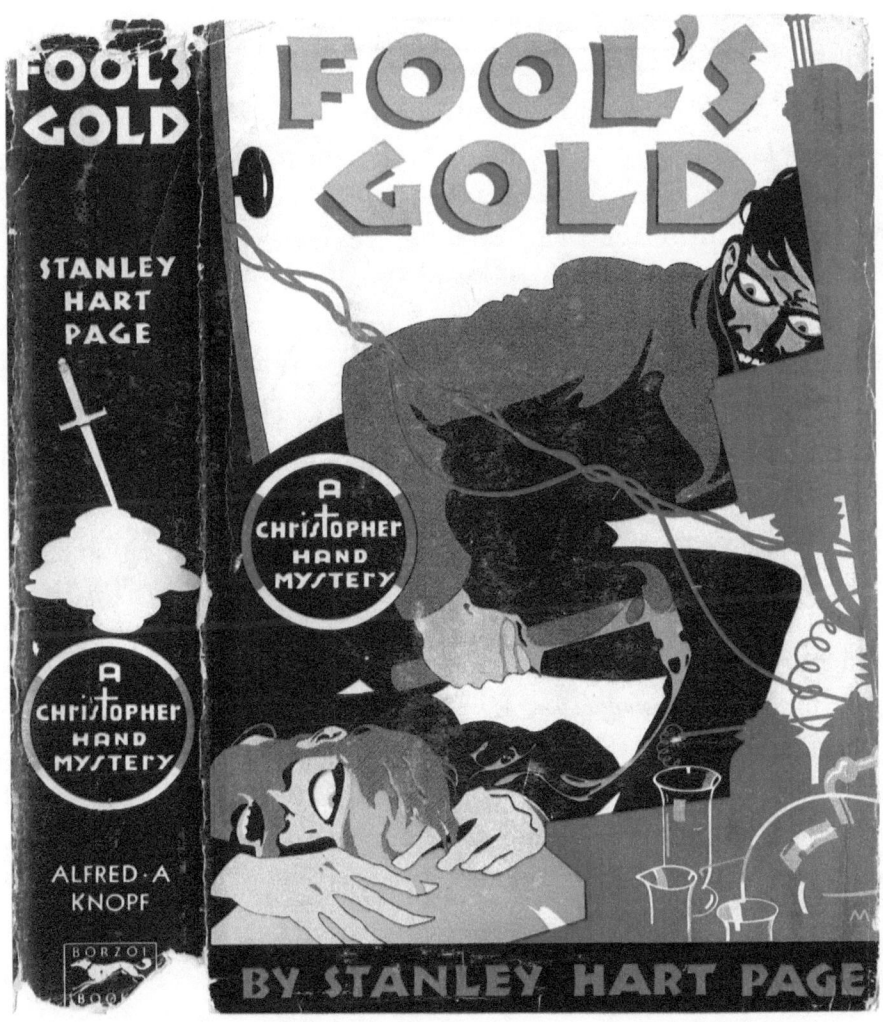

Cover courtesy Curtis Evans

S. Hart Page keeps us in suspense throughout and then gives us the necessary jolt at the end. . . . *[The Resurrection Murder Case]* stamps him as one those few writers who can be relied upon to give us breathless adventure and a mental puzzle."

No less a figure than British mystery writer Richard Keverne lauded *Fool's Gold,* when it was published in England the next year, humorously writing: "Quite early in the story I thought I had guessed the solution to the mystery of *"Fool's Gold"*. . . . but later on the idiot police detective tumbled to the same solution, and of course it was wrong. So it was left to the Sherlock Holmesian Christopher Hand to put us both right, and Mr. S. Hart Page makes him do it in a most agreeable manner." The *Leicester Mercury* pronounced the novel a "really gripping yarn" and the Daily Mirror found it "very readable."

As has been seen above Stanley Hart Page drew upon his own privileged background for his mysteries. His Grandfather George was a noted trout angler in the state of Maine, in 1867 founding, in the remote village of Oquossoc, an angling club on the shores of Mooselucmeguntic Lake. According to *The American Fly Fisher,* George Shephard Page's "reputation and fame as a fish culturist were international in scope." Christopher Hand's detecting companion and chronicler Clark is a devotee of trout fishing, declaring in *The Resurrection Murder Case:* "I had heard of the excellent fishing in the vicinity of Mill Ridge. . . . It was with a light heart that I fell asleep that night. I visualized myself wading in a trout stream." Recalling Philo Vance's enthusiasms in *The Kennel Murder Case* (1933), George Shephard Page was also a breeder of Scottish Deerhounds. With such a background it is perhaps not surprising that one of their scions ended up writing a detective fiction series headlined by a Philo-esque gentleman detective.

Stanley Hart Page grew up in privileged circumstances in Chatham, New Jersey, along with two elder brothers, George Shephard Page and Lawrence Stanely Page, Jr., an elder sister, Elizabeth, and one younger brother, Henry de Bacon Page. Despite their fortune, there was tragedy in the family's life. One Sunday morning in January 1919 Stanley's sister Betty died at the age of twenty-one from the Spanish flu then raging around the world. At her death Betty Page, whose obituary avowed had been "universally beloved" from childhood, was doing Red Cross work and taking a "special course in domestic science" at Centenary Collegiate Institute in preparation for her impending marriage. Less than a year earlier, Stanley's brother George Shephard Page, a professional aviator, had been killed in the Great War.

Described on his 1942 draft card as 5'11", 155 pounds, brown-haired (though balding) and blue-eyed, Stanley Hart Page in late 1931, not long before publishing his first detective novel, wed Beatrice Bayard, daughter of an affluent old-money New Jersey magazine publisher and descendant of Anne Stuyvesant Bayard, sister of Peter Stuyvesant, the ill-fated seventeenth-century Director General of the Dutch colony of New Netherland. Beatrice Bayard, a lovely, doe-eyed twenty-four-year-old actress who had graduated from the American Academy of Dramatic Arts, had acted in traveling company and played small parts in two Broadway plays, the hit 1929 Edward G. Robinson comedy *Kibitzer* (2nd neighbor) and the 1928 revival of John Colton's 1926 melodrama *The Shanghai Gesture* (apprentice mouse). She had spent the summer before her marriage traveling around Europe with an auntly chaperone. She and Page were married in a small private ceremony at the Episcopal Church of the Transfiguration in Manhattan, popularly known as "The Little Church around the Corner," which liberally catered to theater folk and other bohemian types.[3]

Page credited his imaginative wife with having helped inspire him to start writing mysteries and he dedicated his first novel to her. The couple dwelt at the roughly $500,000 (in modern value) Millburn, New Jersey, home of Beatrice's parents, along with her siblings Stuyvesant and Martha. The Bayards employed a single maid, a young black woman from South Carolina memorably named Ida May Neville.

In 1933 Stanley and Beatrice produced one daughter, Martha Pintard Page, and Stanley produced two more

Beatrice Bayard Page

Christoper Hand mysteries, the aforementioned *Fool's Gold* and *Murder Flies the Atlantic,* the latter of which innovatively is set on a zeppelin flying between London and New York. It was published by a rather less distinguished concern, Alfred H. King. Despite Knopf's vigorous pushing in the press and his supposed winning of "many friends," Christopher Hand sadly had not in fact become the Next Big Thing in the way of dilettante detectives. Two years

later there followed from Page's hand, as it were, Christopher Hand's finale *The Tragic Curtain,* which was published by The Dial Press. The author appears then to have laid down his pen, at least as it concerned crime writing.

Page continued to receive press praise for his last two detective novels, however, with, for example, the *Boston Globe* labeling *Atlantic* "a tense and thrilling story that is admirable written" and the *Houston Post* avowing of *Curtain:* "It is well-told, complicated and interesting." With *Curtain* Page provided a fitting end for the series. "There is a certain ingenuity in this work, one which makes it difficult to put it down," reflected the reviewer of the novel in the *Baltimore Evening Sun.* "Mr. Page . . . has thought up a solution to his crimes which pretty completely baffles the reader until the denouement is reached. Moreover, he plays fair and doesn't break the established rules of the game."

Although his detective thus vanished seemingly without a trace ninety years ago, Stanley Hart Page himself lived on for over four decades. For years he and Beatrice were actively involved in the Chatham Community Players, who in 1941 performed Stanley's play *A Welcome Stranger,* which the Chatham Press called a "lively, uproariously funny farce." Hardly in need of money, Page retired relatively young from the news business in 1952 and passed away after a lengthy illness at the age of seventy-seven on August 4, 1979. For nine decades now Page's sleuth Christopher Hand has waited to experience his own miraculous resurrection. While admittedly, despite all the puffing from his first publisher, no Philo Vance, Christopher Hand for a very short time was a name much bruited-about in mystery-loving circles. See for yourself what you think of this clever fella.

ENDNOTES:

[1] On Vapo-Cresolene and George Shephard Page and his children, see the online accounts provided by John Langlois, "On Beyond Holcombe: Vapo-Cresolene," *1898 Revenues: United States Revenue Stamps That Financed the Spanish American War*, 12 November 2012, and by Dan Edminster, "Lamps Designed for Medicinal Purposes: Vapo-Cresolene and Schering's Formalin Lamps," *The Lampworks: An On-Line Resource for Lighting Researchers and Collectors of Oil and Kerosene Lamps, Burners and Other Trimmings*, at http://www.thelampworks.com/lw_vapo_cresolene.htm. On the AMA's 1908 report on Vapo-Cresolene, see *Nostrums and Quackery* (Chicago: American Medical Association, 1912), 626. On the overall dubiousness of Vapo-Cresolene, see James Harvey Young, *The Toadstool Millionaires: A Social History of Patent Medicine in American before Federal Regulation* (Princeton, NJ: Princeton University Press, 1961), 215. George Shephard Page, bluntly notes William D. Eddy *in Stone Pond: A Personal History* (1982; rev. ed., White Plains, NY: Plain White Press, 1988), was "colorful, eccentric and ultimately mad. . . . In the quaint phrases of his obituary, he was 'deprived of his reason and removed to the State Insane Asylum at Morris Plains, NJ'" (p. 51. n. 4).

[2] A 1936 letter writer to *Time* detailed the Lillian White case:

> In April 1922, acting Captain Grant Williams of the New York City police department was imported to Rockland County, handed a skull and other bones found on Cheesecock Mountain and asked to solve the mystery of its presence there. Sterilizing the skull, he placed it on an artificial neck made out of a curtain pole shaved down to fit the opening of the spinal column. Inside the skull on either side of the pole, he wedged two radio tubes to hold the head steady. The other end of the pole he fitted in a stand made of a soap box.

Greasing his fingers, Williams then coated the skull with modeling clay. He spread it thinly, following the contour of the bone evenly. Gradually he applied other layers, feeling his own jowls & forehead for guidance. The length of the nose he determined by measuring the distance between the bridge and the roots of the upper teeth: its contour by following the curve of the nasal bone. To get the fullness of the cheeks he held a pencil from the cheekbone down to the jawbone and allowed a little for normal rounding. He used the same instrument to determine the set of the eyes, holding it slantwise from the eye socket to the cheekbone. . . . The brows he determined by beginning at the inside corner of the eye socket and following around the upper edge of the bone; the fullness of the lips by the protrusions and recessions of the upper and lower teeth. And so on. . . .

Until, 56 hours later, when he had dipped the flesh-colored clay in wax, inserted glass eyes and dressed the victim's original hair, which providentially had been recovered near the skull, he had before him the snub-nosed, sullen face of a temperamental Irish girl.

The rebuilt corpse was subsequently identified as Lillian White, an inmate of Letchworth [a New York residential institution]. The identification was upheld by Justice Arthur S. Tompkins of the New York Supreme Court; and her murderer, Joseph Blunt, was subsequently caught in Maine.

[3] The Church of the Transfiguration was built and consecrated in 1849. During the New York City draft riots of 1863, Rector George Hendric Houghto, gave shelter to African-Americans who were targets of a draft-protesting white mob. Houghton was said to have turned the rioters away, sternly admonishing: "You white devils, you! Do you know nothing of the spirit of

Christ?" The church's nickname came about thusly: In 1870 the rector of the Church of the Atonement refused to conduct funeral services for a deceased actor, airily telling his friend, famed thespian Jefferson Farjeon (grandfather of English mystery writer Jefferson Farjeon), "I believe there is a little church around the corner where they do that sort of thing." Farjeon allegedly responded: "If that be so, God bless the little church around the corner!"

I

A PEARL-HANDLED PISTOL

I awoke with a start. In confusion I gazed into the gleam of the reading-lamp on the table at my elbow. My book had slipped from my fingers to the floor beside my chair. My pipe had fallen into my lap, fortunately right side up. Save for the circle of light cast upon me by the lamp, the living-room was in darkness.

B-r-ring!

That was it, the telephone must have wakened me. I groped for the instrument on the table. Of course it was not there. Reflecting bitterly upon the untidy habits of my lodging companion, I rose complainingly. The telephone I fished out of the crumpled newspapers in the waste-paper basket beside his chair.

"Hello! Hello!" I said sharply into the mouthpiece.

"Is this Mr. Christopher Hand?"

There was nothing unusual about that question. But the tone of the man's voice, charged with repressed anguish, brought me wide awake in an instant.

"Mr. Hand is out," I quickly replied. "If there is—"

"Out!" exclaimed my unseen interrogator. "Where is he? I must get hold of him at once!"

"He is at the Delvers Club. They have a private number that I am not at liberty to give out. If you have a message I shall be glad to give it to him immediately."

"I must get hold of him without delay! There has been a murder committed at my home!"

"Who is this?"

"Robert Garrison. Have Mr. Hand come to my home right away!"

"Is this the Mr. Garrison who lives on Riverside Drive? Hello!"

The man had hung up. His excitement had resulted in my being left with scarcely any information at all. Resisting a desire to call him back, I put in a call for the Delvers Club instead. Hand, I was told, was in the chemistry laboratory. They put the call through to him there.

"I have a case for you," I excitedly informed him. "A murder has been committed at the home of Robert Garrison. The financier, I guess. He—"

"You guess?"

"I was just talking to him on the phone here at the rooms. He was so agitated he just said he was Robert Garrison and that a murder had been committed at his home. He hung up before I could get anything else out of him. He wants you to go right over. His residence is on—"

"Riverside Drive, if that's the Robert Garrison. Well, I suppose I'd better go over there, anyhow. How about you?"

"I'd like to very much. However, I don't want to—"

"I'll meet you at Garrison's home. 'Bye, Clark."

I hustled into my top-coat, snatched my hat from the closet, and quickly left the rooms. A taxi pulled to the curb at my signal.

"Do you know Robert Garrison's home on Riverside Drive?" I asked the driver.

"Yeah; I been there."

"Get me there in a hurry," I ordered, jumping into the cab. "It's worth a five-spot to you if we make good time.

"Okay, boss," sang out the driver. "Hang on!"

As we flashed by a clock, I was astonished to see its hands pointing to twenty-five minutes after one. I hastily glanced at my wrist watch, which corroborated it. I must have napped long in my chair in the living-room.

I climbed out of the cab in front of the Garrison home. I handed the taxi-driver his promised five dollars; then I turned to the house. Somehow, I had expected the place to be all lighted up. Only a faint glow came through the vestibule on the front porch. Had we been enticed there by a hoax? Or was some other Robert Garrison the man who had demanded my friend's services? No cars were parked at the curb.

Determined to find out, I passed rapidly up the walk to the house. Half-way up the front steps I halted. A figure had detached itself from the gloom. Outlined before the glass panel of the front door, I saw the bulk of a policeman. All my doubts about that telephone call vanished. I had come to the right place.

"Stay where ya are!" said a gruff voice. "Who are ya?"

"Mr. Clark," I replied, quietly.

"There's Clarks an' Clarks," the policeman reminded me. "I know some, but they ain't none of 'em supposed to be here."

He moved over to the steps and looked suspiciously down at me. I noticed he held a pistol in his hand.

"By any chance, do you happen to know Christopher Hand?" I asked.

"Ya mean the private dick?"

"Well, I mean the criminologist."

"I just passed him in; he had a badge."

"And so have I," I announced, confidently mounting the steps. "Here it is," I said, taking from my pocket my badge of honorary membership in the New York police department.

The policeman flashed his light on it for a moment. "Well, all right," he muttered. "Come on; I suppose you wanta go in too."

He let me precede him into the vestibule. Then he stepped by me and rapped on the front door. Inside, a lace curtain hung over the glass panel of the door, obscuring my view of the interior. A dark form stepped up to the door and opened it. "Well, what now, Scharf?" was asked.

The policeman started to explain my presence. I brushed by him. "Hello, Tim," I said to the officer in the hall.

"'Tis you, Mr. Clark!" he exclaimed, smiling broadly. "I ain't seen ya since that Farley feller got himself killt."

"Okay, Sergeant?" asked the policeman in the vestibule.

"Sure!" replied Tim. "Didn't I—by jingoes, I forgot to tell ya Mr. Clark was comin'. Mr. Hand told me you'd be here, Mr. Clark. Step right in. Close the door, Scharf; back to the porch with ya."

"So Hand has arrived," I said, stepping into the hall, in which were several other policemen.

"Sure, he was two jumps behind us."

"Where are your cars?"

"Out on West End Avenue; we come in the back way. How are ya, anyhow, Mr. Clark?" he demanded, his hearty voice a jarring note in the quiet of the house. "Yer lookin' younger and handsomer every day! Mr. Hand looks as fine as a church steeple, too. Look here, see them chevrons? That's what Mr. Hand got me. Sure, he give me a fine bust to the commissioner. Two weeks later I got me promotion."

"That's great, Tim; you deserved it. See here, though, what's happened tonight? Is it murder?"

"Murder it is. Ah, the poor little thing! 'Tis a shame, Mr. Clark. Her so young and beautiful, too."

"A woman, eh?"

"Yes, sir. A fine actress she was, so they say."

"Not Mrs. Garrison?" I quickly asked, my thoughts turning to the young musical-comedy star whom Robert Garrison had married a year before.

"'Twas a friend of hern," replied Tim. "They was in the same show together last year, so I heard Mr. Garrison tellin' the boss."

"Who's on this case, Tim?"

"Sure, 'tis Inspector Gerrity himself."

"The inspector, eh? Where is he?"

"They just went into the room where the girl is lyin'. Come on, I'll take ya in."

I followed Tim across the large hall toward the back of the house. We passed along a corridor. At the end of it was a large arched door to our right. Light streamed through it. I glanced in. Three women and four men were gathered in the far corner of a large reception room. Aside from noting that they were all in evening dress, I observed nothing else about them. One of the women was sobbing hysterically. They turned their startled, fear-ridden faces toward me, and I turned away.

Tim was rapping circumspectly upon a door across the corridor from the reception room. Yanked open, it revealed the pugnacious form of Inspector Gerrity.

"Sir, Mr. Clark—" began Tim.

"Oh, hello, Clark," said the inspector gruffly, extending his hand to me. "Come on in. You fellows are right on the job, I'll say. Tim, have you got your men placed?"

"Yes, sir. One at each door. Detectives Madden and Black are here. They're lookin' things over outside, like ya told me to tell 'em."

"All right, Tim," grunted the inspector.

My eyes flickered to the floor of the room. I expected to see the body of the murdered woman sprawled there. I looked in vain. A single reading-lamp, standing beside a chair across the room, illuminated the room meagerly. Beside it stood the tall, spare figure of Christopher Hand. His head was thrust forward, as if he were looking at the floor. "'Lo, Clark," he grunted.

I quickly took in the surroundings. The room undoubtedly was a library. Shelves filled with books lined the walls. Four large chairs stood in the corners, and in the center of the room stood a table covered with magazines. On the far side of the room were two large windows. The room itself, oblong in shape, was about fifteen feet across from the door to the windows and twenty feet long.

The inspector, after closing the door, walked over beside me. "How are you?" he asked, absently.

"Never better," I replied. "You didn't get here much ahead of me."

"How do you know that?" he asked, glancing sharply at me.

"Because I got here ahead of the newspaper boys," I explained, with a chuckle. "You see, I'm getting on to Hand's methods."

"Well, you're right this time, anyway. The ambulance got here first. I got here just as they were leaving, and Hand came in on my heels. You were right behind him. We just came in here before you did."

"Where was she murdered?"

"Right here."

"But—"

"She's over there behind that chair," said the inspector, pointing to the one across from Hand. "See, you can see her hand sticking out."

Almost reluctantly, I walked over beside Hand. I followed his gaze to the floor behind the chair. The sight of murder is always distressing, but this spectacle of a lovely girl crumpled dead on the floor filled my heart with anguish. "Who is she?" I asked, huskily.

"Vera Venora," growled Gerrity. "She's an actress."

Vera Venora! I had seen her in her musical show just the week before—entrancing, beautiful, glorious, the essence of joyous youth. And here she lay, a pitiful heap in her proud jewels and finery. She was half twisted on her side, her legs bent under her, one arm buckled behind her back and the other outflung over her head. Over her left breast the satin of her gown was stained a dark purple.

I glanced at Hand. His penetrating eyes were roving rapidly over every portion of the room where the dead girl lay.

"Well, how about it, put on the lights?" demanded the inspector.

"Yes," said Hand, suddenly straightening. "Let's have a look round."

The inspector pressed a button on the wall over by the door. A large dome in the ceiling flooded the room with brilliant light. The tragic figure on the floor came into sharper relief. I turned away from it.

"No sign of a struggle," mused the inspector. "Everything seems to be in its proper place. Except that girl; I'm hanged if she is! Guess we'd better see what those people can tell us."

"Just a minute," said Hand quickly. "One would naturally suppose that this girl was killed by somebody in the house. Don't you think so, Inspector?"

"Sure it was somebody within the house. There're only two ways to get in or out of this room—through those windows or through that door. The windows are locked on the inside; I noticed that."

"But if there was an accomplice he could have let the murderer out the window and then locked it after him."

"Well, yes. But we're only guessing! The best way to find out is to question those people out there. I don't want to give 'em too much time to think it over. The quicker you can get 'em talking the more likely you are to get the truth out of 'em!"

"Your logic is sound enough. But mine supplements it, Inspector. If we can question them with an ace or two up our sleeves we are in a much better position to judge their answers. It is a wise thing to come to a few conclusions yourself before getting the stories of your principals."

Gerrity looked hard at Hand for a moment. The bull-necked inspector was not without intelligence of his own. But, in my opinion, he owed his present eminence to the help my friend had given him in the past. Long before any of his comrades in the department, he had realized Hand's unique powers in the solution of crime. He had also been keen enough to perceive an unusual trait in my friend, one that I deplored. This was Hand's utter lack of personal ambition, a readiness to let others take the credit for his remarkable work. With admirable foresight Gerrity, then a mere lieutenant, had cemented a friendship with my friend. Since then his rise had been astounding. In regard to Hand, Gerrity had none of the professional law guardian's resentment toward the interference of a private operator. He did more than welcome Hand's co-operation; he sought it.

"Well," he said, with a shrug of his huge shoulders, "what is there to find here? The girl is dead, shot through the heart. Evidently she was standing right where she lies. The doctor examined the wound and said it could not have been inflicted more than a half hour before he saw it—probably a shorter time than that. It's my opinion the murderer was someone inside the house, and I think you agree with me there. The only information we've had about the case is what Garrison told us. He admitted he was in this room alone with the girl when she was shot.

"That's all he told us; he didn't give us any of the details."

"It looks bad for him. Of course, he hasn't admitted doing the shooting, but it looks bad for him. He's your client, and you're trying to get him out of the jam, but—"

"You know better than that, Inspector," interrupted Hand, sharply. "If Garrison's guilty, I'll prove him guilty! But we're wasting time. There are a number of significant details that we have already learned from our inspection here. You touched upon one in your summary of what we know about it. The most significant, however, is that the pistol that this girl was shot with is still in the room."

Gerrity started. Wide-eyed he peered about the room. "Where is it?"

Hand walked over to one of the windows, the one farthest from the corner where the girl lay. At either side of the windows, extending from the top of the window casement to the floor, hung a heavy velvet curtain. Instantly I saw what he had detected. The shiny muzzle of a pistol was protruding from under the curtain at the left of the window! Hand carefully pulled the curtain aside. The pistol, a nickeled, pearl-handled weapon, then lay in full sight on the polished floor. Inspector Gerrity pounced upon it. All three of us stooped over and carefully inspected it.

Whoever had manufactured the pistol had made it as attractive a piece as could be bought. I thought how dreadfully incongruous it was that the bright, shiny little object could have wrought such havoc.

Evidently Christopher Hand's thoughts had run in a different channel.

"Thirty-two caliber," he grunted.

"Covered with finger-prints," observed the inspector, with satisfaction.

Hand reached into his overcoat pocket and pulled out his gloves. After putting them on, he gingerly took hold of the pistol by the muzzle, lifting it from the floor. Using his finger-tips, he broke it. One shell had been fired.

"That's the gun, all right," averred the inspector, as Hand laid it on the table.

My friend was leaning over the table, looking closely at the pistol. "Who is Constance Abbington?" he asked.

"Never heard of her," grunted the inspector. "Why?"

"Her name is engraved on the barrel of this gun," said Hand, simply.

He pulled the switch cord of a lamp on the table. The light glinted upon the pistol. Gerrity and I had no trouble in reading the name engraved along the side of the barrel.

"It's a fairly new gun," said the inspector. "I know the type. They were manufactured first about a year ago. It's fair to assume that this Constance Abbington is still the owner of it."

"I agree with you," said Hand. "It puts a bit of a different color on it. What would Robert Garrison be doing with Constance Abbington's pistol? Garrison is a sportsman, and one of the best pistol-shots in the country. He has pistols of his own, I'll wager."

With a sudden motion he yanked open a drawer of the table. Exclaiming softly, he reached into it and withdrew a blunt automatic. With his gloved fingers he removed the magazine. It was fully loaded. He next worked the action. A loaded shell flew into the drawer from the ejector. Then he held the weapon up so that he could look down its barrel. "This hasn't been fired," he announced. "More complications, Inspector. Why would Robert Garrison shoot that girl with some woman's pistol and then leave the pistol on the floor in here? Of course, a plant can be suspected. But Garrison has already admitted he was alone in this room with the Venora girl when she was shot down. It seems obvious that he is not attempting to throw suspicion on another."

Hand, after reloading the automatic, handed it to Gerrity, who thrust it into his pocket. The inspector placed a handkerchief over the pearl-handled pistol lying on the table. Then he turned impatiently to Hand.

"I think we should get Garrison's version of this shooting right now!" he said.

"Very well, Inspector," agreed my friend, "I think so too."

Once again I glanced at the pitiful figure huddled on the floor behind the chair. To the multitude the taking of that girl's life was to be a sensation seized upon for a few days by the newspapers. To us it was the beginning of an adventure that led to the most amazing plot we had ever encountered.

2

ROBERT GARRISON

Inspector Gerrity crossed to the door and threw it open. He stepped out into the corridor and called for Robert Garrison. Looking into the reception room, I saw the financier step forward. He was a man nearing fifty. Although not portly, his tall figure was rather heavy. His blunt features and bold blue eyes proclaimed his forceful nature. He had long been a captain of finance.

As Garrison stepped into the library, he showed the effect of his harrowing experience. His movements were jerky, and his face was deathly pale. Gerrity closed the door behind him.

Garrison turned and confronted the inspector. "I suppose you are about to put some questions to me," he said, brusquely. "Before I say anything I want to talk this over with Mr. Hand."

"I don't think that is necessary, Mr. Garrison," said my friend. "I am very well acquainted with Inspector Gerrity. I can assure you that he is not the sort of police official who is anxious to pin a murder on the first person handy. He is too thoroughgoing for that. He is as anxious as I am to find the scoundrel who killed that girl, and I understand you are too."

"I certainly am!" thundered Garrison. "This is outrageous! To think that one of my guests, a woman, should be slaughtered right in my own home!"

"Very well," said Hand. "The inspector wants to ask you a few questions. You will greatly assist me if you answer them frankly."

Averting his eyes from the chair that concealed the body, Garrison sat down in one by the door. Hand leaned up against the wall by the windows. The inspector half sat on the edge of the table.

"All right, Inspector," said Garrison. "I intended, naturally, to answer your questions to the best of my ability."

Gerrity concentrated for a moment. "You say you were in this room when that girl was shot?" he asked.

"I was."

"Who else was in here besides the two of you?"

"I don't know who else was here. I wish to heaven I did!"

"You told us a moment ago that you were alone with her."

"I did? I hardly remember what I said. But there must have been another in here."

"What makes you think so?"

"Because someone shot her! Obviously there had to be someone else here."

Gerrity dropped his eyes, but he made no allusion. "Tell us just how this thing happened, Mr. Garrison," he said.

"I will," complied Garrison, firmly. "Miss Venora and I strolled in here. I am backing her show, you know, and I was congratulating her on the success it has already made."

"You had to come in here away from the others to do that?"

Garrison flushed at the implication. "Not exactly," he replied, rather shortly. "Well, I suppose I had better tell you exactly why we came in here. I hope this will be kept confidential."

He waited in vain for some sign from Gerrity that it would be.

"Go on, Mr. Garrison," prompted Hand.

Garrison shifted uneasily in his chair. "All right," he said at length. "This is nothing but a side issue, and I shouldn't care to have you warp its significance into something sinister. I brought Miss Venora in here to get her away from—from one of the other guests who was annoying her."

"Suppose you be more explicit," suggested Gerrity.

The financier thought carefully for a moment. "Well, all right," he said, reluctantly. "I don't see what it has to do with it, but here it is. One of my guests, Dr. Innes, has become infatuated with Miss Venora. She didn't care for him. I don't myself. The trouble is, my wife thinks he is very interesting. We are leaving—we were leaving, rather, for our place in Maine next Friday, and he was going with us."

The inspector's bushy eyebrows raised in astonishment. "Your place in Maine?" he said. "I seem to recollect that your place in Maine is a summer home."

"It was, but I converted it into an all-season house. I planned to spend a good part of the fall up there. Most people don't realize it, but the fall in Maine is the best time of the year. I wanted to go alone, just my wife and I, but she insisted upon taking a lot of people with us."

"Miss Venora, then," said Gerrity, getting back to the subject, "resented the attentions of Dr. Innes. You brought her in here so that she could escape them."

"That's it."

"Perhaps you don't realize it, but that sounds a little silly. Usually a man can't plague a woman with unwanted attentions when there are a lot of people present. She can take refuge in numbers."

"Yes, usually that is the case. But Dr. Innes had—er— taken rather too much champagne."

"Oh, I see. Now, just tell us what happened."

"Well, Miss Venora and I had been here but a short time when it happened. She was leaning against the back

of that chair with her back to the wall. I was standing beside her. She said something that made me laugh; she had
a very keen wit, you know. All at once there was a roar
like a cannon, and Vera collapsed! I was stunned. I stood
looking down at her, unable to believe my eyes. Then I
dropped to my knees and shook her. I called out her name,
but she didn't answer me. Then I got up and ran out to
telephone the hospital for an ambulance. She was dead
when it got here."

"Why didn't you remove her to a bedroom, or somewhere like that? Evidently there was no effort made even
get her into a comfortable position."

"Why, after I had ordered the ambulance I came back in
here. Of course, everyone was terribly shocked. There was
a good deal of confusion. No one had come in here; except
young Innes. He's a medical man, you know, doing research
work over at the foundation. When I got back here, he was
just straightening from examining Vera. He told me she
was dead! I wanted to carry her up to her bedroom, but he
stopped me. He wouldn't even let me put her in a chair. It
was not until then that I realized it was murder. Of course,
I called the police right away. Then I saw what an awkward
position I was in myself. I decided to get Mr. Hand and
called him on the phone. I think you know the rest."

"Let me understand this," said Gerrity. "You were just
standing over in that corner, talking to Miss Venora, when
a shot was fired and she fell. That right?"

"Substantially, yes."

"But you were under the impression that there was no
one else here?"

"I was. There was a light burning over by that chair. It's
still on, you see. All the other lights were out. It would
have been easy for someone to hide behind one of these
chairs. We'd never have seen him."

"Have you any idea how he could have escaped?"

"Well, let's see. I hadn't thought of that. The windows—" said Garrison, raising himself up and glancing at the windows.

"The windows are locked on the inside," pointed out Gerrity. "Were they locked when you and Miss Venora. came here?"

"I'm sure they must have been. It's rather cold tonight; we'd have felt them if they'd been open. They are hinged on the sides, you notice, and you can't keep them closed without locking them with those handles. They were closed and locked, all right."

"It doesn't seem possible, then, that a man could have hidden behind one of these chairs, shot Miss Venora, and then escaped through the window, locking it on himself on the inside. Think so?"

"Of course not."

"Then the only way for him to have left this room was through that door. Were there people in that room across the corridor?"

"Yes, they were all in there. We had been playing bridge there."

"What were they doing, do you know, when this thing happened?"

Garrison thought carefully again. "Well, I know what they were doing just before we came in here," he said. "Some were dancing to the radio. The others were talking. The party was about over."

"Then it is hardly to be supposed that anyone emerging from this room through that door could have done it without being seen. I mean, after the shot was fired. Don't you think so?"

The man hitched his shoulders angrily. "I can't answer for the others," he snapped. "I don't know what they saw."

Gerrity, taking a pencil and pad from his pocket, glanced sharply over at Garrison. "Just give me the names of the others," he said.

Garrison complied willingly. "To begin with," he said, "there's my wife. Then there's Dr. Innes—Dr. Francisco Innes. Henry King, Archibald Flount, Gladys Dykeman, and Mrs. Wallace Abbington."

Gerrity's pencil, scribbling the names as Garrison pronounced them, stopped abruptly at the last one. He glanced up sharply at Garrison. "What's Mrs. Abbington's first name?" he demanded.

"Her first name? It's Constance. She and her husband are separated, but she still uses his name."

The inspector wrote the name on his pad, pecking a vicious dot after it. "Was she in this room tonight?" he asked, without looking up.

Garrison glanced with what I thought was suspicion at the inspector. "I don't want her dragged into this!" he said, thrusting out his jaw.

"Fate has placed things outside your control," retorted the inspector. "Are you going to answer my question, Mr. Garrison?"

"I beg your pardon, of course I'll answer it. Mrs. Abbington and I were both in here shortly before Miss Venora was shot."

"She wasn't in here alone at any time?"

"She was not. She came in here with me, and she left when I did."

"Would you mind telling me what you were doing in here?"

"Certainly not. I am handling some stock transactions for Mrs. Abbington. We were talking the matter over. As soon as I had explained everything to her, we rejoined the others."

Gerrity got to his feet. He took a turn up the room, head bowed and a frown on his face. Finally he stopped before Garrison. "Mr. Garrison," he asked, "do you think the shot that killed Miss Venora was fired inside this room?"

"I'm sure it was fired inside this room," replied Garrison, forcefully. "I should say it was fired right near my head."

"Did you look round to see who had fired it?"

"I'm quite sure I did. I'm rather confused about it, but I think I whirled round. When I saw Miss Venora fall, I forgot all about that."

"You're sure you didn't see anyone?"

"Positive."

Inspector Gerrity took a quick step over to the table. "Have you ever seen this before?" he barked, at the same time flicking the handkerchief off the pearl-handled pistol.

Garrison craned his neck to see. Then he rose from his chair and walked slowly over to the table. If he was acting he was doing a good job of it. From his puzzled expression I would have sworn he had never seen the pistol before. "Where did it come from?" he asked, uncertainly.

"Over on the floor under the window. We found it behind the curtain. Look at the barrel, Mr. Garrison, there's a name engraved on it."

Garrison leaned farther over and peered at the gun-barrel. Suddenly he recoiled. "Connie!" he cried.

"There's one shell exploded in it," said Gerrity, with a shrug.

"But she wasn't in here!" cried Garrison. "I know she wasn't in here! I left her out there with the others; she couldn't have come in here!"

"Well, I guess that's all for the present," said Gerrity, with an air of finality that I could see was maddening to the financier. "Unless Mr. Hand has any questions he thinks should be asked. Have you, Hand?"

"Just a few," said Hand, quickly. Gerrity's face fell. "Just step over to that corner where you were talking to Miss Venora, if you please, Mr. Garrison," went on Hand.

Garrison took a step back. "I'd rather not," he said.

"It's unfortunate that the body hasn't been removed," said Hand. "But we may not have this same opportunity again. I want you to show us just how you and Miss Venora were placed when the shot was fired."

Garrison, taking a deep breath, stalked over to the corner. "I was standing just about here," he said, keeping his eyes off the floor. "Miss Venora was leaning up against the back of that chair."

Garrison was standing out a distance of about two feet from the wall that the windows were in. His back was to it. The nearer window was about three feet to his right. Miss Venora must have been standing with her back to the side wall, her back a distance of four feet from it.

"Had you been in that corner before during the evening?" asked Hand.

"Why, no," replied Garrison, slowly. "No, I'm sure I had not been over here before Miss Venora and I came here. She was mimicking Mr. Flount, and she wanted to be sure he couldn't see her."

"Sure you weren't standing with your elbow resting on that book-shelf?"

"Let me think. I'm sure I stood right where I'm standing now. But—yes, you're right! I burst out laughing at her and leaned back against the bookcase. I did put my arm on it! But how you can tell—"

"Fortunately, your servants aren't very careful about this room. There is quite a layer of dust on the top of the bookcase. In it there is evidence that that book resting on top of the bookcase has been thrust aside. If you will look there, you will notice that the rectangular space formerly covered by the book is the only space free of dust. Similarly, you will notice that something has wiped the dust inward toward that rectangle from the edge of the shelf. Since I notice the right sleeve of your evening coat is powdered with dust near the elbow, I assume that it was your elbow that displaced the book. Now, then, were you in that position, with your elbow resting on top of the bookcase, when the shot was fired?"

"I believe the shot was fired just as I leaned up against the bookcase."

"Just assume that position, will you, please? But first I should like the inspector to notice the evidence that I have just spoken of. If you please, Inspector. An electric torch will aid you to see what I mean."

Grudgingly, Gerrity moved over to the bookcase. Flashing his light on its top, he inspected it carefully. Next he raised Garrison's right arm and peered at the elbow. "You may be right," he grunted. "Go on, Hand."

"All right, Mr. Garrison," said my friend. "Just place your elbow on the top of the bookcase. If you can recollect it, assume the exact position that you were in when the shot was fired."

Garrison placed his elbow on the bookcase, leaned his body against it, and turned his face to Hand. "I think I was standing like this," he said.

"Your body is facing the center of the room," Hand pointed out. "Was your face turned in that direction also, as it is now?"

"No. No, I'm sure I was looking at Miss Venora. Over my shoulder, like this. I saw her give a start, but I had no idea she had been hit. I glanced quickly round. Then I heard her, well, choke. I glanced back just in time to see her collapse to the floor. It was horrible. Horrible!"

Hand told Garrison he need not stay in the corner. With a great deal of relief, the man resumed his seat by the door.

"Can you tell us," went on Hand, "whether Miss Venora had any enemies? Do you know of anyone who might have had reason for taking her life?"

Garrison banged his fist on the arm of the chair. "That's it!" he said, explosively. "That girl didn't have an enemy in the world! There wasn't even any jealousy down at the theater. That means something, if you know anything about the theater. She made her own way, and it was a pretty hard way. Cheap vaudeville first, then bits in the revues, and finally stardom. Everybody down to the chorus was glad to see her succeed. She was unique—the very spirit of youth. She gloried in life, and she never forgot a friend, not even the poor little people she was thrown with at the start. Everybody loved her. And now, just as she reached the top—this! I can't understand it!"

"You have known her for some time?"

"Not so long. My wife was on the stage, you know. Miss Venora had a small part in her last production. I thought she had the makings of a star; so I backed a show for her. She was a success from the start."

Hand turned his back upon Garrison. "I think that's all, Inspector," he said.

"That will do for now, Mr. Garrison," said Gerrity. "I want to question the others. We'll do that—"

He was interrupted by a circumspect rap on the door. He opened it. A group of men, headed by Tim, stood at the threshold. Among them I recognized Dr. Richards, the police physician.

"Hello, Doctor," said Gerrity. "Come right in; we're all through here."

Dr. Richards stepped officially into the library, carrying his little black bag. "Where is she?" he demanded, his eyes roving over the room.

"Over behind that chair," the inspector pointed out. Then he turned to the other men, who I saw were from police headquarters. "Take the pictures and outline the body with chalk on the floor," he commanded. "You can remove her whenever you like, Doctor."

"Hello, Hand," said the doctor, shaking hands with my friend. "Hum-m, too bad, isn't it?" he said, looking down at the girl. "All right, you fellows get your pictures."

Garrison and the inspector, followed by Hand and me, walked out into the corridor. Two men stepped up to Gerrity. "What's the dope, Inspector?" they asked.

"You'll find a pearl-handled pistol on the table in there," replied Gerrity. "Plenty of finger-prints on it. I don't know where you can look for others, but give the room a going over."

As the two men brushed by, the inspector turned to Garrison. "I want to question these other people here, too," he said. "I want to do it individually. Where's the best place?"

"I should think the den would be best," replied Garrison, rather nervously. "You can look it over and see how it suits you."

He led us along the corridor toward the front hall. He opened a door and stepped in, switching on a light. The room was about the same size as the library and was right next to it. A flat mahogany desk stood in the center of the floor.

Gerrity stalked over to the desk and looked round. "This room connected with the library in any way?" he asked.

"The library is on the opposite side of that wall," replied Garrison. "There's no door connecting, however. Will this be all right?"

"Just the place, thanks. I'm going to call them in here one at a time. Saves confusion. That will be all, Mr. Garrison; if you'll just return to the room where the others are?"

Garrison walked slowly over to the door. At the doorway he half turned back to us. For a moment he raised his troubled eyes to us, as if he were about to speak. Then he turned quickly and strode out of the room.

3

A PRELIMINARY INQUEST

Inspector Gerrity laid hold of the desk in the den. He pulled it round so that it faced the door. He then placed the desk chair behind it and sat down. Nodding his head with satisfaction, he leaped to his feet and crossed to the door.

"Step in here, Tim," he called.

The sergeant walked stolidly into the den. "Yes, sir."

"Go into the room where those people are," ordered Gerrity, "and say: 'Is Inspector Gerrity in here?'"

"Is Inspector Gerrity in here? Yes, sir. Same as usual."

Tim strode from the room. Gerrity turned, smiling broadly, and addressed himself to Hand. "I have an ace up my sleeve, too," he said.

"Yes," agreed my friend, "and it's a clever stunt, I must say."

Gerrity returned to his seat behind the desk. Hand and I leaned against the wall behind him. A minute later Stanton, one of the best headquarters detectives, walked in upon us.

"Learn anything?" grunted Gerrity.

Stanton closed the door. "Yes, sir," he replied. "I had a good spot, right behind the curtains going into the next room. I picked something up, Inspector."

"Well, let's hear it."

"At first they were just standing round, not saying a word. I could get a look into the room, and I saw one of the women getting loose from the crowd. She caught the eye of a young fellow and motioned him to follow her. It was all done without the others catching on. She walked over to a chair near me. I could have reached out and touched her. I was on my toes. She no sooner gets sat than she drops a compact, but first she opened it up so's when it hit the floor a lipstick and powder-puff and a cake of powder flew all over the floor. Well, this guy she was signaling to come hopping over to pick it all up. While he's leaning over, the woman was talking to him."

"What did she say?"

Stanton leaned over the desk to his chief. "She said: 'For God's sake, Frank, what did you do it for?'" whispered Stanton, hoarsely. "This fellow started to look up at her, but he caught himself and looked down again. 'What?' he says. 'You don't think I shot her?' She gave him a little dig in the side to start him picking up the stuff again. Then she says: 'Don't worry about me, Frank. I'll say I was talking to you. You say the same thing. Now, don't forget.'

"I could see he was in pretty much of a daze after that," went on Stanton. "She took the compact from him and got right up and walked over to where the others were standing. He stood there for a minute chewing his lip. Then he walked over to one side and stood by himself, looking at the floor."

Inspector Gerrity remained silent for a moment. He picked up the list of guests that Garrison had given him. "Who was the woman?" he asked.

"I didn't get her name at all," replied Stanton. "I think it was Mrs. Garrison, though. I've seen her pictures in the papers."

"The man was Frank," mused Inspector Gerrity. "That must be Dr. Innes. Did you get any more dope, Stanton?"

"No; just the usual reactions. They all keep saying that 'Garry' couldn't have done it. The usual jackass questions and jackass answers. There's one little guy in there, though, that acts pretty suspicious. He's as nervous as a old lady exposed to the flu."

"All right, Stanton. Tell Tim to step in here. You stay here, too. Stand over at the side there. When the woman comes in that you overheard talking to this man Frank, you say: 'Do you want my pencil, Inspector?' Do the same thing when your man Frank comes in. Now tell Tim I want him."

Tim stepped through the door and looked inquiringly over to his superior.

"Put a couple of men in the room with those people, Tim," ordered Gerrity. "Tell them to take it easy; these are highbrows, you know. I just don't want them to talk things over too freely. Ask Miss Dykeman to step in here."

The moment the girl entered the room, I felt sorry for her. She was a pretty little thing. She looked at us with a piteous appeal in her big brown eyes. She stepped timidly through the door and stopped, hesitatingly. I hastened across the room and got her a chair. She murmured her thanks as she sank into it. Twining her fingers nervously, she glanced over at Gerrity. She was surprisingly young

"You are Miss Gladys Dykeman?" he asked, kindly.

"Yes."

"You were present when Miss Venora was shot?"

"Y-yes."

"I suppose you heard the shot. Where were you at that exact time?"

"I was in the reception room. Dancing, with Mr. King."

"You're positive of that?"

"Oh, yes."

"Who else was in that room?"

"Why, I think everybody. That is, everybody but Mr. Garrison and Vera. I mean, Miss Venora."

"Remember, this is a very serious matter. Think hard, Miss Dykeman. Are you positive all the others were there except Mr. Garrison and Miss Venora?"

The girl, striving to conceal her nervousness, looked thoughtfully a the ceiling. Finally, she shook her head of black, bobbed hair. "I—I'm not sure, Mr.—Mr. Chief," she said in a thin little voice.

Gerrity smiled. When he wanted to be, he was a kindly man. "Inspector Gerrity," he corrected, mildly. "Surely you can be certain of some of the people who were in that room with you. You weren't alone with Mr. King, were you?"

"No, but Mr. King and I had just danced over near the corridor. We were right before the door where—where— oh!" she wailed, bursting into sobs.

Gerrity grimaced impatiently, but he got to his feet and walked over beside the girl. "Please collect yourself," he said quietly. "This is a terrible experience, I know. But perhaps you can help us. You want to help us, don't you?"

"Oh, yes," cried the girl hysterically. "But Mr. Garrison *couldn't* have done it! I'm sure he didn't do it!"

"Perhaps not," agreed Gerrity. "But we can never tell unless we get at the truth. You see that, don't you? If you want to help him, the best way you can do it is to help us. Now, then, who were those you were positive were in the reception room when the shot was fired?"

"I can't just say, I'm afraid. My back was to the room, and I hadn't been paying much attention to the others. I'm quite sure Mr. Flount and Mrs. Garrison were there. When I heard the shot, I was *hypnotized!* I just stood staring into the room."

"You could see into the library?"

"Oh, yes. The door was partially open. It was quite dark in there, and I couldn't see anyone. Then Mr. Garrison came rushing out with his eyes all wild and bl-blood on his hands!"

"What did you do then?"

"I couldn't seem to move. I watched Mr. Garrison rush down the corridor. He came in here. Mr. King took my arm and led me into the reception room."

"Who was in the reception room when Mr. King took you back into it?"

"I—I just don't know. I thought everybody was, but—oh, my thoughts were so confused. I know Mrs. Garrison was. She screamed and ran out after Mr. Garrison."

Gerrity leaned forward. "How do you know she ran out after her husband?"

"Because she screamed his name. She screamed his name as she ran by me. Then she turned up the corridor in the direction he had gone."

"You have accounted for yourself, Mr. King, Mr. Garrison, and Mrs. Garrison. Are there any others?"

"Yes. Mr. Flount was there. He rushed over to Mr. King and asked what had happened."

Inspector Gerrity consulted his list. "Then there are left unaccounted for only Mrs. Abbington and Dr. Innes," he remarked.

"Oh, they were there too," cried the girl. "Mrs. Abbington took care of me. Mr. King put me in a chair. I thought I was going to faint—I think I almost did faint. The only thing I can remember clearly was Mrs. Abbington holding smelling-salts to my nose."

"And where was Dr. Innes?"

"Oh, he went right into the library."

"Did you see him go in?"

"N-no."

"What makes you think he went right into the library?"

The girl seemed astonished. "Why, he said he did," she replied, her big brown eyes looking innocently at the inspector. "He must have gone in there right away. I have a hazy recollection of Mr. Garrison rushing back into the library. He came right out, and Dr. Innes was with him, you see. They told us it was V-Vera, and—and that she was dead!"

Gerrity turned to Hand. "Is there anything you want to ask?" he said.

"Just this," he replied, stepping forward. "Miss Dykeman, you heard the shot quite plainly, didn't you?"

The girl seemed disturbed at having a new interrogator. Anxiously she glanced from Hand to me, wondering, I suppose, whether I also would take a part in the terrible inquisition. She folded her hands and swallowed hard. "W-what?" she gulped.

Hand repeated his question. "I say, you heard the shot, didn't you?"

"Oh, yes. It was deafening!"

"Are you quite sure it was fired in the library?"

"Yes, it must have been."

"Very well. Now, how soon after the shot was fired did Mrs. Abbington come to your side?

"I—I don't exactly know. I hardly remember Mr. King putting me in the chair at all. Mrs. Abbington was bending over me—that's all I remember."

"Where do you live, Miss Dykeman?"

"In Greenwich Village. I'm studying art."

"Have you known the Garrisons long?"

"About a year."

"Mr. Garrison was on good terms with Miss Venora, wasn't he?"

"Oh, yes indeed. He and Mrs. Garrison did so much for her!"

"Did you know of Miss Venora's ever having an enemy?"

"Never. Not one!"

"That's all, Inspector."

In a very fatherly fashion Inspector Gerrity ushered the girl over to the door. "That will be all, Miss Dykeman, and we thank you very much," he said, opening the door and revealing the faithful Tim standing just outside it. "Ask Mr. King to step in here," he ordered the sergeant, as Miss Dykeman moved swiftly off down the corridor.

Henry King stepped briskly into the room. He was as straight as a ramrod. In spite of his iron-gray hair, his tanned, pleasant face and athletic figure gave him the appearance of youth. His features were set as he stood expectantly waiting.

"Take a seat, Mr. King," said Gerrity, motioning toward a chair, the one that Miss Dykeman had just left.

King sat down carefully, saw to the crease of his trousers, and glanced up at the inspector. Gerrity lowered himself ponderously into the chair behind the desk. "Mr. King," he began, "you were present when that fatal shot was fired?"

"I was, Inspector. I was right outside the door of the room where it was fired."

"What were you doing?"

"I was dancing with Miss Dykeman. We had just danced out by the corridor when the shot was fired."

"What did you do?"

"My first impulse was to rush into the library to see what had happened. Then I noticed that Miss Dykeman was fainting—or appeared to be. I half carried her back into the reception room and put her in a chair."

Gerrity leaned across the desk. "Who else was in the reception room?"

King frowned thoughtfully. After he had pondered at some length, he looked up. "I want to get this straight," he said. "Flount was there; I remember him perfectly because he bothered me. I had that girl on my hands, and Flount kept grabbing at my arm and asking what had happened. Mrs. Garrison rushed by me as I took Miss Dykeman over to the chair."

"You haven't accounted for Mrs. Abbington or Dr. Innes."

"Hum-m, that's so. Well, I'm afraid I wasn't very obser-vant. You're not, you know, in those circumstances. I told Flount to look after Miss Dykeman and started for the library. I don't like to disparage," he said, with a smile, "but Flount was hardly the man to send to the library while I looked after Miss Dykeman."

"Did you go to the library?"

"I did. Dr. Innes was there, bending over Miss Venora. He told me to go phone for an ambulance. I didn't know just where to find a telephone, but when I came out of the library, I saw Mrs. Abbington looking after Miss Dykeman in the reception room. I knew she could direct me to a telephone. She did, too—told me there was one in here. As I started off to the den, I met Mrs. Garrison. She told me her husband had ordered an ambulance. Just about that time Mr. Garrison and Dr. Innes came out of the library with the news that Miss Venora was dead. I think that's all I can tell you."

"About how soon after the shot was fired did you see Mrs. Abbington?"

Again Henry King concentrated deeply. "It's a little hard to say," he said. "I don't think I could estimate, exactly. Two or three minutes, possibly less."

"Any questions, Hand?" asked Gerrity.

Hand nodded. "When did you first see Mr. Garrison after the shot was fired?" he asked King.

"Why, he came rushing out of the library right after the shot was fired."

"I thought so. You neglected to say so, however. Have you known the Garrisons long, Mr. King?"

"No, I have not. I made their acquaintance just three days ago."

"You never got that coat of tan in the city."

King grinned. "No," he said. "I'm not from the East at all. My home is in Kansas. I'm very fond of these people, though," he added, seriously. "This is an infernal shame! I almost wish I had not come to New York."

"You are staying in the city?"

"Oh, yes. Before you get to asking me a lot of questions," he smiled, "I'll tell you all about myself. It won't take long; I'm not a very interesting person. I live in Emporia, Kansas, and this is my first visit to New York since 1914. I hadn't any friends here, but my stockbroker, Mr. Lessington, undertook to get me into the swim. Through him I met the Garrisons. I was instantly fascinated by them, and they have been most kind to me. They have entertained me constantly the past three days. At present I am staying at the Mockridge."

"Lessington is with the Andrews, Lessington Company, isn't he?" asked Gerrity.

"He's junior partner," affirmed King.

Hand took up the questioning again. "Mr. King," he said, "you stated that you were right outside the library door when the shot was fired. By any chance did you happen to be looking into the library just as the shot was fired?"

"I was looking right at the door, which was partially open."

"Do you think the shot was fired inside the library?"

"I know it was. I didn't see the actual flash of the gun, but I saw the library light up with it. There wasn't much light in the room, you know."

"That is very interesting. Could you see anyone in the library?"

"I saw no one at all."

"Thank you, Mr. King," said Hand, striding back to lean against the wall.

King, at a nod from Gerrity, rose and turned to the door. He hesitated a moment; then he swung round to face us. "I say," he said, suddenly, "of course what I think doesn't interest you much, but I can't believe that Robert Garrison killed that girl. It just doesn't look right!"

"We'll see," said Gerrity, coldly. "Thank you, Mr. King."

Archibald Flount was the next one interrogated. He stopped at the threshold, as if he dreaded to set foot into the room. Tim, who is of average height, towered above him. The little man, primness personified, stood gazing at us through his heavy eyeglasses, much as a goldfish peers at one through its bowl.

"Step inside, Mr. Flount," invited the inspector, quite ominously.

Mr. Flount's entrance was accomplished by a series of frightened hops. Gerrity waved him to the witness chair. Intent upon glancing suspiciously at us, he all but missed the chair. He sat first upon the arm, from which he slid to the seat with an undignified jar. He seized his eyeglasses, attached to a black cord round his neck, and returned them quite resolutely to his nose. "Don't think you can frighten me!" he warned, in a piping voice. "I've heard of your third-degree methods. Preposterous! I refuse to answer questions until I have seen my lawyer. I don't know anything, anyway!"

I turned away to hide a smile, a smile that faded on my lips. It was Mr. Flount whom Vera Venora had been mimicking when her life was snatched from her. I turned back as Inspector Gerrity cleared his throat.

"Mr. Flount," began the inspector, "you are taking a very foolish attitude. I should think you would be glad to help clear Mr. Garrison of the cloud that hangs over him."

"Of course I am!" cried Archibald Flount, shrilly.

"Well, then, you can do nothing better than to answer my questions to the best of your ability. You were in the reception room when the shot was fired, I believe. What—"

"Of course I was!" interrupted Mr. Flount.

"Well, I wouldn't say of course. I guess you were, though. Who else was in there?"

"I was talking with Mrs. Garrison."

"Was there anyone else in the reception room?"

"I don't know. Some of them were dancing. I didn't pay attention."

"Who were dancing?"

"I don't know. Let me think. No, I don't know."

"Were Mr. King and Miss Dykeman dancing?"

"Possibly. Possibly."

"Where were Mrs. Abbington and Dr. Innes?"

"I really don't know; I wasn't keeping track of them."

Inspector Gerrity bit his lip in exasperation. He leaned across the table and growled at Mr. Flount. "Who was in the reception room right after the shot was fired?"

"Hum-m. Let me think. Miss Dykeman fainted. I was terribly upset—not frightened, mind you, upset. I don't know who was there."

Gerrity drew back and barked the next question. "Did you speak to anyone right after the shot was fired?"

"No. Yes. Let me think. It was King. He wouldn't answer me. Uncouth chap, at times; those mid-Westerners!"

"Did you speak to anyone else?" thundered Gerrity.

Mr. Flount looked aggrieved and crawled into his shell. Gerrity threw up his hands in despair. He looked beseechingly toward Hand.

My friend stepped forward and smiled upon Mr. Flount. "Would you mind telling us," he asked, "whether Mrs. Abbington was present at the time Mr. King helped Miss Dykeman into the chair?"

Mr. Flount regarded Hand skeptically for a moment. Evidently he decided that his new interrogator was more to his liking. Opening his mouth to answer, he was arrested by a new thought, his jaw hanging open while he pondered it. Eventually he did answer. "I can't just say whether Mrs.

Abbington was actually present or not," he said. "I believe she went after smelling-salts. I was fanning Miss Dykeman with my handkerchief when Mrs. Abbington stepped up with the restorative. We had her round in no time."

"And Dr. Innes?"

"I didn't see him at all. Not at all. Wait a minute. Let me think. Yes, I did. No, I guess I'm mistaken. I didn't see him. Not at all."

"What line of business are you in, Mr. Flount?"

Flount appeared shocked. "Business!" he said, as if the word were offensive. "I am in no business, sir!"

"Pardon me. Do you live in the city?"

"I have an apartment here. My home is on Long Island. Port Washington."

"Are you married, Mr. Flount?"

The little man glared at Hand. "I'm not going to answer these impertinent questions!" he blazed. "Of course I'm not married!"

"How long have you known the Garrisons?"

"I've known Robert Garrison all my life. Splendid chap, but a little overbearing, at times. He didn't kill that girl."

"No? How can you say that?"

"I don't have to go prying into things to know. I know he didn't!"

Hand smiled understandingly. "You mean you think he didn't."

Mr. Flount flared up. "Nothing of the kind!" he protested, shrilly. "I know he didn't kill her, because she killed herself!"

"Ah, and what makes you think that?"

"They were in the room alone. Robert didn't kill her; so she must have killed herself. Simple, you see."

"Very simple!" agreed Inspector Gerrity, explosively. "Well, Hand, any more questions?"

"No; I guess that's all," grinned Hand.

If Mr. Flount had not entered the room with much dignity, he made up for it when he left. He stalked pompously by Tim and strutted off down the corridor.

"Lord, I hope we'll have no more like him!" growled Gerrity. "Let's have Mrs. Abbington next, Tim."

Mrs. Abbington might have stepped from a magazine cover into the den. She was a tall, willowy young woman. Her blond hair was arranged in an exquisite coiffure; her delicate lips were rouged to just the proper extent; her eyebrows were beautifully penciled; her soft cheek was decorated with a warm flush; her eyes were blue and sparkling.

"Do you want my pencil, Inspector?" asked Stanton, suddenly.

Inspector Gerrity's eyebrows lifted just perceptibly. "No, thank you, Stanton," he replied, "this one is quite all right. Won't you take that seat, Mrs. Abbington?"

Mrs. Abbington gracefully seated herself. For a moment her blue eyes were veiled by their long lashes; then she opened them wide and gazed frankly at the inspector.

"It's unfortunate," began Gerrity, "that we have to subject you to this ordeal, but—"

"Please don't mind that, Inspector," she interrupted, quite brightly. "This whole affair is perfectly horrible, but of course you have to do your duty. Poor Garry, I do hope you'll discover that he didn't do it; I'm sure he didn't!"

"It begins to look as if he didn't," said the inspector, eying Mrs. Abbington narrowly.

Her eyebrows fluttered down, and she clasped her hands a little tighter. But, with an expression of eagerness, she quickly looked up. "I can't tell you how delighted I am to hear it!" she said, and her tone was most convincing.

"Did you know Miss Venora intimately, Mrs. Abbington?" asked Gerrity.

"Why, I met her through the Garrisons. Rather, I met her through Mrs. Garrison. I've known Mr. Garrison a

long while. He didn't know Miss Venora until after he met
his wife."

"Did you know anything about the girl that might have
led to her death?"

"Goodness, no!"

"Didn't have any enemies?"

"Not so far as I know."

"Where were you when the shot was fired, Mrs. Abbington?"

"I was in the parlor adjoining the reception room—toward the front of the house."

"What were you doing there?"

"I was talking with Dr. Innes."

"I see. What were you talking about?"

"Really, I can't see that it matters," replied Mrs. Abbington, haughtily.

Gerrity smiled and waved his hand carelessly. "I don't
suppose you do," he said. "The methods we employ are
usually quite mysterious to everyone but ourselves. To us
they are very simple. Can you tell us what you were talking
about to Dr. Innes?"

I thought the color receded a little from Mrs. Abbington's cheeks. Perhaps I just imagined it.

"Let me see," she said, thoughtfully. "I think he was
telling me something about the foundation. He is doing
research work there, you know."

"What did you do when the shot was fired?"

"Why, I was badly frightened, of course. I walked into
the reception room, and then I saw that Gladys Dykeman
had fainted. I had some smelling-salts in my handbag. You
see?" she said, opening her bag, which she had carried into
the room with her, and displaying the tiny bottle. "I ran
upstairs to get it. Then I ran right down again. When I got
into the reception room, Mr. Flount was waving his handkerchief in front of Miss Dykeman's face. Of course that

wasn't helping much. I administered the smelling-salts, and she responded instantly."

"Where did Dr. Innes go?"

"Why, he walked into the reception room with me. I don't know, to my own knowledge, exactly what he did after that. He said he went right into the library and discovered Miss Venora lying dead on the floor. I saw him come out of the library with Mr. Garrison afterwards."

"Could you tell us where the others were standing at the time the shot was fired? I mean, of course, with the exception of Mr. Garrison and Miss Venora."

Before answering, Mrs. Abbington took a deep breath. The questioning was telling on her.

"I can't tell you," she said. "I was not in the reception room, and I believe they were."

"There is a wide entrance between the parlor and the reception room, is there not?"

"Yes, it's quite wide."

"More of an arch, isn't it?"

"Yes, it's an arch."

"How near to it were you standing?"

"Oh, we were quite near to it."

"In view of those in the reception room?"

"No; we were off to one side. I couldn't see much of the reception room from where we were standing, if that's what you mean. I could just see the side near the windows, and I didn't see anyone over there."

"Mrs. Abbington, do you own a pistol?"

The question did not seem to startle her much. She sat up a little straighter and looked a little puzzled. "Why, yes," she replied.

"Is your name engraved on the barrel?"

Her face, naturally very fair, became a little whiter at that, and the knuckles of her clasped hands showed whitely

through the skin. She did not reply; just nodded in affir-
mation.

"Where is it?" asked Gerrity, shooting the question in
the low, cutting voice he could employ at times.

"Why—why, it's home, in my apartment."

"Sure of that?"

"Why, yes, I think so. I haven't actually seen it for
some time. It should be in the top drawer of my dresser; I
keep it there."

"Could anyone have taken it?"

Her unruffled calm was dissolving. Her replies to Gerrity's questions came as with an effort. I began to feel a
little sorry for her. That is the trouble with me in such
investigations.

"Could anyone have taken it?" she repeated, as I
thought, to give herself time to think. "I—I don't see how.
My servants could have, of course, but I don't see how
anyone else could have taken it."

"How many servants have you?"

"My maid and my cook. I'm sure they would not steal
my pistol!"

"Is there anyone at your apartment now?"

"My maid is there, of course. She waits up to help me
undress."

Gerrity got abruptly to his feet. Quietly he picked up
the telephone from the desk. Its cord reached over to Mrs.
Abbington's chair, and he handed the instrument to her.
"Just call your apartment, Mrs. Abbington," he said. "Ask
your maid to get the pistol out of the top drawer of your
dresser."

Almost as one in a dream, Mrs. Abbington took the
telephone from him. In a toneless voice she gave a number and waited. Gerrity stood very close to her. Presently,
addressing someone over the wire, Mrs. Abbington asked
whether the pistol was in the dresser. I noticed her

respirations increasing as she waited. At length she listened intently, and then, without replying, listlessly handed the telephone back to Gerrity. "It isn't there," she said in a strained voice, looking dully at the wall across the room.

Gerrity slowly replaced the telephone on the desk. Then, with startling suddenness, he whipped about to face Mrs. Abbington. "Your pistol was found in the library near the body of Vera Venora!" he barked.

Mrs. Abbington half rose to her feet, her eyes wild and staring. She opened her lips to speak, gasped, and then slumped back into the chair. With an exclamation I leaped across to her. Tearing open her bag, I extracted the bottle of smelling-salts, pulled the stopper, and applied the pungent neck of the small bottle to her nostrils. She twitched, cried out piteously, and finally opened her eyes. None of us spoke as she stared wildly about her. Hand stepped to the door and ordered Tim off after a glass of water.

Gerrity, a half-savage gleam in his eyes, stepped forward. Hand put out his arm and stopped him. "Not yet, Inspector," he said, grimly.

The inspector glared at Hand for a moment. Then, with an irritable shrug of his shoulders, he slouched down angrily in his chair at the desk. Mrs. Abbington, with the water that Tim brought, refreshed herself. Gerrity peered apprehensively at Hand; then he turned to the woman. "Do you feel that you can answer any more questions now?" he asked, gruffly.

Mrs. Abbington was still quite shaky, but she nodded her head.

"Very well," growled Gerrity. "I have only one question I want to ask you: could Dr. Innes have got hold of that pistol of yours?"

Mrs. Abbington's answer was little more than a whisper. "I'm sure he couldn't," she said. "He has called at

my apartment, but so have a great many other people. He
didn't leave my pistol in the library; how could he? He was
talking to me when the shot was fired!"

"That's all I want to know," said Gerrity, ominously.
"Anything you want to ask, Hand?"

My friend stepped forward, smiling sympathetically.
"Do you feel quite composed now, Mrs. Abbington?" he
asked, kindly.

"Yes," she replied, although her voice did not bear her
good witness.

"I have only one point that I wish to clear up," said
Hand. "You said, I believe, that immediately after the shot
was fired you entered the reception room from the parlor.
You also said that you had been so standing in the parlor that you had seen no one in the reception room. You
merely heard the shot and went into the reception room at
once. That right?"

With a nod Mrs. Abbington acknowledged that it was.

"Now, as soon as you entered the reception room, you
saw that Miss Dykeman had fainted, and you turned and
rushed upstairs for your smelling-salts."

"Yes," she replied, breathlessly, seeming to sense that
she was about to be tripped up.

"What made you so sure that Miss Dykeman was not
the one who was shot?"

"Because I—I—"

"You had just heard a shot from the direction of the
reception room. Immediately upon entering it you saw
that girl being half carried to a chair. Yet you knew she
had only fainted and went after your smelling-salts. How
do you account for that?"

"I—oh, I don't know!" she cried, and immediately burst
into hysterical weeping. Hand, an expression of annoyance
on his face, turned and strode back to his station behind
the inspector.

I stepped over beside the young woman. Looking pleadingly at the inspector, I was rewarded by an impatient gesture from him. I helped the sobbing woman to her feet and guided her to the door. I left her in the hands of her friends, who regarded me coldly as I left the reception room to return to the den.

4

SPITZ AND SPAWN

The inquest, if such it could be termed, might well have continued to its logical conclusion, with all the guests and servants having been questioned, had it not been for a most surprising occurrence. As I stepped back into the den, my feet were arrested by the unmistakable sounds of shooting at the back of the house.

Gerrity leaped from his chair and stood tense beside the desk. "Shots!" he cried. "Someone is shooting out behind the house!

"More than one shooting out there," shouted Hand, as he disappeared through the door.

Gerrity and I rushed after him. Toward the rear the corridor ended at a door. On the other side of it, across a small, dark hallway, a glass-paneled outside door was just discernible. Hand experienced a little difficulty in opening it. Gerrity went to his assistance, flashing a pocket torch on the door. Almost immediately there was the report of a shot from outside. The glass panel of the door flew into flashing splinters. Gerrity swore softly and extinguished the light. The bullet had struck the wall behind us.

A moment later Hand had the door open. He leaped incautiously through it, and Gerrity and I followed. Out at the back, in the gloom, some sort of desperate game in progress. As we emerged, the firing commenced anew.

I could just make out shadowy figures rushing toward the West End Avenue entrance of the property. Here and there the darkness was pierced by the spiteful flash of a pistol-shot. Windows in an apartment house next door jumped into bright squares of light. Cautious heads were poked inquiringly out.

All this I noticed as we raced toward West End Avenue. At the end of the walk we encountered a knot of policemen, some in uniform and some in plain clothes, crowding to get through a small gate in the iron fence.

Gerrity grabbed one of them by the shoulder. "What is it?" he demanded.

"Somebody hidin' in the grounds back here, sir," replied the fellow. "He got Spinelli—shot him from one of those bushes."

As we tumbled through the gate, I heard a shot from up the avenue toward Seventy-seventh Street. A policeman yelped with pain, grasped his shoulder, and leaned swearing up against the fence. His mates fired back at his assailant, who was streaking down the sidewalk. Near the corner he turned out into the avenue. As he passed directly under a street light, the policemen blazed away at him again. He seemed to stagger for an instant, but then he spurted round the corner and was gone. Several of the policemen had left us and were running after him.

"Quick! Here's a police car," cried Hand, running over to a big touring car parked deserted at the curb.

One of the policemen ran round and climbed into the driver's seat. He had the motor going in an instant. Hand leaped into the seat beside him. Gerrity and I plunged into the back seat. The machine leaped away from the curb, swung round in a circle, and headed for Seventy-seventh Street. Hand gave the handle of the siren a twist. The policemen running up the avenue ahead of us scattered in all directions.

Gerrity, as our car rounded the corner, leaned out the side. "There he goes!" he cried.

A long, low roadster careened out into the center of the street a block ahead of us. For a moment, as the driver ran through his gears, we picked up on it; then it shot away, increasing its speed to a terrific pace. Gerrity emptied his pistol at it, but without effect.

The roadster turned up Amsterdam Avenue. At Seventy-ninth Street it turned east. We raced across town after it, flashing by the avenues, Hand keeping the siren screaming. At Central Park the roadster shot into the transverse road. Tearing across the park, we leaned out of the car and sent a hail of lead after the flying roadster. It seemed impervious to gun-fire. Like two things gone mad, the roadster and the police car shot out of the park, leaped across Fifth Avenue, and streaked into East Seventy-ninth Street. A patrolman, attracted by our siren, ran out into the street ahead of the fleeing car. We could see him pull his pistol from his pocket. Before he could use it, the roadster swerved desperately at him. He leaped for his life, and as we shot by him, he was picking himself up from the pavement.

Straight across to East End Avenue the roadster shot. There it executed a hair-raising turn to the left, disappearing round the corner. As we followed after, almost on two wheels, we saw the roadster pulled up to the curb at a rakish angle. Our tires burned as we skidded up beside it. The roadster was empty.

"Where is he?" cried Gerrity, frantically.

He had not uttered the words before a pistol-shot rang out from across the street. I felt a twinge of pain in my left shoulder and fell back a step. Hand grasped me by the shoulders. "Are you hit?" he demanded.

"Just a scratch," I replied, and although I did not believe it at the time, I had spoken the truth.

Gerrity and the policeman were rushing across the street. Hand and I sped after them. A row of dingy brick buildings stood before us. About every thirty feet was an entrance, stone steps leading up to them. Our fugitive was not in sight. Gerrity, it seemed, knew where he had gone. The inspector leaped up to one of the doors. It yielded readily, and we shuffled after him into velvety blackness. There we stopped, expectantly.

"Move off to one side," hissed Gerrity, "I'm going to flash my light."

The beam of light, sweeping over the walls, showed us that we were in a small hallway. A flight of rickety wooden stairs rose before us. To the right a short corridor extended toward the rear. At its end was a door.

"S'pose he went up the stairs?" whispered Gerrity.

"What's this?" said Hand, walking a few steps down the corridor. He flashed his light on the wall. In the center of the brilliant disk was the print of a bloody hand. He rubbed the tip of his finger across it.

"It's fresh," he muttered. "He was facing away from the entrance door when he put his hand there. He was beyond the stairs; so he must have been headed for that door at the end. He was, too. See, he steadied himself with that blood-smeared hand down here, too. He was hit, Inspector."

"Fatally, I hope," growled Gerrity. "See here," he said, turning to the policeman. "You go find a call box and get some reserves up here. I'll tear this blasted section brick from brick to find that devil!"

The policeman, with no show of reluctance, opened the door and passed out to the street. Gerrity and Hand headed for the door at the end of the corridor. About to follow after them, I felt something clutch at my wrist. I spun round. To my consternation, in the fading light of Gerrity's torch I found myself looking straight into a bearded, evil-looking face.

"What's goin' on?" hissed the fellow.

"W-what?" I gulped.

"What's goin' on?" repeated my terrifying interrogator.

Gerrity and Hand heard him then. They directed their torches on us. I saw an open door to the left of the stairs. The man who had me by the wrist had evidently come from it.

"Who in blazes are you?" demanded the inspector in a low growl.

"I'll answer that when I find out who in blazes you guys are," retorted the man. Dressed in shabby, frayed trousers and an undershirt, he stood in his bare feet. He folded his arms over his deep chest and settled back against the door jamb.

Gerrity displayed his badge. "Now, who are you?" he snapped.

"Bulls, eh?" observed the man, with the serenity of his kind. "Who did the shootin'?"

"That's what we're going to find out," replied Gerrity, through his teeth. "Where does that door go?" he demanded, pointing to the one at the end of the hallway.

"Down t' th' basement."

"Do you live here, and what's your name?"

"I live here, and me name's Spawn. Who're ya lookin'—"

"Come along with us," ordered Gerrity. "Show us the way to the basement."

"Yeah?" sneered the man. "If there's a guy down there with a rod, smoke 'im out yerself. I ain't on no police force. Sorry t've bothered ya," he said airily, as he turned to his door.

Gerrity reached out for the man. "Come here!" he said angrily, spinning the fellow round to face him. "You're going to show us the cellar of this place, d'you get me? Come on," he said roughly, giving Spawn a push toward the rear of the hall.

Our new-found, unwilling ally shrugged his shoulders philosophically and started for the basement door. A flight of stairs, not very safe by their appearance, led down into Stygian darkness. The basement was a litter of boxes, old furniture, refuse of every description. We stumbled through it, inspecting the three rooms in the place. Certainly there was no one in the basement other than ourselves, who by then were nearly frantic at the time we were wasting.

Spawn, albeit he was forced into the position of cicerone, was very helpful. He aided us in pulling things aside and peering behind them. At length we were positive that no one could have been hiding in the cellar.

"Any way out of this place except by those stairs?" demanded Hand.

"I never been wild about hangin' out down here," explained Spawn, by way of getting at what Hand had asked him. "This is the second look I've had at it, the first bein' when I chucked that busted chair over there from the stairs. Ya got me, gov'nor; I don't know."

"How long have you lived here?" inquired Gerrity, not very civilly.

"Um-m, three months. I like it here," he explained, as if three months were a long time for him to stay in one place.

"We're looking for a man," said Gerrity, crisply, "who might have had something to do with the murder of a young woman well known on the stage. The shooting occurred tonight. Do you know of anyone living in house who might be the man?"

I thought the question rather foolish. From what I had seen of the house, mean and decrepit, it probably sheltered a half-dozen men who might be the one, including Spawn himself. His rejoinder, however, was surprising as well as enlightening.

"I think I know the guy yer after," he said. "He moved in here three days ago. Funny lad. Bad-lookin' egg, he is. Kept to himself all the time, and if ya spoke to him, ya got nothin' but a cold eye fer it."

"Why the devil didn't you tell us this before?" exploded the inspector.

"Ya ain't asked me, gov'nor," replied Spawn, unperturbed by Gerrity's savagery. "I knew he was a bad hand though, soon as I seen him. Cold!

As the inspector argued angrily with Spawn, I noticed the tall figure of Christopher Hand moving off into the gloom. I was too interested in Spawn to follow him, although ordinarily I should have. Gerrity walked right up to Spawn and shone his light full on the man's bearded face. Spawn's little blue eyes, a puzzle to anyone hoping to read the thoughts behind them, stared unblinking into the rays of the electric torch.

"I don't like people of your kind with beards," said the inspector evenly. "I always have the feeling that they may be a fake."

Spawn grinned and ran his fingers up into his unkempt, stubbly black appendage. "Ya can take a pull at it if ya like," he offered.

The inspector regarded Spawn coldly for a moment. "We'll look you up," he growled, "and we'll look everybody up in this cursed house!"

"Step over here, will you, Inspector?"

Looking round, we saw him over under the stairs. He was flashing his light on several boards forming a panel in the brick wall.

"This looks as if it might be a door of some kind," he said, when we had crowded round him. "At least it offers the only possibility of egress from this basement other than those stairs. Let's see whether we can force it."

"Just a minute," said Spawn, behind us. "I usta live in a place that had a door somethin' like this here. Connected with the cellar of the house alongside."

"Do you know how to open it?" snapped the inspector.

"I dunno; give me a try at it."

Spawn stepped in front of us and stood, with his back toward us, before the panel. He seemed to be manipulating something that was giving him trouble. "No," he said over his shoulder, "I guess this ain't the same kind of a door. I guess it ain't no door at all. I thought fer a minute—"

All at once the rough panel swung sharply outward, Spawn leaped through it, and before we knew what had taken place, it slammed sharply shut again.

With a yelp of rage the inspector emptied his pistol at the blank panel. Hand leaped to it and, with frenziedly exploring hands, tried to find the secret latch. From the opposite side of the wall we heard the hollow, mocking laugh of a man. Inspector Gerrity cursed violently.

Hand whipped about from the panel. "Quick, Inspector, up the stairs to the street!"

Up the stairs we rushed and through the hall to the street entrance. As I passed through the narrow hallway, I vaguely noticed three or four men, in all stages of dress, peering down at us over the banister of the stairs.

Save for the roadster we had pursued to the place, and the police car, the dark street was deserted. Hand led us directly to the entrance of the house next door.

"Unless all these cellars are connected, he's still in this house," averred my friend, as we cautiously entered the front hall. The architecture of the second house was identical with that of the first. With drawn pistols and flashlights we crossed the hall to the basement door. Hand was first as we descended the stairs. He immediately crossed over to the entrance of a room at the side. He stopped at the threshold. As the inspector and I crowded up behind him, he flashed his light over the opposite wall.

"There's that infernal door from the other basement," he growled.

Although the door was made of thick planking, the inspector's bullets had torn right through it. The side we were looking at was all splintered and split where the six bullets had passed through. Hand shifted his light to the floor. There were no blood marks.

"I must have missed him!" groaned Gerrity, in anguish.

Suddenly I felt a pair of hands, strong hands, placed in the small of my back. I found myself, before I could twist away from them, hurtling into the broad back of Inspector Gerrity. The inspector, in turn, smashed into Hand. All three of us pitched headlong to the floor. The force of our fall broke both Hand's and Gerrity's lights. We were left in complete darkness. I heard a hollow thud behind me. Without doubt we had been locked in the miserable place. Again we heard that mocking laugh.

As I was blindly regaining my feet, someone, evidently Gerrity, bumped into me on his way to the door. Presently I heard him hammering desperately upon it.

"Where's your light, Clark?" snapped Hand.

Gerrity, with the butt of his empty pistol, was creating a fearful racket hammering on it. It appeared just about as stout as the last one we had tried to force.

"I don't think you'll open that door, Inspector," said Hand, quietly. "I noticed a pretty heavy bar to be thrown across it from the outside. Let's see what we can do with this other one. Probably the secret of its catch is not so cleverly concealed from this side."

It was, however. Hand ran his long, sensitive fingers all over it. In the meantime Gerrity, in a torture of frustration, literally groaned in despair.

"What can we do?" he cried.

"I believe," said Hand, "the expression is: take it on the chin."

"Where the deuce are those reserves you sent for, Gerrity?" I demanded.

"I hope to blazes they never arrive now!" he replied, bitterly. "Locked up like a rooky here in this damned cellar! Can't you get that blasted door open, Hand?"

Hand stepped back from the door and snatched the light from me. He played it all over the surface of the door. The thing looked perfectly blank and secure. Suddenly, with an exclamation, he leaped over to it again. I had noticed the same thing he had. The door extended from the low ceiling to the floor. It was composed of four planks with two cross pieces. The two planks in the center were short lengths. But whereas one did not quite reach the floor, the other did not quite reach the ceiling. He placed the flat of his hands on them. The one he slid up, the other he slid down, and the door opened.

"Regular sliding bolts, of course!" he growled, as he plunged through the door. Gerrity and I leaped through cellar after him. We were then back in the first that we had visited. Once again we rushed up the stairs. The men in the hallway, whom I had seen on the stairs on our first trip to the street, were by now peering inquiringly down the cellar stairs. We bowled them unceremoniously out of the way as we stormed through the hallway.

"My Gawd, it's the same three fellas!" one of them gasped.

At the sidewalk Hand stopped resignedly. "It's gone," he said simply, pointing across the street.

"What's gone?" demanded Gerrity.

"The roadster. It was alongside the police car."

A man came running like mad down the street toward us. He was making for the police car, and we rushed over to intercept him. As he approached we saw that he was the plain-clothes man that Gerrity had sent to call out the reserves. He was almost exhausted when he reached us.

"The roadster—turned into—Eighty-first Street," he panted.

"After him!" howled Gerrity, leaping into the driver's seat of the police car.

As the policeman sought to get into the car with us, Gerrity stopped him. "You stay here," he snapped. "When the reserves get here, tell 'em to guard these houses until I get back."

We shot away from the place, careened into Eighty-first Street, and sped over toward the park. When we reached Fifth Avenue, Gerrity applied the brakes and brought the car to a stop. "Now which way did they go?" he growled.

"Unless we can find someone who saw him," said Hand, glancing round, "we might as well give him up for lost. The best thing to do is to broadcast an alarm for the car throughout the city. The license number was 71-N-18—"

"I know the number!" interrupted Gerrity, sharply. "I know the make of the car, too."

He started up again, driving over to a call box on Eightieth Street. He barked the necessary details over the wire for a description of the roadster to be broadcast; then he got back into the car. "Well," he said, resignedly, "I suppose the only thing to do is to go back. Maybe we'll find out something about that devilish pair where they gave us the slip."

"I think we could do nothing better," agreed Hand.

The reserves, in charge of a police captain, were overrunning the street when we got back to the house. The captain walked over to Gerrity. Touching his cap, he asked for orders. The inspector told him to keep his men in the street and to see that no one left the block of houses. The three of us then entered the building where we had first encountered Spawn.

Our bewildered spectators, gesticulating excitedly, were still in the hallway. One of them, a tall, lean fellow, apparently had the floor.

"It's jest like you sez, Jake," he was declaiming, "twicet they come up, and they didn't go down oncet! I seen 'em better'n you guys. I was standin' right—holy jumpin'! That's them now! That's all three of 'em! How come you guys don't come bustin' up the cellar stairs this time?"

"Never mind," growled Gerrity. "Here, Bean-pole, step over here; I want to talk to you."

The tall one, with an expression of reproach on his long, lean face, shuffled over before the inspector. "I'm a respectable married—" he began.

"Yes, yes," broke in Gerrity, testily, "with half a dozen kids and all. We'll find out about that later. What interested in right now is a man by the name of Spawn. Know him?"

The tall man brightened. He was about to come into his element, I could see. He inflated his lean chest. With great self-importance he prepared to deliver himself of every scrap of information he had concerning the mysterious Spawn. "Him and that other one are the hardest guys in Noo Yo'k," he declared, his lantern jaw working like a piston-rod. "The minute I laid me eyes on 'em, I sez t' Jake here, I sez—"

"Who was the other one?

"Spitz. Called himself Spitz. Now, I sez t' Jake, an' he'll tell—"

"Shut up!" howled Gerrity. "I don't give a blasted hang what you *sez* to Jake! Were Spawtz and Spin—Spatz and Spawntz—oh, blast it!"

"I think," said Hand, mildly, "the inspector was leading up to asking you whether Spitz and Spawn were friendly with each other."

"Yes!" affirmed Gerrity, explosively.

The angular person's feelings had been outraged. He affected such an injured air that I felt positively ashamed of the inspector. Gerrity, getting more choleric by the minute, brusquely waved his first choice aside. He next selected the person who, evidently, was the slim one's favorite auditor. Jake was more tractable. Through him we learned that Spitz and Spawn had taken the room at the foot of the stairs three days before. Nobody knew much about them. They had been decidedly cool to their neighbors. They had given the impression, without much effort, that they were a bad pair. "Th' kind o' guys that talk to ya after they've pumped ya full o' lead," as Jake put it.

The impression held by the tenants of the house was that the pair were gunmen. Hence their society had not been sought. Jake's description of Spitz was that he was a tall man with a big nose.

Gerrity, gruffly dismissing the men, led the way into the bedroom at the foot of the stairs. The room was furnished barely. A careful search of the place revealed that the men had left little behind them except a few odds and ends of clothing. We found only one article to which even the remotest significance could be attached. It was a coin, a German mark. Hand found it on the floor under the bed.

"I suppose you're thinking," said Gerrity, "that that thing proves these fellows to be German."

Hand smiled and flipped the coin to the inspector. "Maybe it does," he replied, with a shrug. "It's not very conclusive proof, I must say, and I don't think it would be very valuable if it were."

"Well," said Gerrity, with what malicious satisfaction he could muster, "one of those fellows is out on a pretty cold night with bare feet and nothing much besides an undershirt and a pair of pants to keep him warm."

"And the other has a bullet in him," supplemented Hand. "Perhaps that will drive him to one of the hospitals."

"I told 'em to keep their eyes on the hospitals," growled Gerrity. "I hope to blazes he goes to one. He won't, though; those fellows never do. He'll go to some slippery quack who'll keep his mouth shut, and I hope he gets nothing more serious than gangrene. Those fellows are in line for some bad luck; we've had our share tonight!"

Hand smiled and shook his head. "No, Inspector," he said, "we didn't run up against bad luck tonight; we ran up against two of the most astute gunmen, if gunmen they are, that I've ever encountered."

"How do you make that out?"

"By the manner in which we were duped."

"Duped?"

"Precisely. It's not hard to imagine that they picked this wretched house for the very features that enabled them to make their escape tonight. I can even conceive of their having planned the whole thing, exactly as it was enacted. One of them arrived here, wounded and hard-pressed. He got to the cellar door, all right, but we were right on his heels. The other emerged from his room and arranged for us to lose a little time. It was just enough to give his pal a chance to duck through into that other cellar. There was only one ticklish point in their scheme: the escape of Spawn. He managed that very adroitly right before our eyes through the medium of that infernal door. The rest was simple. They waited in the adjoining basement until we had fallen for the bait and rushed headlong into it. Naturally, the first thing we would inspect was the other side of the bewildering door. It was a simple matter, then, to lock us up for safe keeping while they made their escape in the automobile."

Inspector Gerrity swore softly under his breath. Suddenly his features brightened. "Maybe only one of them got away in the car!" he exclaimed. "Maybe the first man went right through to the other cellar, on out to the street, and drove away. That would leave the second fellow still hiding here somewhere."

"I don't think so," disagreed Hand. "There was too much team-work displayed for one of them to run off and leave the other stranded. But perhaps we can make sure of it. That plain-clothes man of yours saw the roadster depart when he was off calling in to headquarters. Perhaps he could tell us whether there was one man or two in it."

We immediately left the building. Gerrity called for the driver of the police car, who made his way to us through the crowd of policemen. In response to the inspector's query, he said he was positive there were two men in the roadster when it passed him. Gerrity, glancing at Hand, shrugged his shoulders in despair. Then he called for the captain.

"Stay here with a couple of men and watch this house," he ordered. "Send word for Lieutenant Dockery and a squad of detectives to come over here at once. Have him put a man on each of the tenants of this house and look up their records. I want a detailed report on each one as soon as possible, and I want the best men working on it. There's a bedroom on the first floor, just at the foot of the stairs. Get finger-print specimens in it. The two we're directly interested in are Spawntz and Span—blast it! Spawn and Spitz!"

"It's easier," murmured Hand, "if you say it, Spitz and Spawn.

5

RECONSTRUCTION

We got back into the police car, and the inspector instructed the driver to take us back to Robert Garrison's house. Gerrity, after we had started, leaned forward and addressed the driver. "Was Spinelli shot very badly?" he asked.

"I think he got it in the stomach," replied the man.

Gerrity once more lapsed into gloomy silence. Finally he turned to Hand. "What do you think of that pair?" he demanded.

"I think Spitz is the man who shot that girl," replied my friend, firmly.

"If he did, he's even slicker than we think he is," growled Gerrity. "If he did shoot the girl, though, he had an accomplice; that's sure. The only way for him to get away was through one of the windows. They were locked on the inside, you know."

"I've been thinking it over," said Hand. "I have a little theory. Perhaps there's nothing to it, but we can see."

The rest of the way we rode in silence. Gerrity kept glancing at Hand, as though he would have liked to ask about that theory. He successfully resisted the temptation. No doubt he was frenziedly trying to think up a theory of his own.

The house, we found, had been cleaned out. Tim informed us that the district attorney had appeared on the scene and whisked everybody off to his office. Gerrity, it was plain to be seen, was rather chagrined. He had lost his opportunity to question Dr. Innes and Mrs. Garrison at first hand. He also reminded us, rather heatedly, that he had had no opportunity to question the servants at all.

We went directly to the library. The body had been removed. My recollection of it was made more vivid by its chalked outline on the floor. Hand proceeded to put his theory to the test. Still equipped with my torch, he flashed it on the window nearest the spot where the body had lain. Both windows were the leaded-pane type, each pane being about five inches square. Over these squares of glass Hand played the light, peering closely at each in turn.

"Perhaps the servants don't dust the bookcases so well," he observed, "but they certainly keep the windows shined. There's not a speck on these glasses."

"What are you looking for?" demanded Gerrity.

"The prosaic finger-prints."

"I should think my men would have looked for them there."

"Perhaps they did. If they found any, they were careful to clean them all off, for I don't see a one on this window."

Hand moved over to the other window. He then stood about ten feet from the outline of the body on the floor. Each square of glass on the right side of the window was inspected individually. Hand shook his head dubiously. He then commenced inspecting the glasses on the left. At one of the lower panes near the center he paused. Placing his head closer to it, he gazed intently at it for a moment. "Come here, Inspector," he said.

Gerrity and I moved over beside him.

"Do you see finger-prints on that pane of glass?" asked my friend.

There were many of them, excellent prints. Gerrity nodded. We both looked inquiringly at Hand.

"It's the only pane of glass in both windows that has finger-marks on it," said he. "The inference is obvious, of course. Wait here."

He turned and whisked out of the room. Gerrity, thoughtfully chewing his lip, stood gazing at the little pane of glass with the finger-prints on it. Soon the rays of Hand's torch were played on the window from outside. All at once his face appeared through the window. Evidently one of the police was holding the light for him. Although the light beam still shone on the window, both his hands were free. They were encased in gloves. In one he held his pocket knife, opened. He inserted the blade between the square of glass bearing the finger-prints and its lead frame. The glass suddenly loosened. Grasping it with his other hand, he lifted it out. "There you are, Inspector," he said.

"What are you standing on?" asked Gerrity.

"There's a convenient ledge here about four feet off the ground," replied Hand. "Now, will you two fellows go over to the corner where the body was? Take the positions that Garrison said he and Miss Venora were standing in."

I took Miss Venora's position, leaning against the back of the armchair. Gerrity stood facing me, with his back to Hand.

"Now move over against the bookcase, Inspector," directed Hand, speaking through the window. "All right," he called; "I'll be right in."

He leaped down from view. Gerrity moved over and, frowning thoughtfully, sat on the edge of the table. I walked over to the window. I was there, inspecting the little open space, when Hand strode into the room.

"You get the idea, Inspector," he said. "Spitz stood on that ledge. He fired the shot through the space where he removed the pane of glass. That operation was done quite easily by forcing back the lead so that it no longer held the glass secure. Here's the glass, covered with his finger-prints. If they match those your men get over at his room, it will definitely link him with the murder. If we apprehend him, and his finger-prints are the same as these on the glass, I'd say it alone would be evidence almost strong enough to convict him."

"I'll call them right away," said the inspector. "Better tell them to redouble their efforts to get prints in Spitz's room."

As he strode from the room, I turned to Hand. "By Jove," I said, "it's a lucky thing Garrison got you on this case when he did. He was certainly in a bad hole and no mistake."

Hand grunted. He commenced to pace up and down, an occupation that he continued until Gerrity returned from telephoning.

"They missed the finger-prints on that window altogether!" sputtered the inspector. "Somebody's going on the mat for this! But see here, Hand, there are just three things—"

"Yes," smiled Hand, turning about to face the inspector. "I can name them for you. Why did Spitz want to shoot that girl? How is it possible that he did it with Mrs. Abbington's pistol? Why did he stick round here after he had committed the murder?"

"That's what I want to know," agreed Gerrity, "and I don't think those questions are going to be easy to answer."

"I think I can give you the answer to the first right now."

"Well, what is it?"

"Spitz neither intended nor wanted to shoot that girl. You know a good deal about Robert Garrison, Inspector; everybody does. He enjoys a laugh just about as much as anybody. A peculiarity of his when he laughs is to throw himself. He puts his whole heart into it. If he's seated, he

throws back his head and usually bangs his hands down
on the arms of his chair; I've seen him do it. If he's standing, he throws his body to one side, twisting it and taking
a step aside; I've seen him do that. I dare say you have,
too. Now, this is my idea of what happened. Garrison
was standing here," explained Hand, taking the position
Garrison had been standing in when he talked with Miss
Venora. "Although he was standing off to one side of the
windows, he had his back to them, you see. It was quite
dark in this corner. Suddenly Garrison, convulsed with
laughter, threw himself aside, up against the bookcase.
At the same instant, or, rather, a split second later, Spitz,
standing on the ledge with his hand protruding through
the hole in the window, fired the shot. It missed Garrison
and struck that poor girl."

"You mean to say Spitz came here to murder Robert
Garrison?" demanded Gerrity.

"I think there's no doubt of it."

"What for?"

"As for that," replied Hand, with a patient smile, "we
can only hope to find out. At present I can give you no
better reason for Spitz's shooting at Garrison than you can
give me for Spitz's shooting Miss Venora."

"Yes, we'd better let the cause go for now. I don't mind
saying that I'm inclined to take your point of view. How
about the pistol, though?"

"That's a plant," snapped Hand, a little savagely. "We
must attempt to discover how that pistol got from Mrs.
Abbington's apartment to this room. In my estimation
that's the crux of the whole situation. If we can find the
person who purloined that pistol, we'll solve the mystery,
Inspector."

"I believe you're right!" agreed Gerrity, forcefully. "It
gives us a starting-point, anyhow. You think Spitz dropped
that pistol into the room after he fired the shot, eh?"

"That's my idea of it. Then he put the glass back and—"

"Yes, and hung round here until the place was overrun with police. That's the thing I can't understand!"

"Well, let's see whether we can find out anything that might help us to understand it. There's a cement walk that runs along under these windows; no footprints, of course. He must have gone directly to the rear of the house, though. That's where he was when he shot Spinelli. Let's have a look out there."

We trooped from the library. Suddenly Hand turned, tapped the inspector on the shoulder, and pointed back to the library table. Gerrity, with a growl in his throat at his own neglect, went back into the room. He picked up the pane of glass from the table, where Hand had left it, and wrapped it in his handkerchief. Gingerly carrying the important piece of evidence, he rejoined us.

Spitz's ambush, one of the policemen showed us, was a small, bushy fir-tree. Gerrity had three of his men direct their torches on the ground all about it. The tree was protected by a low wire fence running completely round it. The fence, on the side toward the house, was badly dented in. Hand and Gerrity quickly stepped over it. They pushed their way in among the thick branches of the tree. I could see them flashing their lights on the trunk near the ground.

"There you are, Inspector," said Hand. "In the darkness he tripped over the wire fence, came hurtling through the branches, and banged his head into the tree-trunk. The evidence is plain enough. He lay here unconscious, at least dazed, and when he came round, your men were all over the place. They were giving the shrubbery a pretty careful inspection, I imagine. When Spinelli approached this tree, there was nothing for Spitz to do but shoot his way out."

"Right you are again," growled Gerrity. "Now, if we can only find out as much about that gun!"

I think Hand would have liked to stay longer. The search, so dear to his heart, for those minute pieces of evidence that one almost always can find at the scene of a crime had not been exhausted. The inspector, however, was impatient to learn the course of the proceedings at the district attorney's office. Hand, I knew, was anxious to remain at Gerrity's side. We all three, therefore, got back into the police car and were driven away.

6

A TWIST

The district attorney's office had something of the appearance of back stage at the theater. Here were the host and hostess, the guests and servants of the gay party of the evening before, transplanted to the severe setting of an office waiting-room. One felt that presently they would walk through the wings and put on the act for which they were dressed.

Actually it was quite different. They were waiting, except those that had already done so, to walk into the inner sanctum of Ulysses W. Hetherton, as excellent a district attorney as ever took office.

With the exception of three policemen, who were regarding everyone narrowly, the assemblage was stiffish and uncomfortable. In a sense, servants and those they were accustomed to serve were all reduced to the same level. The uncomfortable, hitherto imposing butler alone was busy. He glared his staff into their proper attitudes of humility. He got himself assured at regular intervals by his boss that there was nothing he could do for him.

The guests were all quite glum and silent. All, that is, except Mr. Flount. That diminutive glass of fashion had the appearance of a game-cock that had just received the contents of a bucket of very cold water. He fidgeted angrily on his chair, denouncing everybody connected with the enforcement of law, even including the governor.

Garrison, as soon as we entered the waiting-room, jumped to his feet. He crossed eagerly over to us. "This is pretty steep treatment," he said, with a shake of his head. "This man Hetherton—he didn't actually place us all under arrest, but he acts as if he might do that any minute. Of course, we all agreed willingly enough to come over here, but it seems rather unusual. I thought they only carried out this procedure in the case of gangsters and so on."

"This is rather unusual, Mr. Garrison," affirmed Gerrity. "The usual procedure is to pack everybody off to a police station. The district attorney is going out of his way to save you that."

"Well, then, I'm grateful to Hetherton," said Garrison. "By the way, how are you making out, Mr. Hand?"

"Inspector Gerrity and I have identified the assassin," replied Hand. "It's not one of your guests, and neither is it one of your servants"; he smiled, as he noticed an expression of concern come to Garrison's face. "It was an East Side gunman. Removed a pane of glass from one of the library windows and shot through the hole. We'll have no trouble, I think, in convincing the district attorney of that. It should relieve you of further embarrassment here.

The man got away; so the case is not cleaned up yet."

At that moment Hetherton escorted Mrs. Garrison out of his office. I had seen her before, both on the stage and since her marriage. There was a similarity between Mrs. Abbington and her. Both were tall and willowy; both had blond hair. Their features resembled each other's, also, to some degree. But whereas Mrs. Abbington's were stamped with a shrewd intelligence, Mrs. Garrison could lay no claim to that. With her large sparkling blue eyes and soft lips she was the more perfect type of blond beauty.

Hand and Gerrity immediately crossed over to Hetherton. He was relieved to see them and motioned for me to follow them into his office. After he had closed the door, he turned abruptly to us. "Well," he said, "this is a fine mess, isn't it? Garrison will never speak to me again as long as he lives. As a matter of fact, I brought them here to save them as much embarrassment as possible," he declared, lowering his tall figure into the chair behind the desk and turning his lean, shrewd face from us. "I hope you don't mind, Inspector."

"Not at all," lied Gerrity. "I questioned some of them over at the house. All but Dr. Innes and Mrs. Garrison. I didn't get a chance to question the servants, either."

Hetherton grimaced. "Servants don't know anything; nobody knows anything. It looks bad for Garry. I don't think he did it, but he's going to have a devil of a time proving he didn't. What have you fellows uncovered?" he asked, glancing sharply at Hand.

My friend leaned against the wall, crossed his arms and gazed at the floor. Gerrity glanced apprehensively at him for a moment, saw that Hand, as usual, did not intend to detract from his glory, and plunged into a vivid account of the evening. With his head resting on his finger-tips, Hetherton listened quietly. For several minutes after the inspector had finished speaking, he remained in motionless silence. Finally he hitched himself up in his chair.

"Good work, good work," he commended. "This helps us all out. Obviously, the thing to do is to find out how that pistol came to be in the man Spitz's possession. We'll have to iron out this deceit on the part of Mrs. Abbington and Dr. Innes, too. I've had them all sign statements. Here they are, if you care to look them over. Substantially the same things they told you. I noticed that Miss Dykeman, Mrs. Garrison, King, and Flount all corroborated each other, and that Mrs. Abbington and Dr. Innes corroborated only the story of the other."

Hand and Gerrity rapidly glanced through the sheaf of signed statements. At length they glanced at each other and nodded approvingly.

"I think," averred Hand, laying the statements back on the desk, "it is time to get Mrs. Abbington and Dr. Innes here together and lay the cards on the table. Tell them exactly what we know about them and the case in general and see whether they can straighten it out for us."

"That's my idea exactly," said Hetherton, and Gerrity nodded in agreement.

Accordingly Mrs. Abbington and Dr. Innes were summoned. The young woman had herself in better control than when we had last seen her. Dr. Innes, a swarthy, good-looking, stocky young chap, appeared rather nervous. With a show at unconcern, they accepted Hetherton's invitation to be seated.

"These gentlemen," began Hetherton, "have brought to me several facts of which I was unaware when I spoke with you before. Let me tell you before we go any further that they have established the identity of the person who fired the shot. Now, we are all sensible people. Ordinary methods followed in these cases can be laid aside. People, of course, from any walk of life suddenly plunged into a tragic situation are liable to do things that afterwards seem utterly inane and senseless. In the interests of getting down quickly to such bed-rock as we can find, let us remember that and take it into account."

"Pardon me, Mr. Hetherton," said Dr. Innes, "what is the purpose of this preamble?"

"It's this," replied Hetherton, with a twinkle in his eye. "You and Mrs. Abbington forgot, or perhaps you didn't realize, that two of the greatest sleuths imaginable were working on the case that you unhappily were involved in. In such circumstances even the walls have ears," he said, shaking a playful finger at our two victims.

Both Mrs. Abbington and Dr. Innes were plainly disconcerted. The young woman glanced at the doctor, an unasked question in her eyes. He vigorously nodded his head.

Mrs. Abbington, her face flushed, dropped her eyes. "I suppose I was perfectly silly," she said. "I don't know how you found out about it, but evidently you are aware that Dr. Innes and I had a little—a little plot."

"Yes," said Hetherton, still keeping up his jocular attitude. "You made up your minds that you were talking with each other when the shot was fired."

"No; I made up our minds that we were talking together," corrected Mrs. Abbington, with a wry smile. "Dr. Innes, poor man, didn't have anything to do with it. I forced him into it, after a fashion, and he's too much a gentleman to betray me. I didn't know where he was at the time the shot was fired, and, for some silly reason, I thought he might be suspected. I took it upon myself to provide him with an alibi, and of course all I did was to get us both into trouble. I'm frightfully sorry!"

"It's not very deep trouble," laughed Hetherton. "Now, then, let's start all over. Tell us where you were when the shot was fired, what you were doing just beforehand, and right after. Ladies first, Mrs. Abbington."

"Very well," complied Mrs. Abbington, drawing her fine eyebrows down in concentration. "I'm glad our little plot failed, because I know I shouldn't have slept a wink for weeks thinking we'd been found out. I should have expected to bump into a policeman every time I started to go out of my apartment. You see, Mr. Hetherton, I had been talking with Dr. Innes. We were standing in the parlor, just off the reception room. The party was all over, and Mr. Flount was going to take me home when I got ready. I left Dr. Innes to go upstairs for my things, and he—well," she said, hesitating with a nervous little smile,

"I'm going to tell the truth now. Dr. Innes went into the library. I stood out in the hall and watched him go in. I was upstairs when I heard the shot, and of course I ran right down. When I heard what had happened and saw Dr. Innes coming out of the library—oh, it was silly of course, but I thought they might suspect him."

"There," said Hetherton, approvingly. "Now that's all straightened out. Now, Doctor, it's your turn."

Dr. Innes looked over at Hand and Gerrity. The expression on his handsome, dark face was one of listlessness and sorrow. "I'm going to tell the truth, too," he declared. "I'm afraid I made a beastly fool of myself last night. You see, I got hold of a little too much champagne. I didn't over-estimate my capacity, either; I did it maliciously. I'm badly broken up, gentlemen," he said, and I noticed for the first time that his hands were shaking. "I—I had become quite fond of Miss Venora. I asked her to marry me—several times recently. She refused to give up her stage career. But I didn't believe her; I thought she was in love with someone else. Last night I seemed to irritate her. She was quite cool to me. So I, like a fool, proceeded to get drunk. I remember saying a lot of wild things to Mrs. Abbington, who very kindly attempted to quiet me down. I don't remember exactly what I said, but I know I told her I'd go to the dogs if Vera—Miss Venora wouldn't have me."

"Were you saying this just before Mrs. Abbington left you to go upstairs?" asked Hetherton.

"Yes, he was," supplied Mrs. Abbington. "It was just nothing but foolishness. Frank was quite tight and full of injured puppy love. Every young man who ever met Vera fell madly in love with her. The only thing I can say against her is that she was a terrific flirt. They all got over it, but at first they thought that because she turned them down, their lives were wrecked."

"All right, Doctor," said Hetherton, "what did you do after Mrs. Abbington left you?"

"I started to go into the library. I did step into it, but then I saw Mr. Garrison and Vera in there."

"Where were they standing?" asked Hand, sharply. Innes was a little startled by the abruptness of the question. "Why," he said, "why, they weren't standing at all. Mr. Garrison was sitting in a chair, and Miss Venora was sitting on the arm of it, talking to him."

"Was it the chair that had a lamp burning beside it?" asked Hand.

"Yes," replied Innes.

"All right," said Hand. "Go on."

"Well," said Innes, collecting his thoughts, "Vera had been avoiding me all evening. I backed right out, and I don't think they saw me at all. Then I went back into the parlor—where I had been when Mrs. Abbington and I were talking. I felt like being alone. I was sitting in there when I heard the shot. It rather sobered me up. Somebody, Flount I guess it was, kept asking Henry King what had happened in the library. I went in there and—and found Vera!"

Innes choked and buried his face in his hands. Mrs. Abbington, with a little cry of compassion, ran over to him and stroked his hair. She looked appealingly to Hetherton.

"Brace up, boy," said the district attorney kindly, as he rose from his chair and crossed over to Dr. Innes. "We won't bother you any more. Stay there until you compose yourself, and then you may go."

"Thank you, sir," said the young man, raising his strained face to Hetherton. "I'm all right. I'm sorry."

He got to his feet, and he and Mrs. Abbington started for the door.

"Oh, Mrs. Abbington," said Hetherton. "If you don't mind, there is something else we should like to look into."

"You—you mean my pistol?" she asked, the color fading from her cheeks.

"Can I help you, Connie?" mumbled Innes, turning back, almost in a daze.

Mrs. Abbington gathered her composure. She smiled and patted the young man on the shoulder. "You run along, Frank," she said. "I'm sure these gentlemen will be very helpful. You go back to the others. Now, Mr. Hetherton, fire away. I'm even more concerned about that pistol than you are."

Dr. Innes, with an uncertain glance over his shoulder, passed through the door. When he had gone, Mrs. Abbington, who had resumed her seat, looked inquiringly at Hetherton.

"Mrs. Abbington," began Hetherton, uncomfortably, "do you—er—do you think you could give us any different opinion concerning this unfortunate affair now? I mean—ah—any different opinion from the one you gave us before."

Mrs. Abbington veiled her blue eyes. "My opinion before, Mr. Hetherton, was not very valuable, because I could not imagine why Miss Venora was shot. I can't yet. There is utterly no reason that I can attribute it to."

"As I said before, these gentlemen have brought to me some new facts. It now appears that, whereas Miss Venora was murdered, Robert Garrison was the intended victim. He escaped death by a hair."

Mrs. Abbington was palpably startled. She showed it by her wide blue eyes, her parted, lovely lips. "Garry!" she gasped, and her beautiful eyes were suddenly suffused with fear.

"Do you know of anyone who might have had reason to wish him harm?"

"Goodness, no!"

"You understand," Hetherton pointed out, "that it will be necessary for us to go into this rather deeply. It is the opinion of Inspector Gerrity and Mr. Hand, an opinion that I hold in the highest regard, that the solution of this case rests almost entirely upon discovering the manner in which your pistol came to be in Robert Garrison's library at the time of the murder. Since, unfortunately, it is your pistol, naturally you are the first person we turn to regarding it."

Dismay settled over Mrs. Abbington's lovely features.

"I—I hadn't realized the seriousness of—of my pistol's being there," she said, jerkily.

"Are you positive that you haven't missed it lately?"

"I—I don't know."

"I don't quite understand."

"I mean, I haven't seen it for a long while."

"You mean that you wouldn't have known whether it had been taken or not?"

Mrs. Abbington nodded, vaguely.

"Very well. But—I want you to think very carefully, Mrs. Abbington. This is an extremely serious matter. If it is possible for you to answer this next question, I want you to do it! Who might have taken your pistol to kill Robert Garrison with it?"

I thought for a moment that Mrs. Abbington was going to faint once more. She swayed for an instant; then quickly recovering herself, she looked piteously at Hetherton. "Oh, dear!" she wailed, "must I tell you everything?"

The district attorney solemnly nodded his head.

"Well," said Mrs. Abbington, averting her face and speaking as with a supreme effort, "you will realize how very painful this is to me. If it was Robert Garrison he intended to kill, perhaps—perhaps I do know who it could have been."

She hesitated, seemingly to gather her strength, and Hetherton interjected a little help. "The information you give us here," he assured her, "will be received with the greatest fairness by all of us. We will consider it, and if in our opinions it is irrelevant, we will straightway forget it. In any case, we will do our best to keep you from unpleasantness."

"Thank you," she murmured in a weak little voice. "There may be others, but there is only one person whom I can suspect of wishing harm to Mr. Garrison. That is—"

Her voice trailed off to nothing, and she bit her lip.

"Yes, Mrs. Abbington?" prompted Hetherton.

Mrs. Abbington's shoulders stiffened. From then on she spoke in a rapid, clear, strained voice. "I suspect my husband. He would be capable of it—now. He was once a gentleman, or at least I thought he was, but now he is a drink-soddened, malicious fiend. He tried to drag me down with him into the baseness that has claimed him. Thank God, I was too strong for him. I would have dropped from sight, however, had it not been for Robert Garrison. My husband squandered the fortune his father left him; then he began to make inroads upon my small fortune. I was frantic. I loved him, and he loved me; but his love had turned to something—something that I could not understand, except to know that it was dangerous. In my desperation I turned to Garry—Mr. Garrison. He advised me, for Wally's sake as well as my own, to separate from him. He thought if Wally were thrown on his own, it would straighten him out. Mr. Garrison, wonderful friend that he is, took what money I had left and invested it. He has made it grow until now I have quite a substantial income. He positively refuses, though, to allow me to make any advances to Wally."

"Did your husband seek money from you?"

"Many times. At first he tried to keep up appearances, but lately he has been terribly unkempt. He has," she said, twisting her colorless lips into a brave little smile, "gone quite to the puppies."

"Has he ever caused a disturbance?

"Yes, he has. At first he appealed to my sympathy, but when that failed, he staged several ghastly scenes in my apartment. After that he threatened to humiliate me. Oh, he has utterly no pride left! At length, on Garry's insistence, as well as that of one or two of my other wonderful friends, I had to refuse to see him. The last time he came," she said, her voice becoming even more strained, "I had to have the doorman put him out.

"Have you attempted to divorce him?"

"I—I have been persuaded to."

"Mr. Garrison?"

"Yes, as well as some others. The action has just been started."

"Does your husband know of the manner in which Mr. Garrison has influenced you?"

"Yes. Yes, he knows that."

"Does he resent it?"

"Y-yes."

Hetherton leaned across the desk, alert, tense. "Mrs. Abbington," he asked, evenly, "will you tell us whether your husband ever made a threat against Mr. Garrison's life?"

The young woman raised her harassed eyes to the district attorney. "He never did," she said. "If he had, I would tell you."

"He could have got possession of your pistol, couldn't he?"

"I don't know," she replied, dismally. "He might have."

Hetherton plucked a pencil from his pocket, snatched a piece of paper, and glanced over at Mrs. Abbington. "What is your husband's full name, and where is he living at present?"

"Wallace Hyatt Abbington," she replied, tonelessly. "I have his address here," she said, extracting a card from her purse. She turned it in her fingers, glanced at some writing on the back of it, and handed it over to Hetherton.

"I think that is all," said the district attorney.

"Pardon me, Hetherton," said Hand, stepping forward. "If you don't mind, and if Mrs. Abbington doesn't mind," he added, smiling kindly at her, "I should like to clear up just one point. Mrs. Abbington, are you a frequent visitor at the Garrison home?"

"Oh, yes indeed."

"Did you frequently visit the library there?"

"Yes, yes indeed," she replied, wonderingly. "You see, Mr. Garrison insisted that I keep posted on my financial affairs. Although he did as he liked with my money, and I was only too happy that he should, he insisted explaining all my affairs to me. Whenever he made a transaction for me, he would take me off to the library and tell me all about it. I enjoyed it, too; it was so very interesting."

"Thank you, Mrs. Abbington," said Hand, by stepping back signifying that he had no more questions to put to her.

"Do you wish to see any of the others?" asked Hetherton, glancing at Hand and Gerrity.

The pair exchanged one of their understanding glances. "No," replied the inspector. "I think you should tell them to go home."

Hetherton, in his courtliest manner, ushered Mrs. Abbington into the waiting-room. He returned in a moment, closed the door, and resumed his seat behind the desk. "Well?" he said, expectantly.

"Here's another twist," said Gerrity. "We've got to nail Wallace Hyatt Abbington right away! What do you think, Hand?"

Hand, leaning against the wall, shifted his position. "I think you're right," he grunted. "The fellow, no doubt, has drunk himself into a state of aberration. Such people

too weak to place the blame for their downfall upon themselves, fasten the cause of their wretchedness upon those
nearest to them. It's more than possible that Abbington
is obsessed with the insane opinion that his wife and her
benefactor conspired to ruin him."

"Yes, by thunder!" cried Gerrity, smiting the desk with
his huge fist. "He shot at Garrison through the window,
intending to kill him, and then dropped the pistol into the
room to incriminate his wife. A pretty plot! But it didn't
work. I got the significance of the question you asked his
wife, too. He probably knew she was in the habit of being
alone in the library with Garrison. In that darkened room
he probably thought she was with him when he shot at
him. That would have made the plot perfect—she alone
with him, and her pistol the one that shot him. We're getting there. We're getting there!" he said, excitedly. "If we
can nab this fellow the case is complete!"

"Not too fast, Inspector," cautioned Hand. "How about
Spitz and Spawn?"

Gerrity's bubble of jubilation was instantly pricked.
"Oh, yes," he said; almost groaned. Then, with a recovery
of his enthusiasm: "Say, maybe Spitz and Abbington are
one and the same person!"

"I hope so," said Hand, fervently. "That would make
it easier. As you say, Inspector, the case has had a twist.
Let"s go out and see how great a twist it is."

7

THE BEST-LAID PLANS—

Daylight had broken when we left Hetherton's office. As we climbed into the police car, I noted the hour, six thirty. We had not far to go. At six forty we were standing before the mean doorway in Avenue B near East Sixth Street that constituted the address Mrs. Abbington had given us.

"Upstairs, eh?" said Gerrity, peering up the dark staircase inside the door. "Some difference between Mr. Abbington and his wife."

Gerrity had armed himself with a warrant. Pugnaciously, the warrant in his hand, he mounted the creaking stairs. Presently we were standing in a dark, evil-smelling hallway. The odor of cooking food, although not very appetizing, served to remind me that I had been up all night without nourishment.

With a quick glance round at the several doors that opened into the hallway, Gerrity strode up to one and banged imperiously on it. Thirty seconds later it was opened by a burly fellow, backed up by a slovenly woman. The man fixed the inspector with an annoyed stare.

"Man named Abbington live here?" demanded Gerrity.

A long, substantial arm was protruded from the doorway. It pointed to a door directly across the hall. With a grunt, Gerrity walked over to the door and rapped on it. Getting no answer, he rapped again. After a few seconds' wait, he twisted the knob. The door opened, and he passed through, followed by Hand and me.

Abbington's quarters were not even modest; they were mean. A quick glance showed us that the room was empty. The furniture consisted of an iron bed, a chair that I should not have cared to trust my weight to, a small table, and a lop-sided chest of drawers. On the table stood an empty gin bottle and a glass.

Simultaneously we espied a note, scribbled on a dirty piece of paper, lying on the table beside the bottle. We all edged over and peered at it. It read: *"Sam—Be back at seven."*

"Huh," growled Gerrity. "Well, by the time he gets back, if he ever does, I'm going to know what's in those drawers, and everything else there is to know about this residence of his."

He banged the third of the four drawers shut, remarking that Abbington was not endowed with much in the way of worldly goods. The fourth drawer he peered into for several moments. Finally he reached into it. When he withdrew his hand, he held in his fingers a rather large photograph. He held it up, and I saw that it was the picture of an imposing, elderly man.

"I seem to recognize that picture," said Gerrity, looking hard at the photograph. "That face is familiar."

"I dare say it is," said Hand. "That is the late Arthur Hyatt Abbington. The banker, you know. By Jove, I wonder whether this young fellow is his son. He had a son. The old man would rise from his grave if he knew the boy was living here."

With a shake of his head, Hand turned to the table. He reached under its edge and pulled open a drawer. From it he took, gingerly with the tips of his fingers, a thirty-two-caliber automatic. He carried it over to the uncurtained window.

"If the finger-prints on this gun," he said, "are the same as those on the window-pane we took from Garrison's library, I'm prepared to say that Abbington also goes under the name of Spitz, sometimes."

"Quiet!" warned Gerrity.

The stairs outside were squeaking. A moment later there came a soft rap on the door. Gerrity, striding over to it, yanked it open. Framed in the door stood a short, roly-poly fellow carrying a black bag. His small eyes flew open, and a lugubrious expression of dismay enveloped his round features.

"I'll bet that's Sam," said Hand, suddenly. "Come in, we'll shut the door after you."

The little man had other ideas. He turned to go. Gerrity, closing his ham-like hand on his shoulder, popped him into the room and shut the door.

"Vat's da mattah, shentlemens?" cried our startled guest.

"Is your name Sam?" demanded Hand.

It was, by the way he nodded his head.

"What are you doing here?" asked Gerrity, ominously.

Sam swallowed hard once or twice. "I shust come oop to see Mr. Abbingdon," he whined. "Vat's da mattah with that? Ain'd I got no right—"

"What's in that bag?" snapped Gerrity.

"Noddings, noddings!" cried Sam, in alarm. "Socks, neckties, noddings else."

"Let's see it," growled Gerrity, roughly snatching the bag. Sam, because he did not let go, went with the bag. With a desperate effort he re-established his equilibrium; then he volubly demanded possession of his property. His demands petered out as Gerrity lifted a bottle of gin from the bag.

Sam backed away. "Vell?" he said, apprehensively.

"Vell!" mimicked Gerrity, explosively. "You two-bit bootlegger, you! You would walk into this just at the wrong time, wouldn't you? What are we going to do with him, Hand?"

"Kick him out," growled Hand. "No, wait a minute. Abbington will be coming back soon; this fellow might warn him. Let's see," he said, crossing over to a door in the wall. He opened it and revealed a small, empty closet.

"Get in there, you," he ordered Sam.

"And take this blasted bag with you," further directed the inspector. He shoved the bag against Sam's generous mid-section with such force that the man's legs nearly buckled under him. "In you go," he growled. "That gin's safe enough with you; you would drink it because you probably know what's in it. Now keep your mouth shut, understand!"

He slammed the door on the quaking bootlegger.

Hand glanced at his watch. "Almost seven," he said "I hope our friend is punctual."

"He will be," sniffed Gerrity. "He wouldn't take a chance of missing his bootlegger."

As it proved, he was right. A few minutes later we heard the protesting squeak of the stairs again. All three of us stepped aside to be out of sight when the door opened. Presently it swung inward and stopped, half open. Thus it remained for a moment; then it swung farther open.

A man, clad in a shabby dark blue suit, a weatherbeaten hat on his head, stepped slowly into the room. He uttered a heavy sigh. Standing with his back to us, he surveyed the room. He was a tall man. Evidently he had lost much weight recently, for his coat hung from his shoulders like the sails of a ship becalmed at sea. As he turned to close the door, he caught sight of us. The face that he turned slowly toward us was hollow and white. It was hard to tell that it was a young face. His eyes, surmounted by fine brows, were sunken and bloodshot. His loose lips were bloodless, and his cheeks and chin were covered with a stubble of beard. Only his nose, finely molded and aristo-cratic, retained anything that proclaimed this man the scion of one of our first families.

He did not seem surprised. Slowly he smiled, and with the smile much of the dissolute appearance of his face seemed to vanish. "Good morning, gentlemen," he said, with an elaborate bow. "To put the cart before the horse, I am delighted to have you welcome me to my humble abode. I can't ask you to step into the drawing-room, be-cause there is no drawing-room. The servants, too, have all gone for the day."

This was not the man I had expected to find. To be sure, my first sight of him had fulfilled my expectations. But there was something rather winning about him, something debonair shining through his pitiful exterior. Now I could understand his wife's retaining a shred of feeling for him.

"Mr. Abbington?" asked Gerrity, gruffly.

"At your service," he replied, again with the elaborate bow and the boyish smile. "And you, my dear sirs, are from the police. How nice!"

"Might I ask how you know that?" demanded Gerrity, a bit disconcerted.

Smilingly, Abbington raised his hand, holding, I saw for the first time, a newspaper rolled into a cylinder. With a flip of his hand he unrolled it and with a grandiloquent gesture indicated its screaming headlines.

"The press has heralded you," he cried. "My charming wife being involved, I knew you would soon be waiting on me, you see. Before we go into that, though, tell me some-thing. I am expecting a man, a little pumpkin of a man, a friend, I suppose, since he brings me solace. Have you seen such an one?"

"Never mind your pumpkin man," growled Gerrity.

"Oh, very well," said Abbington, dismissing the matter with a wave of his hand. "Before we go into the grilling, you had better take possession of my arsenal. You'll find it in the drawer of that table over there. It's been a harmless article while I've had it. I can't even shoot myself with it; I've tried."

"We've got it," said Gerrity, trying to be rough, and failing. "Sit down, son, there are a few things we want to find out. Now, then, where did you spend the night last night?"

Abbington took Gerrity's invitation, or command, and sought the chair. He was either fatigued or drunk. He thumped down upon the chair, nearly dislodging his hat by the jar. He carefully removed the soiled head-piece, revealing a mop of uncombed black hair, and laid it on the table. Crumpling up the note he had left for Sam, he tossed it on the floor. Then he turned his bloodshot eyes upon the inspector. "Of course I assume you are from the police," he said. "But—"

His pause suggested that we identify ourselves. Gerrity displayed his badge.

"Inspector, eh?" grinned Abbington. "I must say, I'm being signally honored. I had expected a sergeant of detectives, at best. I'm not wholly acquainted with police methods; my sole education in that line being in connection with traffic regulations. Suppose I give you an account of myself; then you can take exception to it afterwards. How's that?"

"Go on," said Gerrity, shortly.

"This murder," began Abbington, "according to my copy of the *Herald,* took place about one fifteen this morning. I'll delve into my past even further than that. To begin with, I supped at Monte's. You'll notice Monte's as you go out, on the corner just below here. Monte's service and cuisine are far from the best, but he's modest as to price and generous with credit. That was about seven o'clock. At eight I was back here, having a few drinks with my neighbor across the way. He's a taciturn sort, but a quart or so of gin will usually move him to espouse the cause of Communism. He was not able to get into form, however, because we ran out of gin. He left me then, and I went out for a walk. My steps took me to the docks; a fellow is not so apt to meet his old, tried and true friends there. And then, as the saying goes, I fell in with evil companions."

Abbington grinned.

"One of them a chap sometimes known as Spawn, by any chance?" asked the inspector, cocking an alert eye at the young man.

"Spawn?" repeated Abbington, with an exaggerated pensive expression. "Odd name, that. No, I'm afraid none of my evil companions was named Spawn. On the other hand, they might have all been Spawns. I didn't and I still don't know any of them except by their first names. There was Soapy, Blink, One Eye, and Dan. The stuff they had with them, and which, generous fellows, they shared with me, was sufficient to make a whole herd of elephants dance the highland fling, even if administered in small quantities."

"I suppose," said Inspector Gerrity, with utterly no credulity, "you are going to tell us you passed out down at the docks and remained there in that condition until early this morning."

"By no means, my dear fellow," declared Abbington, raising his hands in protest. "The fact remains, however, that I was down at the docks with my convivial companions when your murder was committed. It was not until three o'clock that I returned to these elegantly appointed quarters of mine."

"Suppose you were careful to look at your watch?" sneered Gerrity.

"My watch," grinned Abbington, "allegorically speaking, has been drunk up weeks ago. I noticed the time on the clock in Monte's window. It is ten minutes slow. Let's see, yes, ten minutes slow. It loses fifteen minutes a week. I set it each Sunday morning—if I'm up."

"So you came back here at three o'clock, and here you stayed until this morning."

Abbington's grin broadened, showing fine, even, white teeth. "The perception of a police inspector passeth all understanding," he intoned.

"Never mind the perception of a police inspector," growled Gerrity. "What are you doing up so early if you got to bed at three o'clock?"

"Blessed little," sighed Abbington. "I was after a drink. There stands the bottle that Flink and I were at last night, empty. My regular source, the little pumpkin of man I was asking about, was not at home when I got there. I left word with his wife to send him along with some of his socks and neckties when he got back. Then I returned here. I just ask you to notice how detailed this account is, by the way. Then I realized I could go no further without the usual bacon and eggs. I have just returned from Monte's, where the bacon and eggs were consumed on credit. My little pumpkin of a man extends me credit, too."

"How do you ever satisfy that credit?" asked Gerrity.

Abbington winked a red-rimmed eye. "I am a professional man, a man of letters," he said, with a short, mirthless laugh. "Letters is quite correct, about four of them a day. Letters dunning for money, letters ordering goods and complaining about the last shipment. Letters explaining, ah, very adroitly, why the last shipment was not paid for and how it will be paid for in a week or ten days. More letters explaining, also very adroitly, why the payment was not made at the end of the promised week or ten days, and how it will be paid at the end of another week or ten days, provided, of course, that the last order of goods is shipped so that the money can be made. I average fifty cents a let-ter," he informed us, with mock pride.

"So," said Gerrity, summing up, "you ate at this hash-house at seven; came back here and killed a bottle of gin with the fellow next door; went out and got soused with a lot of bums on the dock, came back here again at three o'clock; slept a matter of three hours; went out looking for your bootlegger; didn't find him and came back here again; went out for breakfast; and at last came back here to find us waiting for you."

"My word," breathed Abbington, "that's putting it con-cisely. You have it perfectly correct, however, Inspector."

"Maybe!" snapped Gerrity. "Now, young fella," he snarled, poking his ferocious countenance to within six inches of Abbington's white, dissolute face, "I'm going to tell you what you did. In the first place you stole your wife's pistol! That was some time ago. As for last night, I've no doubt you went out and got drunk, but not with the bums on the docks. Then you called your wife's apart-ment and learned she was at Garrison's house. You had a scheme in that evil, drunken brain of yours! You went to Garrison's house and sneaked round to the library win-dows. You dug a pane of glass out with your knife and waited. Pretty soon Garrison came into the library with a woman, and you thought it was your wife. You stuck your hand through the window and aimed your wife's pistol at Garrison. You were too drunk to make a good job of it; Garrison stepped aside and you shot the girl, who wasn't your wife at all. Then you dropped that blasted pistol inside the room and streaked for the rear. You tripped over a little wire fence and smashed your head into the trunk of a fir-tree. When you came round, the police were all over the place. One of 'em came over to the tree you were under and you let him have it—let him have it with the gun we found in that drawer, didn't you, you mutt! Let him have it without warning! Then you made your get-away in a car you got somewhere. If you tell me that isn't right I'll smash your blasted face in!"

Abbington blinked at Gerrity's blazing eyes. Either he had no fear or he had reached that stage where nothing matters. He grinned. "Sounds like a movie thriller," he remarked, dryly.

"One minute, Inspector," said Hand, who up to then had taken no part in the proceedings.

His intervention, I knew, was occasioned by the choleric condition of the back of Gerrity's neck, presented to us as he bent over Abbington. Gerrity, bred in the police school, always resorted to violence when an investigation reached the stage to which we had brought this one. Hand never forgot to be clever.

"Mr. Abbington," he said, quite suavely as compared to the inspector's roarings, "you seem to be a young man of some intelligence. You will see, I am sure, that for you to be candid at this point will gain you far more than an attempt at elusiveness. To be quite frank with you, I think you have brooded to the extent that you are far from yourself. I think that you lost your reason temporarily last night. In such cases the perpetrator of a crime is by no means in a hopeless situation. There are cases on record of men who, having killed while in the grip of temporary dementia, have been cured and later set quite at liberty."

"So," said Abbington, with a much soberer countenance, "you think I went off my bean last night and tried to fill Garrison full of holes?"

"We know it," replied Hand smoothly. "You see, you left your finger-prints on the pane of glass. They are also on your wife's gun; also on the one we found in your table drawer. They have also been found at your hide-out in East End Avenue. So you see you can't hope to escape detection. The story you tell us now will have the greatest weight of any. I've been through many a case such as this, and I can tell you that the straighter the story you tell now, the more chance you will have. It's hard for you to see that now, I know, but you will later on."

For a moment I thought Hand had won. Abbington's chin sank to his chest. His eyebrows came down in a straight line over his nose, and he chewed at his under lip almost desperately.

A silence quite terrific was shattered by a piercing scream from within the closet. We stood there galvanized. The closet door burst open and swung back with a shivering crack against the wall. Sam, eyes extended whitely, mouth agape with horror, literally flew from the closet. He clutched his precious bag under his arm. His round, compact body smote Inspector Gerrity in the curve of his back was hurled to his hands and knees. Sam, like an acrobat, balanced for a moment with arms and legs in the air on the inspector's broad back. His bag had flown from his grasp, striking the wall opposite the closet. It descended to the floor at the same instant as its owner.

Gerrity gasped desperately for his lost breath. Sam stared dismally at his bag. It took no such prolonged glance to tell that it was leaking furiously. Sam raised his hands and spread his pudgy fingers in an eloquent gesture of deep grief.

The inspector got shakily to his feet. "What in—damnation—is the blasted—idea?" he gasped.

Sam, the cause of his horror recalled, leaped up beside the inspector. He pointed wildly into the dark recess of the closet. "Th-there's an a-animal in there!" he chattered.

As if called forth to bear witness, an animal appeared for an instant, timidly, on the threshold. Then it scampered back into the gloom.

"A mouse!" howled Gerrity, after the manner of an injured bull. "A mouse! You blithering blatherskate, you stove me in on account of a mouse! I'll put you away for this!"

On a face less lugubrious, Sam's distress would certainly have evoked pity in the coldest heart. His hands were beyond expressing his emotions. They fluttered up, but then fell resignedly to his side.

"I think," said Hand, "we have had this fellow's company far too long. Let's bid him adieu, Inspector. There's nothing much you can hold him on, anyway; your evidence against him is all seeping through the floor. You can't convict a man on a lot of broken bottles, you know."

"You might," I suggested, in a voice strained from repressed laughter, "you might charge him with atrocious assault and battery, Gerrity."

"I'd rather charge him with dynamite!" spat the inspector. "Get out of here, you—you cannon-ball! If I wasn't so busy, I'd railroad you!"

He took a threatening step toward Sam, sufficient to send the little man scurrying out of my life forever.

"Well," said Hand, turning once more to Abbington, "now that the interruptions are over, are you ready to tell your story, my boy?"

"I'd rather let you provide the entertainment," replied Abbington, weak from unkind laughter. "Lord, I haven't laughed so much in months!"

"Shut up!" snapped Gerrity. "Will you talk now or later?"

"Later."

"All right, you're out of the letter-writing business. You're going to the Tombs. If it hadn't been for that blasted mouse—"

8

CLEARING THE SMOKE

Abbington was lodged in the Tombs. Inspector Gerrity went to his office, there to set the huge wheels of the police department into motion on the new angle of the case. Hand left to see his client. I returned to our rooms. Fortified with a breakfast, I peeled off my clothes and fell into bed.

I awoke to find Hand's angular form towering above my bedside. "W-what time is it?" I yawned.

"Noon," he grunted. "The inspector and I are going to hold a conference. Thought you might like to sit in on it."

"Give me a minute for a cold shower," I pleaded, hopping out of bed wide awake.

When I emerged into the living-room the floor was a mountain range of untidy newspapers. Hand's long legs were balanced on the edge of the table. The rest of him, enveloped in his easy chair, was completely obscured by a copy of the *Morning Herald*.

"Ready?" he cried, tossing the paper among its fellows.

He was out of the room before I had picked up my hat and coat. I caught up with him on the curb, just in time to climb into the taxi he had hailed.

"I see the newspapers are making hay while the sun shines," I observed. "I suppose, as usual, you've been making yourself unpopular with the scribes."

"All but Garthwaite," he grinned.

Hand has a private arrangement with Garthwaite, the best man on the *Herald*. Garthwaite's stories frequently are the most complete ones to appear first on the street. Hand's name never appears in them, but there is always much reference to Inspector Gerrity. Gerrity, I am aware, secretly wonders at this. He often wonders, too, how it is that Garthwaite knows so much about a baffling case. It is generally believed among the newspaper fraternity that Garthwaite is very close to Gerrity. The truth of it is that Gerrity hardly knows the reporter at all.

Smiling Sergeant Tim ushered us into Gerrity's office. Tim was never to be found far from the inspector. By the expression of Gerrity's blue eyes when he raised them to us, all had not gone as he desired. With an impatient gesture he ruffled a pile of papers on the desk before him. "I hope you have better news than I have," he growled.

Hand and I drew chairs up to the desk.

"Let's hear the worst," said Hand.

"Abbington's and Spitz's finger-prints don't check," complained Gerrity, as if that were somebody's fault. "At least, Abbington's finger-prints are certainly not those left on the pane of glass. We can't find his finger-prints on his wife's pistol, either. And here's another blow," he added with emphasis, "there are finger-prints on that pistol, plenty of 'em, but the finger-prints of the man who moved the pane of glass are not among them!"

"Hum-m, that is a blow," agreed Hand. "Yes, that upsets a number of calculations. We're in the dark, of course, with but a few glowing lights to guide us. I'd be willing to swear, though, that those lights illuminate the picture sufficiently to show us the man who removed the window-pane firing that pistol. On the other hand, it's inconceivable that he would be so careless as to leave his finger-prints all over the glass and then put on gloves to keep them off the pistol. Did you get any prints at the East End Avenue house?"

"Plenty of 'em," replied Gerrity, swinging round on his swivel chair to gaze at the window with a disgruntled stare. "Nobody stays long in that room our two friends were in. They were there three days, and in the space of the past month, Blake found out, there have been four other tenants in it. They did find, though, a set of finger-prints that match those on the window-pane."

"That's something," said Hand, in the same even tone he always utters. But I could see by the gleam in his eye that the information was more than welcome. "That establishes a very important point, Inspector," he added. "We are now positive that Spitz was at the window and was the one who removed the glass. He must have fired the shot. Sad as it may be, he is not Abbington. See what I have here."

He took from his pocket a small leather case. Opening it, he extracted several curious glass slides. These, seven in all, he ranged in a row upon the top of the desk.

Gerrity hung his head over the slides for a moment, then he peered inquiringly at Hand. "What's the idea?" he demanded.

My friend's thin lips broke into a smile. "More finger-prints for you," he said. "It's an idea I've been waiting to put into use. Gives people the chance to supply you with a specimen of their finger-prints unconsciously. In the center of each of these slides you will see a sort of blur. In reality it is a portion of a gnat's wing, semi-transparent, glued to the glass. Looks mysterious, that's all. I look mysterious, too, when I hand one of these slides to someone and ask him whether he's ever seen it before. I hold it by pressing my finger-tips to its edges. My unsuspecting victim, however, grasps it by pressing his fingers to the flat of the glass. First he holds it to his right eye and inspects it carefully. The result is that he is only more mystified than ever. He hands it back, but I offer it to him again with the suggestion that he inspect it with his left eye. In that way he has used both hands on it. In the end, he is profoundly puzzled, and I have the prints of most of his fingers."

"Pretty complicated way of getting them."

"Yes, but sometimes it is helpful to have a man's finger-prints without his realizing it. I must admit that I tried this out pretty much as an experiment. I dare say any one of those people would have willingly supplied me with his finger-prints had I asked for them. Fortunately, they were all gathered at Garrison's house when I got there. King was the only one who saw through it."

"Why, they're nothing but glass, aren't they?"

"I don't mean the glass, Inspector; I mean the deception. I got him off by himself, as I did the others, and gave him his slide. He peered at it with his right eye, all right. When I handed it back to have a look at it with his left eye, he laughed, placed the glass flat on the table, and pressed the fingers of his left hand to it. 'There you are,' he said. 'Now you have a much better set of fingerprints.' That's his, right there; see how broad the prints are where he pressed his fingers to it? This is Flount's; you can see how daintily he held it. Each plate has a number etched in the corner, and I remember who held each one. Let's have your men compare them with the prints on the pistol. Mrs. Abbington's, at least, should be there."

Gerrity pressed a button on his desk. When Tim opened the door, he asked to see one of the Bertillon men. While we waited, he picked up two or three of the slides. Holding them up to the window, he looked through them. "Pretty good," he chuckled.

The door opened to admit Saunders, one of the best finger-print experts in the department.

"Still working on that gun, Saunders?" asked the inspector.

"Yes, sir," he replied. "I can give you a different report on it now, or, rather, a changed one. We found some prints that check up with Abbington's."

"You did!" cried Gerrity, half rising from his chair.

"Yes, sir. They aren't very good, and perhaps they wouldn't stand up in court. They're pretty well obliterated by other marks on top of them."

"Oh," said Gerrity, settling back with a disappointed mien into his chair. "Where were they? Could they have been made when he held the pistol to fire it?"

"Don't think so, sir. They were on the barrel. They're pretty faint and are pretty well rubbed off anyway. They're his, though."

"Haven't found any like his on the window-glass?"

"No, sir, I'll swear his are not on that."

"Well, Saunders, here are some more to compare with 'em," said Gerrity.

He carefully piled Hand's glass slides on top of each other. Using both hands, he held them out to Saunders.

"Pay particular attention to number four," said Hand. "That's Dr. Innes's," he explained to us.

Saunders carried the slides away with him. When he had gone, Hand turned to Gerrity. "What else, Inspector?" he asked.

"Well," replied Gerrity, "we've found that roadster. Abandoned down by the Brooklyn Bridge. Belongs to a chap by the name of Alfred Henderson. He's a respectable accountant, and he was home last night. He reported the car stolen yesterday afternoon at the sixth precinct. He has some bullet-holes in it now to remember the experience by. And, Hand, there were blood stains in that car. The fellow was hit, all right."

"Yes; no doubt of that. But the car doesn't tell much. I hardly thought it would, unless the pair were in it when it was found. What did you find out about the inmates of the East End Avenue house?"

"Found out plenty about all of 'em except that Spitz and Spawn pair. Spitz has never been arrested here, because we haven't his finger-prints. At least, we haven't found them so far—still working on it. The others in the house don't amount to anything. A couple of them have been in for small offenses. Not a desperate character in the lot."

"Well, anyway they have pasts that are tangible. Spitz and Spawn seem to have dropped out of thin air to plague us. Couldn't get a line on either of them, eh?"

"Not a thing. Nobody knows where they came from, or where they went, which is worse. The fellows are still working on them, of course."

"Maybe they did come from Germany," mused Hand. "That coin, you know."

"Maybe they came from most any place," growled Gerrity. "I'm checking up with the Ellis Island records, anyhow.

We were interrupted by Tim, who, after a sharp rap on the door, advanced into the room. He handed Gerrity a long, white envelope.

"Ah, here's Professor Hertzog's report," he cried, snatching the envelope from Tim's fingers. "Now we'll find out about that bullet."

Tearing open the flap of the envelope, he produced a typewritten sheet of paper. As he quickly read it, his eager expression melted into one of perplexity. When he read it, he tossed it over to Hand; then he settled back into a gloomy reverie. My friend read it through with inscrutable countenance. Then he handed the letter to me. I took it eagerly and read the following:

Dear Inspector:

After a careful microscopic inspection of the bullet submitted to me by Lieutenant Gannon (at your instruction after it had been extracted from the body of Vera Venora deceased) and a painstaking comparison of the fatal bullet with two others fired from the pistol bearing the name Constance Abbington on its barrel, I am now ready to make a report. It is my opinion, concurred in by Major Andrew Dangerfield, U. S. A., who collaborated with me in the examination, that the bullet which killed the deceased was not fired from the Abbington weapon. At my request Lieutenant Gannon (with due regard for the finger-prints on the weapon) discharged two of the bullets in the cylinder of the pistol into the pad in my laboratory. The rifling creases on the two bullets fired in my laboratory coincide perfectly with each other, of course, but neither of them bears resemblance to the creases on the bullet taken from the body of the deceased. The only similarity between the bullets fired from the Abbington gun and the murder bullet is that they are of the same manufacture (Remington) and the same caliber (thirty-two). Both Major Dangerfield and I are convinced that the murder bullet was not fired from the Abbington pistol.

I make this informal report in accordance with our telephone conversation of this morning, and hope that I have not held you up too long with it. We wished, however, to make as exhaustive an examination as possible. The importance of the people involved in this unfortunate affair impressed us with the desirability of eliminating every possibility of an error in our findings. We will submit to you a report in full detail very shortly.

I glanced at my companions. Hand sat on the small of back, legs spread wide at either side of the desk folded, and chin sunk on his chest. Gerrity had taken to pacing up and down the room. Finally he stopped and glared down at the top of my friend's head.

"Well," he growled, as if Hand were to blame for the latest development. "Well, what do you make of this?" he demanded, leaning over and banging his fist on the obnoxious report where I had laid it on the desk.

Hand, at the risk of slipping to the floor, stirred in his chair. "I make of this," he said, "what I had hoped was not the case. I was afraid of this."

"You were afraid of it?" asked Gerrity, incredulously.

"Yes. There was something vital missing in the evidence that supported our former theory. We assumed the murderer shot Miss Venora with Mrs. Abbington's pistol and then dropped the pistol into the library to incriminate its owner. The pane of glass that was removed from the window is a good four feet off the floor. If the pistol had been dropped from there it would certainly have made a dent in the polished floor."

Gerrity once more seated himself, slowly, like a man whose brain is at grips with a problem. Finally he nodded his head. "That's right," he agreed. "You're sure there wasn't such a dent?" he asked, glancing sharply at Hand.

"Positive. The rug extends no nearer than three feet from the wall under the window. I looked very carefully for such a dent. There wasn't one."

"Then how in blazes did that pistol get there?" cried Gerrity, suddenly leaning forward across the desk. "It wasn't used to commit the murder, and it wasn't thrown into the room by the murderer. What connection has it with the blasted murder, anyway?"

"My opinion of its connection with the murder remains unaltered," replied Hand, slowly shaking his head. "It's not its connection with the murder that's bothering me; I still think it was put there to incriminate its owner. But it becomes evident now that it was placed in the library by someone *in the house.*"

"By Jove, that's right!" cried Gerrity. "Someone in the house," he mused, once more pacing the floor. "Who could it be?"

Once more we were interrupted. Following his solitary rap on the door, Tim stalked into the office again. "They got the feller they picked up down at the flop-house out here, sir," he said.

"Who's in charge of him?" snapped Gerrity.

"Sergeant Stuart, sir."

"Tell Stuart to step in here," ordered Gerrity. Then, turning to Hand: "This fellow is supposed to be one of the bums Abbington was drinking with last night. Hello, Stuart, how did you make out?"

"Not much one way or the other, sir," replied the sergeant who had replaced Tim. "This guy's a regular 'bo. The only name I can get out of him is One Eye, which is just what he's got, one eye. He's been up for vagrancy and intoxication so often he ain't had a chance to see the Empire State Buildin' yet. We put Abbington in a line-up and this guy couldn't pick him out. He says, though, that he and some other bums were drinkin' down on the docks last night where Abbington says he was. He says maybe another guy did get in the party, but he was so lit up he don't remember. They were drinkin' smoke; we found some of it on him. He's sufferin' from alcoholism right now."

"Could you find any of the rest of the gang?" asked Gerrity.

"One," grinned Stuart. "We got him at the morgue. He took just one drink too many and fell in the river. One of the launches fished him out this mornin'. I tell you, Inspector, if Abbington was on that little tea-party last night, he'd oughta be in worse shape than he is right now."

"I know it," growled Gerrity. "Do you want to see One Eye, Hand?"

"I think I'll forgo the pleasure," smiled my friend.

"All right, Stuart, lock him up," ordered Gerrity. "When we follow a lead," he said ruefully, "we just seem to trip ourselves up. Unless we can find someone in that drinking-bout last night who was sober enough to know whether Abbington was there, he's got an alibi we'll have trouble to shake."

"I think it extremely improbable that you'll find any more," Hand gave as his opinion, "unless they all fell into the river but One Eye. The others are probably all on freight trains headed in every direction. The word passes along very rapidly down there."

"Well, let Abbington go for the present, blast him!" said Gerrity. "Let's get back to the pistol. How about the servants?"

"Of course, it's possible one of the servants planted that gun. It was pretty carefully hidden under the curtain so that it wouldn't be found until after the murder had been committed, you see. You can't very well arrest all the servants right now, but we should investigate each one very carefully. I understand from Tim that each one was finger-printed this morning."

"Yes; but I didn't like to do it to Garrison and the others. Even the help put up the deuce of a row over it. We have the finger-prints of the others now, anyway, with that trick stunt of yours."

"We have more than that. I looked them all up this morning. I suppose you've been at that, too. I bumped into your men once or twice."

"I have a report on every one of them. Not very complete yet, though."

"All right, this is what we'll do. I'll give you what information I've gleaned. You check it with your reports and supplement it wherever possible."

"Good! Fire away. Who's first?"

"We'll take Garrison first," began Hand, as Gerrity selected from among his papers the report on the man. "We won't have to go into his past very deeply; it's too well known as it is. Born in the city; old New York family; father noted financier before him; club man; sportsman; first wife died ten years ago; no children, married Dorothy Devore, musical-comedy star, about a year ago; forty-nine years old; immensely wealthy; agreeable but forceful personality; popular with everybody, including the masses. That do for him?"

"Sure," grinned Gerrity. "Next?"

Hand tilted back his head and quoted from memory. "Mrs. Garrison next. Born twenty-three years ago in Rochester; named Dorothy Dugby; working-class family; orphaned at ten; no brothers or sisters; brought up by uncle, fairly well off, in contracting business, name James Dugby, of Rochester; theatrical education and vocal training; assumed name of Devore when she entered theatrical career at sixteen; well liked by associates both before and after stage success; inclined to be temperamental; popular with set she married into; strong, continuous effort, so far frustrated by her husband, on the part of her old manager, Isidore Gutzbaum, office Forty-ninth Street, to win her back to stage; quite devastatingly beautiful; many admirers. That do for her?"

"Right," grunted Gerrity. "Next?"

"Constance Abbington. Born twenty-eight years ago in Boston; maiden name Smythe; family, once wealthy, now not so rich; private and finishing-school education; popular débutante; married Wallace Hyatt Abbington; stormy married life, ending in separation from profligate husband; taken under the wing of the Garrisons; small fortune enlarged; apparently no enemies, with possible exception of husband; evidently on good terms with deceased. Got anything else on her?"

"I haven't got that much," growled Gerrity. "Where'd you get the dope about her family?"

"She has an old servant," laconically replied my friend. "Next we'll take Miss Dykeman. Born nineteen years ago in San Francisco; came East a year ago to study art; took up Bohemian life and rapidly getting sick of it; father, Ralph Dykeman, is friend of Robert Garrison and asked Garrison to keep an eye on his daughter; is considering giving up art and going home; evidently on good terms with deceased. That's all."

"That's enough," smiled Gerrity. "Next?

"Dr. Innes," announced Hand, rather thoughtfully. "Unusual chap. I haven't discovered much about him. According to himself, he was graduated in three years from Harvard University; M.D. degree from Harvard Medical School three years ago; interned at Bellevue and since has done research work at the foundation here in the city; says he was born in France; parents dead; introduced to Garrison circle by Mrs. Abbington three months ago; known Mrs. Abbington eight months, at the foundation said to be industrious, brilliant, and taciturn; bachelor apartment East Ninety-sixth Street; old French manservant who gives absolutely no information; evidently went quite giddy over Vera Venora as soon he met her, two weeks ago. Got anything else on him?"

"Well, let's see," mused Gerrity, perusing the paper he held in his hand. "He entered this country nine years ago at the age of sixteen. That'd make him twenty-five now. Must be a bright cuss! His parents were Garcia and Maria Innes, Spaniards living in Paris. Before coming over here to study at Harvard, he was educated in England. There's a polyglot history for you. We got that information from the immigration officials. Who's next?"

"Let's take Henry King; we can dispose of him without much trouble. I saw Richard Lessington, his stock-broker. Lessington, although he has conducted a lot of transactions for King, had never met him before he came on four days ago. It seems that King made arrangements with Lessington's father, the late Kenneth Lessington, back in 1914 to handle his financial affairs in Wall Street. According to Lessington, King has been quite a large stockholder ever since. As soon as he got to New York, King more or less foisted himself upon Lessington, who, as you know, is not a tremendously congenial chap. Lessington passed him along to his friend Garrison and was, if I'm any judge of men, most wholesomely relieved when the contact struck fire and the Garrisons took King up. I found Lessington mournfully wondering whether this upheaval would jar King loose from his new friends. That would throw him back upon Lessington, you see. Not that Lessington does not fancy King—he describes him as a likable fellow—but he has no appetite for showing a mid-Westerner the town. I wired an inquiry to the police out in Emporia and requested them to wire a reply immediately to your office. Did you get it?"

Gerrity picked up a yellow telegram form lying on his desk. "Henry King bachelor gentleman farmer," he read. "Left here month ago to travel through East. According to his bank now in New York. Chairman Emporia Community

Chest. One of our best citizens." Gerrity tossed the telegram back on the desk. "There's the answer to your telegram," he said. "If that's all you have on him, I can tell you this much more: he registered four days ago at the Mockridge from Emporia, Kansas. Now, then, what have you got on this little pepper-pot, Archibald Flount?"

"He's immensely wealthy," smiled Hand. "No near relatives; lavish Park Avenue apartment; country home in Port Washington; has a line of degrees after his name a block long; according to himself, a profound thinker; author of the monographs *Bacon versus Shakspere, The Decline of the Social Graces,* and *Man—Still the Brute.* A little bookworm of a fellow, with a dull, self-centered past. Unless you have something further, Inspector, I think that cleans up our biographies of the living. Now let's have an obituary of the dead. Get anything to go on concerning Vera Venora?"

"Nothing, except to check up on Garrison's version of her. The poor kid was all that he said she was. Her right name's Violet Mintz. Lived with her mother. Father's dead."

A rap on the door, followed by Gerrity's barked invitation to come in, produced Saunders in the office. "We checked up on these new prints, sir," he said. "The prints on that number six plate are all over the pistol."

"Not surprising," said Hand. "That's Mrs. Abbington's. Could you find any prints to match those on the other plates?"

"No, sir. There are only three different prints on the pistol. Most of 'em are the same as those on number six plate. Then there are the few faint ones that check up with Abbington's. The third print don't compare with anything we got. They're pretty faint, too, and mostly rubbed off. They're still trying to match those fingerprints on the pane of glass from the files, Inspector. No luck yet."

"All right, Saunders," said Gerrity, dismissing the man with a wave of his hand. "Well, where have we got to?" he grumbled. "We're worse off now than we were before."

"No," disagreed Hand. "I'll admit we haven't constructed anything resembling a case yet, Inspector, but we've cleared away considerable smoke. In my estimation we have made progress. From now on we can look ahead." And then, as if an afterthought: "Should you mind very much if Mr. and Mrs. Garrison and their guests of last night were all to leave town?"

Gerrity glanced sharply over at him. Then he dropped his eyes. There is no one who knows Hand better than Gerrity or I. And after years of association with him, there are only two things that we can be sure of about him: he always has a reason, and he never tells what the reason is.

"No," said Gerrity, at length, "I shouldn't mind at all."

9
PUPPETS

Back at our rooms Hand slumped into his chair, cocked his legs up on the table, and set his pipe a-bubbling.

"Unusual case, Clark," he said to me through the cloud of tobacco smoke that enveloped him. "We have a number of motives, but only one seems strong enough to warrant murder."

"Abbington?" I asked, making myself comfortable in my own chair.

Hand nodded. "I'm inclined to scout the theory, too. If he was the man, he made elaborate plans. Cost him a lot of money. He had to hire the assassin, and he had to bribe someone to plant his wife's pistol in that room. It's just as inconceivable that he was able to bribe someone to plant the gun as it is that he sneaked into the house to do it himself. Where would he get the money to hire an assassin? No, it doesn't ring true to me. If Abbington wanted to kill Garrison, he'd have done it himself."

"I agree with you. How about Dr. Innes? He's a Latin type. Hot-headed, probably. Unrequited love will drive a man to almost anything."

"To build a case against Dr. Innes we must abandon the theory that Garrison was the intended victim. We must assume that in drunken desolation the man decided that if he couldn't have the girl, nobody else would, and all that rot. Hardly possible, Clark. In the first place, this crime was carefully premeditated. Although it actually didn't, it was supposed to work with a deadly precision. Besides, a man driven to distraction by unrequited love usually shoots himself along with his victim, or else doesn't care what happens to him afterwards. He'd only known the girl two weeks; a man of his intelligence would make a better stab at winning her. But the greatest stumbling-block is Spitz. He was certainly there, he was certainly armed, and he certainly removed the pane of glass. It could have been a coincidence," he said, his voice trailing off into a thoughtful silence. And then: "But no, that's altogether too far-fetched."

"Again I agree with you. King, Flount, and Miss Dykeman are hardly to be considered, I take it. Mrs. Abbington wouldn't plant the crime on herself. She certainly would have no reason to destroy her benefactor, and unless she's a lunatic, she wouldn't shoot the girl. That lets her out. The only one left is Mrs. Garrison, excepting her husband, of course."

"Excepting her husband, provided he was not intended to be killed," amended Hand. "Also excepting her manager, Isidore Gutzbaum. His motive is pretty faint. I put the Gutzbaum bug in Gerrity's ear so he'd look him up. As for Mrs. Garrison, she is in the best position to have carried out the plot. She is also the least likely to have done it. On the other hand, Clark, who knows the undercurrents beneath the seemingly placid exterior of that group? A few of them have risen to the surface, and we have seen the direction and strength in which they flow. There may be others, much stronger than any we have detected. It is our business to sound for them."

"Rather a delicate job, I should think."

"Yes, but it can be handled, and you are the man who is going to handle it."

This announcement brought me bolt upright in my chair. "You don't mean me!"

"But I do," chuckled Hand. "I can't think of anyone better. Transplant you into a new setting, among new people, and, lo and behold, three days later you are the bosom friend of everyone. It is because you are a sympathetic listener, my boy. You are a sphinx with a sympathetic, understanding smile."

"Bosh! Such a person would be an ass, not a sphinx!"

"By no means! A wise countenance and a silent lip are the two requisites of a reputation for wisdom. Man is by no means so profound as he thinks he is, and it's through his mouth that he gives himself away. There, does that smooth your ruffled plumage?"

"You've only made it worse. It seems now that if I keep my mouth shut, I may pass as normal, but if I dare speak, I reveal myself as an idiot."

Hand laughed softly. Then he sobered. "As a matter of fact," he said, quite seriously, "you have an unconscious knack of impelling others to confide in you. I have maneuvered you into position to use it before this."

"And so I am to play the role of Judas."

"Rather the opposite. You are to discover the motive that drove one person to take the life of another."

"How am I to do it?"

"If I'm not mistaken, you will learn for yourself very shortly. That is by far the preferable way to find things out. If you don't mind, Clark, will you just tidy up a bit—those papers on the floor and so on? I'm about to have a go with my razor; I feel uncomfortably like our friend One Eye."

He left me to straighten up the mess he had made of the room earlier in the day. The job having been completed to my complete satisfaction, I dropped once more into my chair. I was there, sucking meditatively on my pipe, when someone gave our door buzzer a push.

I opened the door to discover Robert Garrison standing in the hallway. His eyes, heavy-lidded and dull, attested to his lack of sleep. Altogether, his features looked even more pinched and drawn than they had when I had last seen him. He managed a smile as he accepted my invitation to enter. Somehow I had a premonition that my future was about to be divulged.

Hand entered the room as sleek and spruce as if he had not been up all night. "Right on time, Mr. Garrison," he commended. "Have a seat."

Garrison lowered himself slowly into my easy chair. He passed his hand wearily over his brow. "Just been to see that poor girl's mother," he said dismally. "I think this has taken ten years off my life."

"You're lucky it didn't take the last twelve hours with it," growled Hand, throwing himself into his chair.

"That's another thing I wanted to have you straighten out for me," said Garrison, quickly. "I didn't get a chance to ask you about it this morning, but I understand you've formed the opinion it was I who was the intended victim."

Hand explained how he had arrived at that conclusion. He went further by telling his client exactly what had been done on the case thus far. Garrison, listening shrewdly, sat forward on his chair and asked quick, intelligent questions from time to time. As the recital continued, a flush came to his cheeks. Some of the despondency left his face.

"Now, then," said Hand in conclusion, "after a fashion we have a distinct advantage in this case. Suppose this plot had succeeded and you had been killed last night. We should now be searching for your murderer. We should be thinking, too, that were you alive, you undoubtedly could tell us the name of the person who wanted to kill you. As it is, although we are looking for the person who killed Miss Venora, we know that it is the person who wanted to kill you. Surely you must have some idea who it is."

Garrison smiled wryly. "I feel like the corpse rising up to give testimony," he said. "Your logic is sound enough, Mr. Hand. You have just convinced me that it was indeed I who was singled out for the victim. But even before that— in fact, ever since I first learned from Mrs. Abbington and Dr. Innes that you thought it was I—I have been wondering who the deuce could bear me such ill will. There is the man whose wife was killed by my car. But she was drunk, the insurance company paid him a huge sum, I endowed his children with some more, and it struck me at the time that the fellow was only too glad to be rid of her anyhow. One naturally makes a few business enemies, but I swear there's not one who could wish me the slightest harm."

Hand took a pencil and note-book from his pocket. "What's the name of the bereaved husband?" he asked.

"Hum-m," mused Garrison, gazing thoughtfully at the ceiling. "His name was Patrick Donahue, I remember that all right. It was some time ago—ten years. Here," he said, fishing into his coat pocket for a wallet, "here's my insurance company. They could give you his address; I've forgotten it."

Hand accepted the proffered card. "All right," he said. "Now what about business? Would your death be an advantage to anyone?"

"I can't see how," replied Garrison, with a shake of his head. "My affairs right now are such that no one would profit by my death. As for the market, my death would have no effect upon it."

"Well, let's get to Abbington. There seems to be—"

"I can't think that he would do it!" interrupted Garrison, abruptly.

"I was about to say there seems to be some reason for a man of his type to imagine a grievance. Actually, there is no reason for him to wish you harm. But you have interfered between husband and wife, than which there is nothing more intrepid. Of course, your going to the aid of that poor young woman was admirable and beyond reproach, but you did persuade her to go after a divorce."

Garrison gave a slight start. He opened his mouth as if to speak, but apparently thought better of it. After a few moments of frowning silence he said: "You may be right, but I hate to think it. You've seen Abbington, and you know how he's thrown himself into the ash-can. But I have never given him up for lost. I was fond of the boy; I still am. I have done my best to help him. First it was money, but I soon realized that was the wrong track—he drinks up every penny he can lay his hands on. Then I thought the proper course was to let him sink to the bottom of the heap. A little of that sort of thing should bring him to his senses, do you see? I thought, and I still think, he has the stuff in him to straighten himself out. I've done everything in my power to induce him to rehabilitate himself. If he shows a willingness, I am anxious to help him succeed."

"Does he know that?"

"Absolutely."

Hand placed his finger-tips together and, resting his head on the back of the chair, gazed at the ceiling. "There seems, he said, "to be a little incongruity here. You seem to have altruistic hopes that young Abbington will yet find himself and be a man. Then why," he demanded, "did you persuade his wife to divorce him?

Garrison had seemed uncomfortable, but now he was downright nettled. His face flushed, and he shifted irritably in his chair. "What has that got to do with this?" he demanded petulantly. Then he dropped his eyes before Hand's cold stare. "Well—er—I'll tell you. I thought it was the thing to do. The boy has disgraced himself; you can't get away from that," he explained, rather lamely.

As if satisfied with the answer, Hand once more took up his idle inspection of the ceiling. "So much for that," he said. "Now, Mr. Garrison, you told us you wanted to take your wife to Maine. How does she feel on that subject now?"

"Why, I suppose she feels as I do. The trip is off."

"Well, how did she feel about it last night?"

Garrison essayed a wry smile. "She had agreed to go, but she insisted upon taking a lot of friends with us. That isn't what I want," he said, gazing wistfully at the wall. "I want a chance to have her all to myself. It's beautiful up there at this time of year. The pure, spicy air, like wine; the fairyland islands, all fringed with fantastic rock and gossamer spray; the clean blue of the heavens meeting the deeper, white-flecked blue of the sea; the rose and gold of the sun on the fleecy clouds at evening; and a soft carpet of pine needles under your feet as you watch it all. Even the raging storms that howl and lash and pound at the islands are a boon from heaven. They tear a man's soul out of his body and hold it up for him to look at. The fog, too, has its peculiar charm—puts you in a little world all your own to think things over. I know I could get her to love it! If only—"

The unfinished sentence left him in a gloomy reverie. As he had spoken of his wife and his beloved Maine he had seemed a rather pitiful figure—still seemed a pitiful figure as he sat there, everything else forgotten, his thoughts turned inward. Hand glanced at me. I shook my head, for somehow I thought it would be a sacrilege to break in upon his meditation. Garrison, sitting there, was a far different man from the brisk, decisive, everlasting youthfulness that Wall Street knew him to be.

Hand cleared his throat. "Sorry to—" he began.

"Oh, great heaven!" exclaimed Garrison, with a start. "I beg your pardon, I let myself be carried away, I guess." He smiled, still with a trace of that wistfulness about him.

Hand hesitated, just for a moment; then he plunged into a delicate subject. "You and your wife are quite happy?" he asked.

Garrison frowned. "I suppose I had better disabuse your mind of any suspicions on that score," he said gruffly. "My wife and I are very happy together! She is all the world to me. There's a difference in ages, yes; but she's devoted to me!"

"Fortunate man!" sighed Hand. Then, suavely changing the subject: "We were speaking of your going to Maine. I believe your home is on Ghost Island, which you purchased twelve years ago."

"Where did you get your information?" asked Garrison, quite sharply.

"I didn't trust to my memory," smiled Hand. "I had a look at the files in the *Herald* office."

"Oh, yes, they made the mistake. It isn't Ghost Island," he corrected, with considerable warmth; "its right name is Arrowhead Island, and that's the name for it you'll find on the chart. Ghost Island is a name the natives gave to it. Something to do with a shipwreck years ago. It gets its proper name from its shape, an arrowhead, pointing straight out into the sea. It's the farthest island out in Casco Bay."

"Three miles off shore, and fourteen miles northeast of Portland, isn't it?"

"Yes. It's three miles from the mainland, but there are other islands nearer to it than that. There are two right near us, but neither one is inhabited. The island has six acres, mostly covered with pines. There are cliffs to the seaward, but on the landward side there is a snug little anchorage. Oh, it's a jewel! Wish I could show it to you."

"I think you can," said Hand, with an enigmatic smile.

"Eh?" ejaculated Garrison, in astonishment.

Hand ignored his client's puzzled glance. "What is the nearest island to you that's inhabited?" he asked.

"None, at this time of the year," replied Garrison. "The nearest one that has a summer home on it is about a mile and a half away. The two islands near us, as I said before, are not used for anything. One is very small. Thumbcap, it's called. The other, Barren Island, is mostly a swamp."

"Splendid!" said Hand, to Garrison's further bewilderment. "Now, then, I think the thing for you to do is to take your wife, Mr. King, Mr. Flount, Dr. Innes, Mrs. Abbington, and Miss Dykeman and go down to Ghost Island, or Arrowhead Island, as you prefer to call it, and spend at least a month."

Garrison gulped. "What? Why—why such a thing is out of the question!"

"Not at all," corrected Hand, serenely. "Such a sojourn might clash with your own desires, but your wife would certainly agree to it. If I'm not mistaken, there's nothing to prevent the others I named from going. Mrs. Abbington, Miss Dykeman, and Mr. Flount have nothing to keep them in the city. Mr. King is foot-loose. Dr. Innes was going with you anyway."

"Yes, but—"

"I shouldn't include anyone else in the party. Servants, of course. But I'd take along the most trusted ones from your Riverside Drive home. How soon can you get started?"

"But, my dear fellow, I haven't—"

"It's important that you get off as soon as possible. How about the day after tomorrow? Tomorrow would be better if you could make it."

Suddenly Garrison lost his temper. "See here, cried, angrily. "I can't allow you to take charge of my affairs in such a high-handed fashion!"

Hand, a compelling gleam in his pale gray eyes, leaned forward and tapped the man on the knee. "Oh, yes, you

can," he said. "You can because you are an intelligent man.
You've engaged me not only to find the person who murdered Miss Venora, but to protect you and your friends as
well. I absolutely refuse to go any further unless I have
your co-operation!"

Garrison thought the ultimatum over very carefully.
Finally a sickly sort of grin appeared on his lips. "I surrender," he said. "You cleaned up a mess for my friend
Colonel Warren once. Warren said you were the most
infernally secretive man he ever knew in his life. He also
said that if he hadn't been so infernally stupid, he would
have understood everything you did. Well, I suppose I've
got to walk through this thing blindfolded, just as he did.
Only, after it's all over, you will take the blindfold off,
won't you, now?"

Hand sat back with a merry laugh. "Absolutely!" he
promised. Then, more soberly: "How will you go down to
Maine?"

"We'll go in the *Dorothy;* that's my yacht. I'm not so
sure about being able to get off so quickly, though," said
Garrison, with a concerned expression.

"What's to prevent it?"

"Well, in the first place, I don't just know how I'm
going to bustle all these people off like that. And then,
there's the house. The others who were going down with
us were all right, but I don't know how these people will
stand to rough it. I've had the very deuce of a time with
the natives down there. They are afraid to go on that
island. Think it's haunted by those chaps who were drowned
in that old shipwreck I told you about. Imagine that! I had
the same trouble with them when I first built the house,
and now I'm having it again. They don't mind going out
there to work in the summertime. There are people on the
near-by islands then, or we're there ourselves. But in the

fall, when there's nobody nearer than those on the mainland, it's almost impossible to get them to go out there at
all. We weren't down last summer. We were in the Bahamas looking for an old pirate ship that's supposed to be
sunk there. I had the natives start converting the house in
Maine into a year-round residence. As soon as the summer
people left, they wanted to lay off until next summer. I
had to threaten to bring a gang of men down from New
York before they'd go on. Of course, if I'd done that, I'd
have got in wrong with the natives, and you must stand in
with the natives. They went back at it, anyway, and were
just about finished up last week, but they set fire to the
place. By accident, of course."

"Phew!" whistled Hand. "That makes it bad. Did it do
much damage?"

"Not much. It was just luck that the whole place didn't
go. They had finished work for the day and were on their
way home in their boat. Then they realized they had left
one of their comrades behind. Oh, they're a great bunch!
Mel Dibber, who wrote me about it, said the man had
taken sick in the afternoon and gone off for a rest. Most
likely he got drunk; I know Arty Johnson pretty well.
Anyway, they turned back for him. When they got to the
island, they found the basement of the house afire. After
a good deal of heroic work, Mel said, they got it out. He
said if they hadn't gone back, Arty Johnson would have
burned up with the house."

"I suppose," said Hand, "Mr. Johnson dropped a match."

Garrison laughed. "That's my idea of it, too," he said.
"But Mel has a different one. He was unusually vague when
it came to that. I gathered the impression, however, that
he thinks either the house set fire to itself, or the spirits of
the old shipwreck crew at last took stringent measures to
rid their haunt of outsiders. He also intimated that since

the fire there have been other ghostly manifestations on the island. At any rate, he simply can't get any of the boys to go back to work there."

"And there the matter stands?"

"Well, nearly there. I sent a man down to give Mel and his merry men a pep talk to see whether he couldn't get them back to work. He failed quite signally. He has, however, carried out my orders and posted himself on the island. He's living in the house now. Good man, Mapes. Used to be a policeman."

Hand rubbed his chin reflectively for a moment. "Well," he said, "I can't see that this alters matters much. You can go right away. The reassurance your presence on island would bring should enable you to get the men back to finish the job. You could live on the yacht a few days if necessary. There's only one more thing."

Garrison waxed suspicious. "What's that?" he asked,

"You have forgotten to invite Mr. Clark to go with you."

"What?" said Garrison, feebly. Then his face broke into a smile. "How beastly stupid of me! A thousand pardons, Mr. Clark, and I hope you'll be able to go."

"Errah—ah," I stammered.

"Mr. Clark accepts with thanks," said Hand, briskly. "Now, the thing to do is to get right off. We'll have to leave that to you. You shouldn't have much trouble; all these people should welcome the opportunity to get away and escape all this publicity. Better get started on it right away. Let Clark know the particulars of your departure."

Garrison seemed just a trifle dazed when he left. He smiled gamely, however, and promised to do everything possible to speed our departure. When he had gone, I turned to Hand. I looked more or less injured, I imagine, at the way he had manhandled my destiny.

"Now, don't look so reproachful, Clark," he said, his eyes grinning at me over the match he had applied to his pipe. "Here I've arranged a capital holiday for you with a group of charming people, and you have the cheek to stand there looking at me with the dying glance of a man that's been betrayed. But see here, Clark, you get the idea, of course."

"You're going to coop those people up together on isolated island on the coast of Maine, and I'm supposed watch the lids blow off!"

"That's it exactly! Can you imagine how submerged passions would incubate under such conditions? No outlet for emotions. All thrown together from morning till night. You're going to be in a delicate spot, my boy. It will be just as much up to you to see that no further harm is done as it will to discover who was responsible for the last. You can't relax a minute! Keep your ears open wide, and don't forget a thing you hear. There's something in that Garrison-Abbington triangle that hasn't come to light. Garrison seems jealous of his wife, too. Maybe she's tired of him. Dr. Innes may be your man. There seems to be nothing more to implicate Flount, King, and Miss Dykeman except their misfortune to have been present when the crime was committed. But watch 'em, Clark, watch every one of 'em! Gerrity and I will work on the case from here. But I don't mind telling you that I'm pinning my greatest faith on you!"

10

THE SECOND ENCOUNTER

An agonizing atmosphere of embarrassment pervaded the drawing-room at the Garrison home the following evening. I was there at Garrison's invitation to take dinner with them. Final plans for our departure for Maine were to be made.

Everyone who had been present when the tragedy occurred, with the exception of Mr. Flount, was there. In order to cover up a painful silence, the guests were making a great display of the ordinarily perfunctory business of accepting cocktails from a footman. Everyone had made arrangements to go to Maine but Mr. Flount, who was the only hold-out. It appeared that he preferred the comfort of New York to a coldish island down East. Nevertheless, he was expected at the dinner, and his arrival was something of a sensation.

The footman, who was about to become unfortunate, was offering me his tray of cocktails where I sat near the entrance from the hall. Bursting through the portières, Mr. Flount darted into the drawing-room like an enraged whippet. He took the footman in that portion which extended as the man bent obsequiously before me. The courageous fellow saved the rest of us from a drenching. He clasped the cocktails to his bosom as he descended to the floor.

Mr. Flount, who had bounced violently aside, regained his balance. His eyeglasses, swaying violently at the end of their ribbon, he snared with an expert finger. With much hauteur he replaced them to his nose and glared the hapless servant out of countenance. The footman gathered up his wreckage and sheepishly departed.

"Clumsy fellow!" exclaimed Flount. "Standing right before the door in that fashion!

With a newspaper he held in his hand, he indicated the spot where the minor catastrophe had occurred. Evidently his astonishing experience had caused him to forget that he held the paper. The sight of it, when he brought it into evidence, appeared to recall something unpleasant to his mind. His face took on that angry brick-color that one sees on the face of a sorely tried policeman. "There!" he shrilled, clasping the paper as though he were choking the life out of a snake. "I am outraged! No respect! Here, look at this!"

Jerking the paper open, he spread it angrily at arm's length. Trying, some of us vainly, to appear solemn, we crowded round him. What I beheld in his trembling grasp was a tabloid newspaper, the front page adorned with a large, bellicose likeness of Mr. Flount. With raised umbrella he was evidently set out to commit mayhem upon the taker of the photograph. The picture appeared under the caption: "LOVE SLAYER?"

"Damaging!" Mr. Flount informed us in an angry falsetto. "My character is defamed! I'm libeled! I'll demand a retraction, I tell you! I'll sue! A pretty state of affairs when one can't put one's nose out one's door without having dozens of those disgusting snapshot fellows pounce upon one!

"Then," said Garrison, "you should come to Maine with us, where they can't get at you."

Flount snorted fiercely. "And let the world think I ran away from this?" he cried. "I'll see my lawyer! I'll start an action at once!"

"You'll play right into their hands if you do," warned Henry King, grinning most shamefully. "That question mark after the 'LOVE SLAYER?' saves their bacon. They're just asking the world whether it thinks you got into a love-affair. Of course the world will think that's ridiculous."

Flount stiffened. "What do you mean, ridiculous?" he demanded.

"I mean ridiculous that a gentleman of your intelligence would kill anybody," explained King, unconvincingly.

"Oh. Well—well, I'll see my lawyer. I'll—let me see, what is it you do? Yes, I'll wreck this paper! This yellow journal! Don't you think so, Robert?"

"I don't think so," advised Garrison. "They'd only make capital of you. Better to let it be forgotten. And better for you to come to Maine with us, where they can't repeat the—er—atrocity."

Flount thought the matter over carefully. "You may be right," he conceded at last. "I may let them off, I don't know. At any rate, Robert, if that invitation is still open, I shall accept it and go to Maine with you. Beastly newspaper! Yellow journal!"

"Of course it is," Garrison heartily assured him. "You're acting very wisely, Archie. Come, now, have a cocktail. Oh, they're all on the floor."

"And the footman," snickered Henry King.

"There'll be more in a minute," smiled Garrison. "Come, Archie, sit down and—forget it."

Another footman soon appeared with a fresh set of cocktails. Flount, if he had done nothing else with his

amazing entrance, had dispelled the restraint that had laid
hold of everybody. Miss Dykeman, who was sitting next to
me, prattled about the kindness of Mr. Garrison. From her
I learned that he had induced them all to go on the pretext
of escaping publicity. The room buzzed with conversation.

At length the butler stalked into the room and announced dinner. I glanced up from my conversation with
Miss Dykeman. Mrs. Garrison, apparently, had been in the
act of leaving the room. She was standing in the doorway,
with a servant, the same whom Flount had capsized, holding the portière back for her.

"Just a minute, Garry," she called to her husband. "I've
got to see someone for a moment; be back almost instantly."

She made a charming picture standing there, with her
shimmering white satin evening gown and her golden hair
against the dark background of the velvet curtain. With a
little smile and a flippant wave of her hand, she walked
gracefully out into the hall.

Once again I lent my ear to Miss Dykeman, who was
describing the advantages of living in California. She
struck me as a delightful young person; not very sound in
her arguments, but, among men at least, able to get others
to agree with her. Finally I saw Garrison frown at his
watch and walk resolutely from the room. A moment later
I heard him cry out.

I leaped to my feet. For a moment I stood peering nervously at the portières that hid the hall from view. Then I
heard Garrison's hoarse voice again. I ran for the hall.

A man lay prone on the rug by the front door. Garri-
son was leaning over him, shaking him by the shoulders.
"Boynton! Boynton!" he cried. "What's happened here?
Where's Mrs. Garrison?"

Evidently the man was unconscious, for he did not stir.
Mrs. Abbington, white of face, brushed by me and rushed
up to Garrison.

"Here," she gasped, fumbling in her bag, "my smelling-salts."

Once again the tiny bottle played a role in the case. Garrison applied the neck of the bottle to Boynton's nostrils. I saw then that the man was the servant who had ushered Mrs. Garrison out into the hall. The others crowded round as the pungent fumes began to restore Boynton's senses. Finally his eyes opened. He stared blankly into the face of his employer.

"Boynton!" cried Garrison, in anguish. "What's happened?

"Wurr—wurr," mumbled Boynton. "Mizzer Garrison?"

"Yes, yes; what's happened!"

Once again Garrison jammed the smelling-salts bottle under Boynton's nose. The man recoiled; then he sat up and felt tenderly of his head. "Mr. Garrison," he said, very reproachfully, "I really can't stand this, sir. First a ducking from Mr. Flount, and now a pegging from some ruffian! I'm afraid, sir, that I shall have to give notice."

"Hang you and your notice!" said Garrison, fiercely. "Where's my wife?"

Boynton sat with his hands flat on the floor at either side of him. With a blank expression on his own, he gazed up at Garrison's agonized face. Suddenly his eyes flew wide open. He twisted about to look at the door. Then he leaped to his feet, swayed, and would have fallen had not Garrison caught him.

"Mrs. Garrison!" he gasped. "They must have taken her away!"

"What!" cried Garrison. "What's that you say, Boynton? Who must have taken her away? Speak up, man!"

"Those men. One of them came to the door, sir, and asked to see Mrs. Garrison. I told her she was giving a dinner, but he insisted. He gave me his card and told me to give it to her."

"That's right," broke in Mrs. Abbington, excitedly. "Boynton came into the drawing-room with the card. Connie read it and went out into the hall. You remember, Garry, she asked us to wait."

"Yes, yes," said Garrison quickly. "Then what happened, Boynton?"

The footman passed his hand before his brow. "The man was standing over by the door, sir," he said thickly. "Mrs. Garrison walked up to him, and I started back to the pantry. Suddenly Mrs. Garrison called to me. She looked rather frightened, sir, as I walked up to her. The man was smiling and telling her not to be uneasy. Then all at once another fellow jumped through the door and struck at me with a blackjack. I didn't have time to bob out of his way, sir, but I did see the other man clutch Mrs. Garrison by the throat. Then I guess I went down."

"Oh God!" groaned Garrison.

I stepped up. "See here, Boynton, what sort of man was this?"

"A thickset, stocky man, sir. Clean shaven and appeared a gentleman."

"Where's that card he gave you?"

Boynton looked about on the floor. "It was on my tray, sir," he replied. "Here's the tray, where I dropped it. And here's the card."

He stooped over to pick up the oblong piece of cardboard, but he was so dizzy that he staggered back. I leaned over and quickly picked it up. "M. Henri Ardette," I read. "Who's he?"

"That's the fellow with a style shop," said Garrison, quickly. "She had ordered some dresses from him."

"Well, come on," I cried. "Let's see what we can find outside."

I rushed out on the porch. The darkness was just as deep as it had been the night of the murder. We scattered aimlessly throughout the grounds. I wondered what had happened to the two men Gerrity had detailed to watch the Garrison house.

Finally I stopped to think, certain that we should get nowhere without some sort of system. As I was pondering, a man walked up to me in the gloom. "Well, what do you think of it?" he asked.

I recognized the voice as Henry King's. "King," I asked, "what would you do if you were abducting a woman from this house?"

"Ye gods!" he exclaimed. "If I—you've got me."

"Well, I'll tell you what I'd do. I wouldn't take her out the front here. The back is the logical way; shady with all those shrubs and the hedge along the sidewalk. The only risk would be getting across the sidewalk, and that's quite a risk, too. No doubt they'd have a car waiting there. Let's see what we can find out back there."

We turned and ran back alongside the house.

"Garrison's gone after a policeman," panted King, as we ran, "and Flount is calling the police from the house."

Reaching the gate, I saw evidence that my deduction had been correct. A small knot of people were standing on the sidewalk. In the center of the group was a policeman. Before him stood a messenger boy, talking excitedly and gesticulating toward the Garrison house. King and I burst through the gate.

The policeman caught sight of us. "Hey, what's goin' on here?" he demanded.

"There's been an abduction—Mrs. Robert Garrison," I hurriedly explained.

"You ain't kiddin' me, are ya?"

"I am not! We've got to find out whether anyone saw her taken away."

The messenger boy forced his way over to us. "I was just tellin' him, mister," he said. "I seen the lady. They lugged her through that gate and carried her over to a sedan standin' right here at the curb. And what's more, I know one of the guys that took her."

"Who was it? Quick!"

The policeman thrust himself before me. "Just a minute," he said pugnaciously. "I'll handle this!

Angrily I shoved my badge before his eyes. "You'll take orders from me," I said, severely. Forcing my way through the crowd that was collecting, I went out into the street and hailed a cab. "Here, boy! King! You, officer!" I called. The three of them ran out to the street and over to the taxi. "King, you and the boy get in there," I commanded. "Officer, you stand on the running board and get us through traffic. Where does this man live, sonny?"

"Same house that I do," piped the youngster, from within the cab. "Least, he's rented the basement there."

He gave me a number in West Fifty-sixth Street, and I ordered the cab-driver to proceed to it as quickly as he could get there. Then I hopped into the cab.

"Now, then," I said, turning to the boy as the cab sped down the street, "who is this man?"

"I dunno, sir," replied the lad. "He rented the basement of the house we live in, Mother and me. Him and another fella have been fixin' it up, somehow. I went down there the other day, but they threw me out."

"My boy," I said, "I think you are going to earn a great big reward tonight."

As we flew along, I got out a pencil and note-pad and scribbled a note to Hand. "Here," I said, thrusting it into the boy's hand. "When you have directed us to the place, go out and phone this message. Try the number you see written there, but if you can't get it, call police headquarters and ask for Inspector Gerrity. If he's out, and he probably is by now, give this message to whoever is there. Do you get it?"

He had it, all right, and with such a bright youngster I had no fear of his not carrying out my instructions.

The boy directed the driver over Fifty-seventh Street to Eleventh Avenue. There we turned left. Near the end of the block on the east side a narrow alley cut between a fish-market and a dingy tobacco-store. Into this the boy directed the driver. As the cab lurched into the alley, the headlights fell upon the back of a sedan, standing a hundred feet from Eleventh Avenue.

"That's the bus they used!" whispered the boy excitedly.

"Show us the cellar," I said, eagerly.

The taxi came to a stop behind the sedan. We tumbled out. Through the murk we followed the boy, who intrepidly led us over toward the black row of buildings that lined the alley. He pointed to a sunken door. It was accessible by four or five stone steps.

"That's it, sir," he whispered.

"The place is cut up into rooms, I suppose," I said, using a cautious voice.

"I don't know, sir," replied the boy. "We ain't lived here so long. First time I was down here was the other day, and then they kicked me out. I didn't get to see much."

"All right. Go telephone that message. When you get it through, go to police headquarters and wait for me there."

The boy sped off into the gloom; the rest of us descended the steps. As we halted uncertainly before the door, I turned to King. "Are you armed?" I asked.

"Good Lord, no," he replied.

I got out my light and flashed it about the pit. In one corner was a pile of fresh lumber. I selected a good-sized stick and handed it to King. The policeman tried the door. It was locked.

"Come on," I said, "we'll break it down."

We stood off a pace. At a signal from me all three of us hurled ourselves at the door. A splintering crash heralded our precipitate entrance into the basement. As we stood in the dank blackness inside, I could hear my companions breathing, but I could hear nothing else. Once again I got out my light. Bracing myself as if against an attack, I sent its beam cutting through the darkness ahead. We were in a sort of vestibule. There were three doors for us to choose from, one ahead and one on either side.

"Three doors and three of us," said Henry King, significantly.

"I don't like to send you off with nothing but that stick to protect yourself with," I protested.

"I'm not so good with a pistol, anyway," he said, and I could see that he was grinning. "But I've killed many a rattlesnake with a stick, and I guess I can do for a few more." This last was quite grim.

"All right," I agreed. "I'll take the door ahead, and you two take the one nearest you."

My door was not locked. Turning my light to see how King was faring, I found he had already disappeared through his door.

There was one door in the room that I entered, one, that is, besides the door to the vestibule. A heap of refuse was piled against it. The heap had the appearance of having been piled there recently. I set to work to remove it. Suddenly I paused in my work and listened. Surely there was somebody on the other side of that door! I redoubled my efforts. About to yank the door open, it flew back toward me, and the policeman leaped through it.

"Oh, it was you," I said, with a good deal of disappointment.

"Yep," he replied, flashing his light about the room. "This room's empty, too. So's the other one. Guess there's nothin' here."

"Then let's go look up King," I said, a bit nervously. "I'm worried about him, with no light or gun, nothing but that stick."

We turned toward the door to the vestibule, but a hoarse, muffled shout brought us to a halt. "Mr. Clark! Clark! Cla—"

The voice was King's, and it stopped with terrible suddenness!

With an oath, I leaped for the door to the vestibule. The policeman behind me, I rushed through the door King had taken. We found ourselves in a small, bare room. Directly across from us was a heavy door, standing ajar. Warily approaching it, we flashed our lights through it. The room on the other side had the appearance of living-quarters. A carpet, with a table standing in its center covered the floor. With a gasp I saw the body of a man lying face downward on the other side of the table. I leaped over to it. It was Henry King, lying with his head in a pool of blood!

I dropped to my knees and rolled him over. There was a gash on the side of his head, and his face, except where it was spattered with crimson, was a deathly white. As I rolled him over, though, I was relieved to hear him moan.

The policeman, paying no attention to my proceedings, was inspecting the room.

"Is there any water round here?" I called to him.

"Water?" he said. "Yeah, there's a wash-room over here."

He approached me with a glass of water in his hand. I set my light on the floor and dashed the water on King's face. Taking my flask from my pocket, I poured some of the spirits through his teeth. He coughed feebly and a moment later opened his eyes.

King showed himself to be a man of good vitality. In a few minutes he was able to stand erect. He gazed, quite bewildered at first, at the policeman, who was inspecting the walls with his light. Suddenly King clutched me by the arm. "They didn't get away, did they?" he demanded.

I brought myself back with a start. "By Jove!" I exclaimed, "I forgot all about them! Any trace of them?" I asked the policeman.

"Not a sign," he growled. "Beats me, too, because the only way out o' this joint is the door we come through. They couldn't have made it through there before we got to it. And how about the woman, too?"

"Wait a minute," I said, grimly. In the right wall I had seen something familiar. It was a boarded panel, identically like the one that had been the means of Spawn's escape over at East End Avenue. I amazed my companions by walking up to it, manipulating the center boards, and thrusting it open.

We went through into a large room. At the back of the building a door opened out into the alley. The policeman helping King, who was still very shaky, we stepped outside. For a moment I blinked in consternation and amazement. Both the taxicab and the sedan was gone!

"Now where did that infernal taxi-driver go?" I asked, uselessly and heatedly.

"Beat it," replied the policeman, with a shrug. "Those guys are wise; they ain't gettin' themselves mixed up in nothin'!"

"Why didn't we order him to stay here?" I cried, bitterly. "They couldn't have escaped in their automobile then!"

In spite of our protests, King accompanied us as we explored the alley. It turned a short way on and, passing between the buildings, ended in Fifty-fifth Street.

"No telling where they went from here," observed King gloomily.

Except that it's a one-way street," I said, "and they'd hardly take a chance going the wrong way on it. They must have gone over to Eleventh Avenue."

"That doesn't do us much good," grunted the policeman.

We turned and retraced our steps dejectedly into the alley.

"By the way," I said to the policeman, "what was that room where we found King. I didn't take much notice."

"That room had a table and a couch in it," he replied. "There was another little room off of it with a bed and a bureau and a mirror. Then there was the wash-room."

"Then that's the place where they intended to hide Mrs. Garrison," I declared. "By Jove, to think they got away from us! Say, what happened to you, King, do you know?"

King grunted. "You bet I know," he replied, with feeling. "I stepped into a little room off that sort of hallway we were in first. Then I struck a match. I saw a solid-looking door across from me. I walked over to it and tried it. It was locked—tight. My match went out and I struck another. Imagine my surprise when I saw by the light of it that the door had opened! I put the match out in a hurry and stood there wondering what in the devil to do. All at once somebody grabbed me by the wrist and yanked me into the room. That was when I shouted for you. I started to put up a fight, but they clouted me with something. Boy, my head's still full of fireworks!"

I put my light on him. "It's still bleeding pretty badly, too," I said. "We've got to get you to a doctor."

Suddenly the lights of an automobile, turning recklessly in from Eleventh Avenue, flooded the alley with brilliance. The car rolled up to us and stopped, immediately disgorging policemen. Another car followed it. From somewhere in the crowd Gerrity and Hand rushed up to me.

"What about it, Clark?" demanded my friend.

"We traced them here," I explained, gloomily, "and then they got away through another of those trick doors. They're gone!"

"Gone?" cried Gerrity, despairingly.

"How about Mrs. Garrison?" asked Hand, sharply.

I merely shrugged my shoulders dejectedly and shook my head.

"Gone!" exclaimed Gerrity again. "It'll take us a year to find 'em!"

"I'm not so sure," said Hand, grimly. "Our friends Spitz and Spawn did this; I don't think there's any doubt of it. And—I have a plan."

11

MR. FLOUNT SHOWS HIS METAL

Inspector Gerrity set the telephone down on his desk with a thump. "Nothing doing yet!" he growled. Then he resumed his restless pacing of the office, chewing angrily on his cigar. Hand, tipping his chair farther back, inhaled deeply from his cigarette.

"What was it this time, another brewery?" I asked.

"Storage," grunted the inspector.

This disgruntled conversation had to do with the plan Hand had put into motion. Convinced that Spitz and Spawn were the abductors of Mrs. Garrison, he had hit upon an idea. It had to do with the cellars where the wily pair had twice outwitted us. Hand reasoned that they probably had other cellars, doctored up in just such a fashion as the two we had found. His plan was to find out what other cellars in the city had been rented recently and raid them all. As soon as the real-estate offices had opened in the morning, Gerrity's detectives had started making the rounds.

Up to then, two in the afternoon, several distilleries, two breweries, and an opium den had suffered, but not a cellar had been found that suggested Spitz and Spawn at work. We sat in Gerrity's office, waiting for the investigators to report. If a cellar appeared in any way suspicious to them, they called us and we went right out and led the raid.

Finally Gerrity came to roost in his chair at the desk. Slowly he removed the mangled cigar from his mouth and glanced searchingly at Hand.

"The thing that beats me," he said, ponderously, "is the craziness of this whole thing! Where's the motive? One woman is shot to death, another is kidnapped, and a man is lying in his hotel room with a cracked head. What's the idea? If it's ransom they want, why did they shoot the Venora girl? It isn't robbery. The only person with any cause for revenge was locked up at the time Garrison's wife was whisked off. If we only knew what the pair we're after are up to, we'd have something to go on. But—what's the blasted idea?"

"The newspapers," I said, "have figured it all out. They call our men the Star Slayers, and—"

"The newspapers and their Star Slayers!" scoffed Gerrity. "That's crazier than ever. Besides, Mrs. Garrison has left the stage."

"But there's been talk of her going back to it. At any rate, the producers have taken it to heart. I understand every female theatrical luminary in the city goes about with an armed guard."

Gerrity sniffed disdainfully. "Yeah," he affirmed. "They got permits this morning, dozens of 'em."

"How have you made out with that fancy dress man, Ardette?"

"Well, he had a rock-bound alibi, you know all about that. I thought I told you about the card, but I guess you were up at Garrison's. We finally located the shop where it was engraved. They got an order to make the plate and a sample card. A man came in and got the sample; said he'd let 'em know if it was all right. Of course he's not been back. The thing that I can't understand is how Spitz and Spawn knew Ardette's firm was making dresses for Mrs. Garrison."

He glanced hopefully over to Hand, who seemed not to be listening to us.

"There must be somebody besides Spitz and Spawn in this," I said.

Gerrity slapped the table. "I know there is!" he snapped. "Those two never pulled off that job last night alone. Two good detectives blackjacked right in Garrison's grounds! There must have been a whole gang. On the other hand, neither Flannery nor Bowen saw the men who cracked 'em on the head. It's a tough world!"

Gerrity's telephone bell rang again. He snatched up the receiver and answered it. The eagerness on his face melted to annoyance. He placed the flat of his hand to the mouthpiece and turned to Hand. "It's Garrison again," he said. "Wants to speak to you."

"Oh, good heaven!" groaned Hand. "Tell him I'm out."

The inspector got rid of Garrison as adroitly as was possible with him. "My gosh, he's in bad shape," he said, as he put the telephone down.

Hand's chin sank deeper on his chest, and his eyes seemed to sink deeper into his head.

Sergeant Tim rapped on the door and stepped into the office. "Miggs's here, sir," he announced.

"Send him in," ordered Gerrity.

A ratty, shifty little man stepped inside the door. He stood fumbling uncomfortably with his greasy cap. His eyeballs seemed to bounce from object to object in the room.

Gerrity regarded him with an expression of repugnance. "Miggs," he said, "did Lieutenant Copley tell you what we're after?"

"Yeth, thir," lisped the man. "Theyth a couple o' guyth what might be them two. You know, Maloney and Naper."

"They're both up the river, and you know it!" snapped Gerrity. Suddenly he shot out of his chair and strode truculently over to Miggs. "You know East End Avenue," he snarled. "Where did that pair come from? Speak up!"

Miggs cowered before him. "They ain't none o' the N'Yawk boyth," he whined. "They're thtrangerth, Inthpector. I ain't never hoid of 'em before."

Gerrity glowered at the little man for a moment. "Get out of here!" he commanded, with a jerk of his head. "If you get a line on those fellows, you let me know, understand!"

Miggs, without waiting to reply, scurried from office.

"You won't get anywhere with your stool-pigeons, Inspector," remarked Hand. "I think Spitz and Spawn are strangers. Clark, will you do me another favor?" he asked, almost pleadingly. "Go up and see Garrison again, will you, old man? It's not pleasant, I know, but try to bolster him up. Jove, there's nothing worse than seeing a strong man go to pieces. How he must love his wife!"

I left them with a good deal of reluctance. A little fresh air seemed in order before my ordeal at the Garrison home. I set out, therefore, to walk over a few blocks before hailing a cab. As I was striding along, quite deeply absorbed, I was suddenly conscious of my name being called in a piping high voice. Glancing up, I beheld Archibald Flount waving a closed umbrella at me from the opposite sidewalk. I halted.

Mr. Flount advanced to the curb, peered searchingly in the direction that traffic was not coming from on the one-way street, and stepped blandly forth, directly into the path of an onrushing taxicab. To the nerve-racking tune of screeching brakes, a portly gentleman slid from the back seat of the cab and disappeared below the windows.

I closed my eyes on the frightful tragedy that I was sure must follow. A moment later I wrenched them open again and heaved a sigh of relief. The cab was slued round in the street. Four wide marks on the pavement and the odor of burned rubber attested to the driver's frenzied application of the brakes.

Flount stood before it, resting easily on his umbrella. He was glaring at the chalky-faced driver. The stout gentleman in the cab raised his bulging eyes to a level with the window. He gazed incredulously upon Mr. Flount. Then, evidently seized with rage, he popped up and protruded his head through the window.

"Hey, you little nincompoop!" he bellowed, shaking his fist at Flount. "What do you mean by stepping out into the street like that?"

Flount, with a disdainful toss of his head, turned his back on the cab and greeted me effusively. The taxi-driver's neck swelled double its size, to allow, no doubt, his heart to drop back to its proper location. Thereupon he unburdened himself concerning Mr. Flount with such extraordinary fluency that a truck-driver parked alongside nearly fell from his cab in ecstasy.

"Pay no attention to them," Mr. Flount soothingly advised me. "Come, my dear fellow, let us be off."

He took my arm and, with great dignity, escorted me off down the sidewalk, followed by the beratings of the taxi-driver.

"Where are you bound?" he asked me.

"Why, I was on my way to see Mr. Garrison," I replied. "Hand wanted me to see whether I couldn't console him somewhat."

"Poor fellow!" sighed Flount. "It was to see what I could do for him that I came down this way."

"Ah, you propose to do something?"

"I most certainly do. I shall see that Inspector Gerrity and tell him that something must be done!"

"Oh," I murmured. "That would be nice of you, but I really think he is out."

"Then I shall wait for him to return," declared Flount, firmly.

My heart dropped for Gerrity.

"You see," confided Flount, "the police need a snapping up once in a while. The newspapers seek to do it from time to time, but the newspapers, bah! What are they? One good, respectable citizen—"

"Hold on!" I interrupted, throwing a restraining arm across Flount's chest. "I think I know that fellow looking in the window ahead there."

We halted, and Flount adjusted his glasses, "Can't say that I share the pleasure," he said. "Although, of course, he has his back to us."

I was staring hard at the man's broad back. One of his shoulders was peculiarly broader than its fellow, and that was suggestive. Spawn, I well remembered, had just such a peculiar set of shoulders. The back of his head, as much as I could see of it under his hat, also appeared familiar.

The man, standing about twenty feet from us, turned languidly in our direction. Although my pipe was burning to the best of its ability, I hastily applied a match to it. Over my fingers I surreptitiously observed the man's face. The beard was gone, but there was no mistaking those cold, almost colorless eyes. It was Spawn!

He was dressed in the best of taste. He appeared like a successful business man wasting a few minutes in an out-of-the-way part of town. I pretended, at the expense of scorched fingers, to have trouble with my pipe. I reflected with some satisfaction on the way I had handled Flount, or, to be more exact, his umbrella. As he had leaned nonchalantly upon his umbrella, staring fixedly at Spawn's back, I had kicked the thing from his grasp. He had regained his balance with a weird, upward motion of the arms and a violent twist of the body. As Spawn had turned toward us, he was protesting volubly, at the same time industriously brushing the dirt from the umbrella. It saved me from being given away by the bold inspection of Spawn that Flount would otherwise have given him.

I turned quickly to my companion, presenting my back to Spawn. "So sorry!" I exclaimed, as if I had just noticed my clumsiness. "I hope I haven't damaged your umbrella."

"It is a very valuable one," grumbled Flount. "I always carry it with me; you never know when a shower will come up, or something. You have got the case all covered with dirt. Really, sir, that was unpardonable!"

"I insist that you let me have it cleaned," I said, noting with satisfaction that Spawn had walked right by us without recognition. I grasped Flount by the wrist and hissed in his ear: "There goes the abductor of Dorothy Garrison!"

I had expected Flount to be frightened and amazed. He showed no such emotions; quite the opposite, in fact. Grasping his umbrella resolutely by the tip, he thrust forward what jaw the Lord had given him and set out after Spawn. Fortunately, I still had him by the wrist and was able to pull him back.

"Easy," I cautioned. "If we nab him here, we may never find the lady. If we follow him, no doubt he will lead us to her."

Flount flattered me with an appreciative glance. We set out after Spawn. The man walked along with an easy stride, looking neither to right nor to left. Frantically I was debating what I should do. I had bungled the affair of the night before, and I hoped fervently not to repeat the tragedy. Should I dispatch Flount after Hand and Gerrity? Surely that would avail us nothing, for then they would never be able to find either Spawn or me. We passed a policeman. Desperately I resisted an impulse to enlist his aid. That would have ruined whatever chance we had of finding Mrs. Garrison. Clearly it was up to Flount and me to handle the affair alone. Otherwise we might capture Spawn, but that would be as far as we should get.

For one who was wanted so badly, Spawn was remarkably careless. It would have been easy, with the street all but deserted, for him to detect that he was being followed, but he walked straight on, with never a glance round. To my amazement, I suddenly realized that he was headed in the direction of police headquarters. In fact, the headquarters building was but a half block ahead. That was rashness for you!

Without slackening his pace, Spawn suddenly turned and entered an alleyway off the sidewalk. Motioning Flount to be cautious, I stole up to the alley and peered carefully round the corner. Spawn was half-way down the passage, swinging along as nonchalantly as ever. At the end of the building he again turned to his right and disappeared. Flount and I, as quietly as possible, quickly followed after him. At the other end I peered round the corner. I was just in time to see a door close at the other side of a dingy courtyard.

I turned to Flount. "Did you see that door close?" I asked.

"Yes."

"Then run to police headquarters. Bring Hand and Gerrity back here as quickly as you can. Show them where that fellow went. I'm going after him."

Flount clutched me protestingly by the arm. "But, see here, I don't—"

"Do as I say!" I said, roughly; then I quickly crossed the courtyard.

The door was not locked. Softly I opened it and stepped inside. Before me were two flights of stairs, one going up and the other going down. Remembering Spawn's past propensity for subterranean chambers, I selected the stairs that descended to the basement. At the foot I was faced with another problem. Here was a door that I soon found was locked. I got out my skeleton keys and, doing my utmost to work silently, commenced to try them. The third one turned the bolt. Slowly I opened the door.

The long, narrow room that I was in was filled with boxes, neatly piled in rows along the wall. I could just make them out in the faint light that filtered through the door. Down the center of the room a narrow passage had been left between the boxes. Pistol in hand, I proceeded along it, feeling very much as if the floor might drop out from under me at any moment.

As I approached the other end, I made out the faint outline of another door. I could imagine what lay behind it, but I meant to make sure. Gingerly I felt for the knob, found it, and cautiously turned it. The door was not locked. As it gave inward, a shaft of light fell through it. That was disconcerting. To delay meant disaster. I gave the door a shove and stepped back to shield myself by the jamb.

I was looking into a room very similar in appearance to the one where Henry King had come to grief the night before. As far as I could make out, it was empty. Slowly, keeping my pistol before me, I advanced into the room. I determined quite definitely, then, that there was no one besides myself in it. As I reached the center of the room a calm, serene voice, all the more terrifying because of its serenity, froze me up like a pillar of ice.

"You might lay your pistol on that table before you."

I realized I had been enticed into a trap. Decidedly, there were but two courses for me to take; either I had to whirl about and blaze away, or I had to comply with the order of the man standing behind me. I realized, too, that what I should have done was to remain outside. I should have stood guard at the entrance until my friends arrived.

"I suggested," repeated the ominous voice, "that you lay your pistol on the table before you."

Quickly I expelled the bitter realizations from my mind. I still held a trump. The man did not know half a hundred bluecoats were due to descend upon his den any minute. My play was to stall for time. I reached out and dropped my pistol on the table.

"That was very sensible," purred the voice. "I dislike firing indoors; it leaves such a pungent odor."

I turned about to face him. It was Spawn, standing half-way between me and the door. How he had arrived there was too puzzling for me to consider.

"You are using up all our cellars," he complained. If you don't stop following us, we shall be all out of them shortly. But then, you will not follow us any longer."

He held an ugly-looking automatic in his hand, and when he said that, he had a nasty, oily grin on his face.

"You fellows have been rather clever," I said, "but your luck can't hold out forever, you know. This is the third time we have come to grips with you, and the third time is usually considered very treacherous."

"Ah, but for whom?" he inquired, in his silky, insidious voice.

I thought it best to ignore the question. "The thing that baffles me," I said, "is what you fellows—"

I paused momentarily, for over Spawn's shoulder I saw the pinkish face of Archibald Flount!

"The thing that bothers me," I went on, desperately, "is what you fellows are up to. There doesn't seem to be—"

This time I stopped outright. Flount had raised his umbrella and brought the handle down with a thwack on Spawn's head. The man's hat flew from his head, and he collapsed to the floor without so much as a groan.

"Good work!" I commended, hoarsely, at the same time taking possession of Spawn's pistol. "Here, take this."

Flount drew back from the proffered weapon. "I feel safer with my umbrella," he said.

"Did you get to police headquarters?" I demanded.

"No; I came back. You forgot to tell me where it is. I was lost when you met me in the first place."

"Did you get a policeman?" I asked, wildly. "Didn't you tell anyone we were here?"

"Of course not!" replied Flount, stiffly. "You told me to go to police headquarters. Of course I couldn't find it without directions."

"It's only a half block away. Run, man! When you get to the street, turn to your right. It's just across to your right when you get to the corner. Hurry up!"

"That won't be necessary," said a grim voice behind me. The place seemed full of voices always ready to burst out of the silence to my rear.

"You can just drop my friend's gun; I have yours," said the voice.

Flount was glaring indignantly over my shoulder. There was nothing for me to do but drop the automatic. Then I turned about to face the new menace. It was a tall, stringy-looking man. In one hand he brandished an automatic, and in the other hand he held my pistol. He had beady little eyes; an amazingly long nose, that in other circumstances I should have thought lugubrious; and an undershot jaw.

All at once I heard a buzzing sound. Flount and I paid little attention to it, but its effect upon our captor was instantaneous and startling. Keeping his sharp little eyes on us, he leaped across Spawn's recumbent body and quickly closed the door. He shot two bolts, one at the top and the other at the bottom.

"See that door?" he rasped, with an automatic indicating one at the side. "Get through it—quick!"

Flount was for standing his ground. I saw the hopelessness of it. I dragged him across the floor, wrenched open the door, and pulled him through it.

"Shut it!" commanded the tall person.

As I was complying, I heard Flount cry out: "Dorothy!"

I whirled about. The sight that met my eyes filled me with a mixture of pity and joy. On a cot in the small room, lighted by an unshaded electric light bulb, lay Dorothy Garrison, bound and gagged! I leaped by Flount, got out my pocket knife, and had her free in thirty seconds. Flount and I helped her to rise, but her muscles were so stiff that she could not stand. We placed her back on the bed.

"Archie!" she cried. "Mr. Clark! Where are the others? Where is Garry? He's not hurt!"

"Robert is home safe and sound, Dorothy," replied Flount, chafing Mrs. Garrison's wrists, where the impression of her bonds showed cruelly in the white flesh. "He's just about frantic, but he's all right."

"Please take me home," she pleaded.

"Well—er—in just a minute," I stammered. "Just rest a moment."

Mrs. Garrison, wild-eyed, clutched Flount by the arm. "Aren't we free?" she asked, piteously. "Are you prisoners, too?"

Flount and I looked dismally at each other. We could say nothing.

Her lips trembled, and a big tear coursed down each of her lovely cheeks. Had I faced Spitz and Spawn at the moment, I could have torn them to shreds with my bare hands. Mrs. Garrison shook her head, smiled through her tears, and patted Flount's dejected shoulder.

"Never mind," she said bravely, although there was a little catch in her voice. "I feel safe now with you two here. I—I can't tell you how grateful I am."

And then there came a sound that caused my heart to leap with hope. I heard a thumping. It grew in volume, ending with a splintering, jarring crash.

I leaped over to the door. Placing my ear to it, I heard gruff, excited voices in the outer room. A moment later I recognized one of them, crisp, cold, commanding.

"Hand," I cried joyously, pounding frenziedly on the door. "Hand! In here! We've found Mrs. Garrison! Unlock the door!"

I heard exclamations; then the door opened. Hand and Inspector Gerrity bounded into the room.

"Mrs. Garrison, good!" cried Gerrity. "Clark, what happened to Spitz and Spawn?"

"I don't know," I quickly replied. "They were out in that room there; one of 'em unconscious. They locked us up in here."

"Stay with Mrs. Garrison, Clark," commanded Hand. "Come on, Inspector."

When they had left us, I turned to Mrs. Garrison. "Well, you're safe at last," I smiled.

Now that the danger was past, she seemed disposed to cry. The sight of her agitation alarmed Flount.

"Now, now, now, now," he cooed, hopping uncomfortably about before her. "Please don't cry, Dorothy. The sight of feminine tears always unmans me."

"I—I won't," sobbed Mrs. Garrison.

I thought it best to get her mind occupied. "How did you get here?" I asked.

"I—I don't know," she replied, getting control of herself. "I remember only one thing, some horrible-smelling cloth they put to my face. It was right after they carried me out to an automobile up at the house. The next thing I knew, I woke up in this terrible place. Won't you take me home?"

"As soon as the inspector and Hand return," I promised, wishing I could comply with her request without delay.

We waited half an hour before they did return. I could tell by Gerrity's face that their search had been disappointing.

"Escaped?" I asked, more or less uselessly.

"They had at least three avenues of escape," replied Hand. "By the time we were able to explore them, they could have been blocks away, and probably were. Honeycombed the basements. There's a cordon of police round this block. Perhaps one of them will pick them up, but I doubt it."

"Whatever brought you here, anyway, a message from heaven?"

"Just got a line on the place. Spitz and Spawn rented it direct from the owner. Pretty cute, sneaking right up to the shadow of police headquarters. Last place you'd think of looking for them."

All at once I felt overwhelmingly contrite, "Of course," I said, hanging my head. "I can't tell you how delighted I am that your scheme worked, Hand, but in a way it makes me feel worse. If I hadn't bungled it up for you, that pair would be in our hands this minute!"

Hand clapped me on the back. "On the contrary," he declared, "it might very well have failed altogether. We have Mrs. Garrison, you see, and otherwise they might have got away with her again."

"But you can thank Flount for that," I said warmly. "He's a very devil of a fellow." And I proceeded to tell them about our experience.

"Spitz!" said Hand, snapping his fingers, when I told him about the tall man with the lugubrious nose. "I saw a man like that disappear into a cigar store on the corner as we left police headquarters. You see, he was acting as look-out. Probably raced through the cellars intending to remove Mrs. Garrison before we could get here. The way you fellows had done for Spawn put a different color on it. The best he could do was to revive Spawn and get the pair of them away."

"That," said Archibald Flount, impatiently, "is neither here nor there. What I set out to do was to return Mrs. Garrison to her husband before he goes out of his head. Come, Dorothy, I shall see you home."

12

A BIRD IN THE HAND

I need not describe the joy with which Garrison and his wife were reunited. But it did, much to Hand's satisfaction, influence the course of events. Garrison swore he would stay in the city not one minute longer than was necessary. He was for boarding his yacht that very night. He would take his wife, he said, out of any remote possibility of further danger to her. We persuaded him to wait long enough to give the others a chance to get ready.

At first it was thought Henry King would be unable to go. The man himself set us right about that. Although he had three stitches in his scalp, the courageous fellow bullied his doctor into allowing him to sail with the yacht. X-ray pictures had shown that his skull was intact.

We were to sail at noon on the day following the return of Mrs. Garrison. At ten that morning I was closeted with Hand and Gerrity at police headquarters.

"I can't impress you too strongly with the importance of your mission," Hand was reiterating, for my benefit. "In fact, I am more than ever of the opinion that the success or failure of this case hinges directly upon it."

Inspector Gerrity, dark of brow, glowered over his desk. "I'm hanged if I am," he growled. "I'm bound to admit— blast it all!—that New York seems no safe place for the Garrisons. But why take all the rest of them away, too?

We're going to have precious little to go on after they've left. Suppose something turns up that we need information on, what then?"

"I think we have all the information we need," replied Hand, coldly.

Gerrity hitched his shoulders petulantly. "If only one or the other of that pair would go after that car," he said, ardently.

He referred to the sedan that had been used to abduct Mrs. Garrison. The machine had been located, with the aid of the license number supplied by the messenger boy. It was in a public garage in Forty-eighth Street. The car had been stolen the afternoon before. A reputable clothing merchant had reported it stolen and was anxiously waiting to get it back. Two of Gerrity's detectives were watching over it. Spitz and Spawn, once more engulfed in the maelstrom of New York life, had failed to come after it.

A silence ensued, each one of us occupied with his own thoughts. After announcing himself with his perfunctory rap, Sergeant Tim came among us.

"Mr. Garrison here, sir, wantin' to see you."

Hand glanced sharply up. "Garrison?" he said. "What's he doing here?"

"I'll show you," said the man himself, brushing by Tim.

"Where is Mrs. Garrison?" demanded Hand.

Garrison waved his hand, in which he held a piece of note paper, toward the door to the outer office. "Right out there in the waiting-room," he replied. "I'm not letting her out of my sight for a minute!" he declared vehemently, although it seemed he could not see her then. "We came down with the escort the inspector so kindly placed at our disposal. Just before we left the house to go to the yacht, I received this. This! Now what do you make of that?" he demanded, laying the piece of paper on Gerrity's desk and banging it with his fist.

Gerrity and Hand read it. Then I got it. It ran thus:

Robert Garrison, Esq.

Dear Sir:

We feel that you are making a mistake by leaving the city. Inasmuch as we expect to have
urgent business with you in a day or so, we
must request you to remain at your Riverside
Drive home. Should you ignore our request,
we regret to inform you that you will hence-
forth be in the most deadly peril.

Spitz & Spawn

As if by a given signal, we all looked at Hand. To our
astonishment, my friend's face broke into one of the few
wide grins I have ever seen on it. He rubbed his long
hands together with satisfaction.

"I feel that we have struck at the very roots of their
plot, Inspector," he said. "Now if they will only become
desperate enough to attack Mr. and Mrs. Garrison before
they leave the city!"

Garrison gave a start. "Er—how's that?" he asked, nervously.

"We must give them every opportunity," went on Hand,
as his client's color faded. "Of course they know Mr. and
Mrs. Garrison are here at police headquarters. It would be
senseless to remove the police guard for the remainder of
the trip to the yacht. That would give us away."

"That would be the finish of us!" corrected Garrison,

Hand's eyes, alight with a disturbing gleam, suddenly
came to rest upon me. "I have it!" he cried, delightedly.
"I've noticed it before. Stand over there, Clark, beside Mr.
Garrison. There, you see; same height, same build. Not a
very close resemblance about the face, but that won't matter. They'll probably take him from the rear."

I cleared a certain huskiness from my throat. "I don't like to be bothersome," I said, "but what exactly do you intend doing with me?"

"Change hats and coats with Mr. Garrison, Clark," ordered Hand, ignoring my plea for enlightenment. "Now, Mr. Garrison, just walk across the office, away from us, that's it. Watch him, Clark, watch him closely!"

Garrison, looking very mystified by it all, walked across the office. At the wall he turned about and glanced inquiringly at Hand.

"Did you get it, Clark?" asked Hand, eagerly. "All right, now let's see you imitate it."

Garrison's gait was not hard to imitate. Although almost imperceptible, he walked with a sort of limp, a slight drag of the left foot. He stood apart and, like an antique dealer inspecting a piece of chipped china, watched me as I walked across the office.

"Good!" he commended. "I rather fancy that's my limp exactly. Got it on a hunting trip; I was the only thing we shot."

I was becoming distinctly nervous. Garrison, on the other hand, was brightening.

"By Jove, this is clever of you, Mr. Hand," he cried. "I mean, thinking a way out so quickly, and all. Just what do you intend to do?"

That was what I wanted to know.

"Your hat is a little small for Mr. Garrison, Clark," observed Hand, critically. "That doesn't matter, but his is a trifle large for you. We can fix that up with a little paper under the band. It'll be all right. Look here, Inspector, have you a bullet-proof vest?"

"I have one I invented myself," replied Gerrity, with pardonable pride. "It's almost certain to stop a bullet," he added, reassuringly.

"Good. I want Clark to wear it. Just go with the inspector, will you, Clark? Put it on and rejoin us here."

"I don't want to appear unduly curious, but—" I began.

Hand had left the office with Mr. Garrison. I started resolutely after.

"The vest is right here," cried Gerrity, clutching me by the arm. "It's the latest thing," he assured me, as he got it out of a cabinet in the corner. Laying it on the desk, with eyes alight with enthusiasm, he gave the thing a sort of caress. "My own idea," he acknowledged. "Very light and pliable. The Armstrong people, who made it for me, were inclined to be skeptical, but that's only natural."

"Er—have you tried it out?"

"Not yet. Haven't had time; I got it from them the very day this case came up. You may have my word for it, though, it'll work."

His word or no, I did not like it. The thing seemed entirely too light. As he eagerly helped me into it, I kept hoping some objection would occur to me, but none did.

"Comfortable, isn't it?" cried Gerrity, as I was rebuttoning my coat.

"Um-m, yes. Awfully light, though, don't you think? It doesn't seem—"

"Light? Yes," interrupted Gerrity, "that's the beauty of it. Its flexibility is its chief standpoint. Bullet might give you a bit of a jar, but it'd never penetrate. Happy to have you wear it, old man, mighty happy."

It was nice of him to say so, and I knew he meant it in the proper spirit. Nevertheless, I should have preferred another one. The thing was altogether too light. And, besides, I could have got along quite well enough without this mysterious necessity of wearing a bullet-proof vest.

Hand and Mr. Garrison abruptly returned to the office. "Here, Clark," said my friend, "put Mr. Garrison's overcoat and hat on again. We must get you going, my boy; we'll have to hustle. Ah, that hat! Give me some scraps of paper, Inspector."

He inserted a few folds of paper under the band and handed the hat back to me. It fitted more snugly. Hand nodded in approval. He quickly reached up and, with a neck-snapping tug, pulled the brim down low over my eyes.

"There you are," he said. "And keep your head down, too."

I drew myself up. "Would I be going too far," I asked, stiffly, "if I should inquire about this business? As matters stand, I feel more or less like a clay pigeon!"

Hand closed the door. "You are going to our rooms," he said, speaking deliberately. "When you get out of the car—"

"What car?"

"The Garrisons' car. When you get out of it before our door, get across the sidewalk in a hurry. Don't run, but don't waste any time. Go immediately up to the rooms and stay in the living-room. Go directly over to the souvenir-case in the corner and examine the articles nearest the floor."

The souvenir-case, I might say, is a child of my own brain. It grew out of my friend's deplorable tendency to cast off all thoughts of neatness the moment he enters the rooms. It is all very well, and a trait that I am in hearty sympathy with, for a man to surround himself with the mementos of his past deeds. Hand's souvenirs, mostly gruesome objects, recall a successful investigation. To be sure, there are many that recall unsuccessful ones as well. But when a bullet, once used to cut short the career of a foreign diplomat, is to be found nestling in the sugar-bowl, or when one opens his razor-case to find in it a poisonous dart, devised by a Chinese gentleman of murderous instincts, obviously something must be done about it. I had made Hand a present of the souvenir-case. He had been delighted with it. After waiting several weeks for him to utilize it, I had given up hope and put the souvenirs into it myself.

To get back to the instructions Hand had been giving me, I agreed to go to the souvenir-case and examine the articles nearest the floor.

"Then what?" I asked.

"Nothing," he replied. "Absolutely nothing. Just remain there, examining the articles nearest the floor, that's all."

"Sounds more as if I should get into the souvenir-case myself!" I grumbled.

"Better be off, Clark," said Hand, abruptly. "Here, I'll show you how to go."

He took me by the arm and led me out of the office. Partly because I was quite nettled, and partly because I knew it would do no good, I asked no questions. He led me quickly along the hall toward the stairs. As we were about to go down, Miss Franklin, one of the women detectives, stepped up to us.

Miss Franklin was looking particularly attractive. She was wearing a smart costume, and her blond hair was tucked under a saucy little hat. I raised my hat, or perhaps I should say Garrison's.

Miss Franklin, with a bright smile, stepped right up me and slipped her arm through mine. My expression of pleasure was somewhat marred by Hand, who clapped Garrison's hat back on my head and yanked it down over my eyes.

"See here!" I objected. "You've got that so low I can hardly see."

"Miss Franklin is going with you," he said. "She is wearing the clothes in which Mrs. Garrison arrived here. You two are Mr. and Mrs. Robert Garrison, now don't forget. All right, follow me."

At the foot of the stairs we were joined by a squad of six detectives. In their midst we made our way to the front entrance of police headquarters. Hand left us just inside the door.

Descending the broad steps outside, I hoped fervently that no one intended to pot Garrison with a rifle bullet at that stage. Still, with our body-guard surrounding us, it would have been a difficult feat to accomplish.

The Garrison limousine, a huge affair, was drawn up at the side. The chauffeur, sitting stolidly behind the wheel, leaped out and opened the door as we approached. He recognized me, or, rather, did not recognize his employer, just as I got in. He started to object. One of the detectives silenced him with a curt order to drive us to the address where Hand and I have our rooms.

Settling back on the cushions, I saw with relief that the shades were drawn over the windows. It gave me the feeing that I was less like the actual bull's-eye of the target. Two of the detectives got into the car with Miss Franklin and me. The odds were three to one that I would not be hit *en route*.

Off we went, motor-cycle escort and all.

"I feel like the Queen of Sheba," remarked Miss Franklin, with a rippling little laugh.

I regarded her somberly. "I feel like the fatted calf," I said.

"My goodness!" she exclaimed, in mock horror. "Poor man, you do look so hot and bothered! Now all I have to do is to take a little ride from headquarters to Mr. Hand's house in this lovely big car. Then I just sit tight for a little while, and then drive right back again. Not only that, Mrs. Garrison told me to keep these perfectly heavenly clothes. Isn't this a nice job? What are you going to do?"

"If I carry out my orders, and I will," I replied, "I shall go up to my living-room and get all out of shape looking at some souvenirs that are too near the floor."

"Yes," said Miss Franklin, brightly, "that sounds like Mr. Hand's orders; you never understand them. What do you expect will happen then?"

"Anything from mayhem to murder." My smile, intended to be cheerful, I am afraid was quite sickly.

"Take it easy, brother," growled one of the detectives, through the speaking-tube to the driver's seat. "We ain't in no hurry."

"But I have to be on board a yacht at noon," I objected.

"The yacht won't sail without you, sir," he reassured me.

I tried to detach my mind from what was about to take place. It only made me more nervous to wonder. I found it difficult. That wretched bullet-proof vest of Gerrity's kept reminding me that I was nothing more than a rabbit one leap ahead of the hounds.

Miss Franklin prattled on. She always seems quite vacuous. As a matter of fact, she is the cleverest woman detective in the department. She hides her shrewdness behind a mask of frivolity.

At last we arrived. The detectives in the car kept well out of sight. The chauffeur held the door open for me. With a feeling of dread I descended to the pavement. Before I had taken one imitation of Garrison's step, I expected to be mowed down in the best approved gangster fashion. Nothing happened. I entered the building and, flinching slightly, glanced up the stairs. The battery of machine-guns that I had expected to see there did not materialize. I quickly mounted the steps and bobbed into the living-room. Even that erstwhile haven of refuge had an odd appearance of insecurity.

Absently, I started to remove Garrison's hat. I caught myself and, with a quick look round, strode quickly over to the souvenir-case. The thing stands on the floor, the lowest shelf being but a few inches off it. I therefore was required to squat on my haunches to inspect the articles laid out there. They were an odd assortment—half an egg-shell, a twisted piece of wire, a gold cuff-link, a torn patch of cloth, and a dozen other objects just as incongruous. I knew their histories by heart.

Time passed. I thought my knee-caps, cramped in the awkward position, would surely break. It was, therefore with some relief, as well as a good deal of another emotion that I heard a voice break the stillness of the living-room.

"Get up, and be quick about it! Let's see the backs of your hands—reaching for the ceiling."

I responded as rapidly as my cramped muscles would permit. I had recognized that voice, and the recognition had brought with it no reassurance. It belonged to Spitz!

"We warned you not to try to get away," went on Spitz, speaking to my back in his cold, clipped voice. "You'd have been all right if you'd stayed where you were. Keep your hands up and turn round here!"

The effect of my about-face was almost comical. Spitz and Spawn both stood just inside the door to the back hall. They each held an automatic leveled at me. For a ghastly moment I thought the weapons would go off as a result of the agitation the sight of my face produced upon the men who held them. After the first shock they just stood and regarded me dumbly.

"I don't recall a warning from you gentlemen," I said, as steadily as I could. "Perhaps you have the wrong address."

Out of the side of his mouth Spitz spoke rapidly to Spawn. What he said I could not tell, for he spoke in a foreign tongue. I had no doubt that my fate was being decided then and there.

One would naturally suppose, I should think, that a man in my predicament would have felt the icy fingers of awful fear squeezing about his heart. Nevertheless, I awaited the outcome of their grim conference with the greatest aplomb. I say that with no feeling of pride.

Immediately behind Spitz and Spawn I had caught sight of Christopher Hand and Inspector Gerrity.

Hand's face was adorned with an expression of pleased interest, such as one sees on the face of a biologist examining a new bug. Gerrity was grimly determined.

Whatever Spitz and Spawn would have decided to do with me will never be known. I think they had about reached an understanding—one that boded me no good.

An explosion, reminiscent of Hand's target practice in the living-room, crashed through the apartment. It seemed to come from Gerrity. I expected either Spitz or Spawn to pitch headlong to the floor. Neither did anything of the kind. Both leaped a foot into the air. That was all I saw. My eyes became blinded with tears; my nose and throat were suddenly choked up.

Exactly what happened next I was quite beyond knowing. I floundered forward. At the first step there was a second explosion, much more terrific than the first. With it came the kick of a horse to the pit of my stomach. The floor flew up and struck me. There I lay, perfectly certain that my last moments were at hand.

Vaguely I realized a desperate struggle was going on before my tearful vision. I gave little interest to it. A man preparing to meet his Maker loses interest in paltry affairs of that kind. There were shots and hoarse voices, and then the sound of breaking glass. At length there was quiet.

I lay there wondering whether I was to die without the pressure of a friendly hand in mine, without a word of pity welling from the heart of a sorrow-stricken friend. This was not to be.

"Clark."

It was Gerrity's voice.

"H-hello, old man. I—I'm done for!"

"What's the matter with you?"

"Shot. I'm shot through—through the stomach."

"Get out! You have my vest on, haven't you?"

"It didn't work. Don't—don't feel badly about it, old man. I—I don't blame you. My own fault."

"Didn't work, hey?" cried Gerrity, in the tone Robert Fulton must have used when he saw his steamboat push up the river. "Here it is—the bullet! Right beside you here on the floor. It worked. It worked! By thunder, I knew it would! Here, let's see," he cried excitedly, as he ripped my vest and shirt open. "There you are. That's where it struck, and it never got through! It never got through! You don't understand, Clark, but this means a lot to me. By thunder, it worked!"

"You mean to say I'm not shot?" I demanded, almost irritably.

"Of course not! How could you be with my vest on?"

"Well, then I'm blind. I can hardly see a thing!"

"Tear gas," said Gerrity, laconically. "Here, get up and go over to the window. I smashed it. The blasted stuff's got me crying again, too."

Gerrity helped me to my feet. He guided me over to the window and pushed my head through it. Getting my handkerchief into play, I mopped at my eyes. Sniveling dismally, I essayed a look at the world. A large crowd in the street was watching me sorrowfully. I hastily withdrew my head.

"You're sure I'm all right?" I asked, apprehensively. "I'm not shot?"

"Absolutely not! Couldn't be. That vest would stop a cannon-ball."

"Perhaps it would," I said, spiritedly, "but I just want to tell you I had something to do with stopping that bullet. I never got such a whack in the stomach before!"

"Of course! Of course! The vest is pliable. It gives, and the force of the bullet is taken up by the body within it.

But the bullet can't penetrate. Oh, it's a beautiful idea. I can't tell you how glad I am that it worked!"

"Neither can I," I sniffed. "By the way, what happened to Spitz and Spawn?"

Gerrity shook a lingering tear from his eye and frowned. "I'm afraid Spawn got away," he growled. Then, brightening: "But we got the other one, Spitz! He's the one who shot the Venora girl. The other fellow was just his accomplice, anyway. We'll get him too before we're through with this!"

"Well, we won't get him just yet awhile," said a disgruntled voice.

Although my vision was still quite blurred, I looked up to see Hand walk into the living-room. He was frowning.

"Was that your tear-gas pistol that went off, Inspector?" he asked, icily.

Gerrity turned a lively crimson. "Er—I'm afraid so "he muttered. "It must have become loose in my pocket when we climbed over that fence out back. There it is over on the floor by the door."

He went over to the spot where he and Hand had been standing behind Spitz and Spawn. Bending over, he picked up an object that had the appearance of a large fountain pen.

"There it is," he said, striving to strike a cheerful note. "Arthur Anderson gave it to me on my birthday. Looks like a fountain pen, doesn't it?"

"You're too old to have birthdays," growled Hand. "Well, Spawn's got clean away. How he did it I don't know. He must have been blinded by that gas, and the place is surrounded by police."

"Where's Spitz?" I asked.

"Packed him off to police headquarters in a patrol car," replied Hand. "You all right, Clark? Good! Let's get on up to headquarters, Inspector, and see what Mr. Spitz has to say for himself."

13

SPITZ

Garrison's car with Miss Franklin had departed. We climbed into a police car and set out for headquarters.

"I suppose," I said, turning to Hand with something of an injured air, "that now it would be all right to ask how this all came about."

Hand took his cigarette from his lips and grinned. "Sorry you were kept in the dark," he said, unconvincingly. "But your part should have been clear to you."

"It was. I knew perfectly well that I was nothing but a decoy. I might have enjoyed it had the game not been so desperate."

"But you had the protection of my bullet-proof vest," pointed out Gerrity.

"And now I have a bruised mid-section," I added. "But that's not what I meant. Hand, how the deuce did you know those fellows could be duped into going right into our rooms?"

"I didn't know it, but I felt pretty sure that they could. You see, they visited the rooms last night; they were familiar with the ground."

"Visited our rooms last night!"

"Yes. Fortunately, we were out all night. For the inspector's benefit I'll explain how I knew it. I picked those rooms because they have a front and rear entrance, although they are on the second floor. I have found it useful at times to walk languidly into the house from the front, only to skip energetically out the back way and down the steps. But the back door, besides being a convenient means of leaving the house unobserved, is also a hazard. An enemy might use it. I have therefore installed a burglar alarm on it. But when Clark and I are both away from the place, I disconnect the alarm. Instead, I unlock the door and fasten a thread from the knob to the door jamb. If, when I return, the thread is broken—well, somebody has been paying an illicit call. It's a help to know when to be on your guard. This morning the thread was broken, and who would have been more likely to break it than Spitz and Spawn?"

Gerrity still seemed perplexed. "But how did you know they'd go to the rooms at just the right time for us to grab them?" he demanded.

Hand smiled again. "I just told Clark that I didn't know it," he reminded the inspector. "But I had a fair idea that they would. It was pretty clear that they were hot on Garrison's trail today. They wanted to get him, and the time to do it was before he left the city. Not much chance after he boarded the yacht. Once on that island in Maine, it would have been practically impossible for them to get at him. Yes, they were looking for a chance to get him before he left the city."

"What for?" exploded Gerrity. "What in blazes do they want to get him for?"

"Perhaps Spitz will tell us," said Hand.

There was something else I wanted to clear up. "The idea, then," I said, "was that they trailed Miss Franklin and me to the rooms, thinking we were Mr. and Mrs. Garrison. Then they sneaked up the back way and stuck me up in the living-room. But why didn't they shoot me down before they even found out who I was?"

"They couldn't have, anyway," insisted Gerrity. "As you crouched before the show-case, with your head thrust forward, the only target they had was your back, and that was entirely protected by that vest of mine."

"Not altogether," I murmured, reflecting upon what the effect of a low shot might have been. I refrained from pointing out, too, that neither Spitz nor Spawn was aware that I was equipped with his precious vest.

What Hand had to say on the subject was more reassuring. "They wouldn't have shot you, Clark," he declared, "because we should have prevented it. But it was evident at once that if they did intend to kill Garrison, they meant to have words with him first."

"Yes," agreed Gerrity, "from the way they nodded to each other and so on I could tell that. But what did they want to talk to him about?"

"Aha! If we knew that, we'd have the riddle solved. If we had only sent Garrison up to the rooms instead of Clark, we'd have found out. No we wouldn't, either, that infernal gas-pistol birthday present of yours would have spoiled it. It's just as well Clark did it."

I felt tenderly of the pit of my stomach and thought otherwise.

"Well," said Gerrity, grimly, as the car pulled up beside the headquarters building, "there's an individual in there who can tell us, and by thunder, he will!"

We went up to Gerrity's office, and the inspector ordered Spitz brought before us. The man was escorted in by four detectives. Spitz, his arms shackled behind his back, strode to the center of the room. Placidly he regarded the ceiling. Gerrity, with malice in every line of him, glared at the prisoner. He motioned the detectives to leave us. Then he walked menacingly over to Spitz and halted before him.

"Got you!" he spat. "A nice specimen of manhood," he observed, scornfully eying Spitz up and down. "Shooting women through windows at night and carrying them off to your filthy cellars! Shooting honest policemen from under a bush! The chair's too good for an animal like you!"

Spitz looked down upon Gerrity and grinned, a crooked grin that made his face even more singular. "Really, Inspector," he said, in a cultured voice, "I suppose you must indulge yourself a little. You've had several bad days, according to the newspapers. Now you will be a hero. Splendid!"

"If we address you as Spitz," asked Hand, quietly, "will you know to whom we are speaking?

"Spitz will do."

"Very well, then, Spitz; you realize, of course, you are in a bad position; it couldn't be worse. It could be a good deal better, however, and perhaps you can improve it yourself. For some unknown reason a person or persons, also unknown, have placed Robert Garrison's life in deadly peril. Perhaps his wife's as well. You have made one certain attempt upon his life. But we believe the hand that fired that shot was hired to do it. If you tell us the name of your fiendish employer, it might save your life."

Again Spitz grinned, and this time shook his head. "You might try a little third degree," he suggested. "Although it wouldn't work, either. Too bad!"

"Am I to gather," asked Hand, "that you refuse to tell us?"

"You may gather from that," replied Spitz, "just exactly what you please."

"You realize what you are headed for?"

"I'm sorry, I don't. You seem to infer that it was I who did that shooting the papers have been full of. I mean the Venora girl."

Gerrity glared at the man for a moment. "Do you deny it?" he thundered.

"Of course," replied Spitz, with an amused chuckle.

The inspector stamped over to his desk and pushed a bell-button. Sergeant Tim, as though personally connected to the button, popped into the office.

"Ask Saunders to step in here," ordered Gerrity. "Tell to bring the finger-prints of this fellow and all other data he has on him."

Saunders, apparently, had been waiting to be summoned. He entered the office carrying a wire tray. On it were a finger-print card, the pane of glass from Garrison's library window, a china mug, an automatic, an electric light bulb, and some photographs. He laid the tray on Gerrity's desk. At a nod from the inspector he picked up the finger-print card.

"This is a set of his finger-prints," he said, indicating Spitz. "They check with those on the window glass from Mr. Garrison's library. They check with those on the mug, taken from the room over in East End Avenue. They check with those on the automatic, taken from him when he was captured. They check with those on the electric light bulb, taken from the cellar where Mrs. Garrison was found. These photographs are of finger-prints on the steering wheel of the roadster used by the gunmen the night of the murder. They check."

"Good!" said Gerrity. "Has a bullet from that automatic been given to Professor Hertzog?"

"Yes, sir. The gun was taken right up to the professor's laboratory, just as you ordered. As soon as a couple of bullets had been fired from it, Lieutenant Gannon brought it back here and gave it to me."

"All right, Saunders, ask Lieutenant Gannon to step in here."

We waited in silence for Gannon to join us. Covertly I watched Spitz. Once more he was gazing serenely at the ceiling. The mass of evidence, of a most damaging nature, that Saunders had marshaled against him seemed to leave him unmoved.

Lieutenant Gannon stepped briskly into the office.

"You took this fellow's gun up to Professor Hertzog's?" asked Gerrity.

"Yes, sir."

"What did he say about the bullets?"

"I didn't stay long, Inspector; had to get the gun back here for the finger-print men. But before I left, the professor compared the two bullets under a magnifying glass. He's funny, you know. Won't say anything definite until he's compared them atom for atom. But in this case he said he was sure he'd find the bullet that killed Miss Venora was fired from that automatic," said Gannon, indicating with a fateful forefinger the weapon that had been taken from Spitz.

"That will do, Gannon," said Gerrity, grimly.

When the lieutenant had withdrawn, Hand turned once more to Spitz. "You see," he said, significantly.

"And I'll tell you one more thing!" snapped Gerrity. "The bullet that killed Miss Venora and the bullet that wounded Patrolman Spinelli were fired from the same gun; we've determined that. If you shot the one, you shot the other!"

Spitz smiled, almost benignly, first upon Gerrity and then upon Hand. "You don't seem to realize," he said, "that all the evidence against me is purely circumstantial."

"We'd have no difficulty convincing a jury that you killed Miss Venora," retorted Hand. "Circumstantial evidence is weak only when it is insufficient or unsupported. There is a man right in this room who saw you in the act of keeping Mrs. Garrison a prisoner. We have enough right here to convince any jury of your guilt, never fear. It would be much better to have the district attorney asking for a conviction of second-degree murder than first. We're offering you a chance to save yourself from the chair. Are you going to take it?"

Spitz maintained his exasperating air of amusement. "That is very good of you," he said.

"You seem to think this is funny," growled Gerrity. "You won't think it's so funny when they're strapping you in the chair with all the bright lights on you!"

"Policemen are habitually boring," observed Spitz, with a sigh.

Hand looked long and narrowly at Spitz. "I think this fellow needs time to consider," he said. "He's too fresh from his accustomed liberty to realize what he's up against. We'll let him stew in his own juice for a day or so, eh, Inspector? Before you go back to your cell, though, Mr. Spitz, where do you hail from?

"Your own little old New York," grinned Spitz.

"You lie, my friend," said Hand, evenly. "You are German."

Unexpectedly, to me at least, this simple, apparently unimportant statement found a chink in Spitz's armor. He gave a slight start, and, for the first time, a gleam of fear came into his eyes. He quickly recovered himself and smiled as blandly as ever. "What makes you think so," he asked.

"You and your friend Spawn," replied Hand, "were conversing in German when you were deciding what to do with Clark this morning. By the way, Clark, they had just about decided, when the inspector's birthday present got obstreperous, that you have lived long enough."

"Spawn is a German," explained Spitz, hastily. "He has trouble with the English language. That's why we were speaking in German."

"Is it?" said Hand, skeptically. "Well, I'll assure you of one thing, I am going to find out why you don't care for your nationality to be known, and why you make uncalled-for explanations for having spoken in German. I might tell you that Spawn had no trouble with English when he talked to Clark at the time Mrs. Garrison was found. His grammar was not perfect over in East End Avenue, but he knew the English language, all right. Have him locked up again, Inspector. And now, Clark, I don't think you should keep that yacht waiting any longer."

14

COMPLICATED EVIDENCE

The yacht *Dorothy* slid peacefully through the waters off the New England coast at half speed. The port motor was out of commission. Like everything else that had happened since Hand took up the Garrison case, the defection of the Diesel engine was a mystery.

According to the engineer, the engine had been all right just before the start from New York. Both port and starboard engines had been all right. But when the order to get under way was given, neither would start. After much fussing, the starboard engine had started. Nothing could induce the port engine to function. Ever since, it had remained no better than so much ballast.

Garrison had refused to postpone the trip. In this he had been heartily seconded by Hand. We had put off at reduced speed and run under it the entire twenty-four hours that had elapsed since our departure.

A bridge game, played by Mrs. Garrison, Mrs. Abbington, Henry King, and Dr. Innes, was in progress in the reading-saloon. Garrison, Archibald Flount, and I were onlookers. Miss Dykeman was below in her room with a bad case of *mal de mer*. She had feebly announced, right after luncheon, that the Atlantic was by no means so nice an ocean as the Pacific.

I felt sorry for Miss Dykeman. Just the same, her indisposition was something of a relief to me. She had, for what reason I am at a loss to find, taken quite a fancy to me. I am one of those men who get no enjoyment from regarding themselves in a mirror. I am twice her age, and my friends, I know, although they do not think I do, consider me a rather dull but amiable fellow. Not exactly the sort of qualifications to cause a fluttering of the female heart, even when it is in its teens. Nevertheless, Miss Dykeman's heart had evidently fluttered. As a result I had got nowhere with my investigation. At last I was free to pursue my shady duty, that of eavesdropper.

Garrison, muttering something about the engines, got up and left us. Soon after, remarking that I had something to attend to in my room, I also left the reading-saloon. After waiting round for the best part of a quarter-hour, I met Garrison as he came up from the engine room.

"Still a total loss?" I asked.

"Can't do a thing with it," he replied, a little irritably. "Simply won't go. Never had any trouble with it before. Can't understand it!"

"Well, one motor will get us there. When do you expect to raise the island?

"Captain says tomorrow morning. About ten. We'd have been there by tonight with both motors working."

I steered him off to the lounging-saloon up forward. "This is a beautiful yacht," I said.

"Comfortable," said Garrison, absently.

He seemed preoccupied. He dropped into a wicker chair, stretched his legs out, and drew his eyebrows into a thoughtful frown. I decided to find out what was troubling him.

"Strange, that motor going dead just at this time," I remarked.

Garrison gave me a quick glance. "More than strange," he said. "I don't like it. Somebody tried to put those motors out of commission."

"Who could it have been, a member of the crew?"

He shook his head. "The same crew has manned this yacht for the past three years," he pointed out. "They are trustworthy seamen, from the captain down."

"But who else was aboard her? She's been in port, but I suppose there's been a watch on her."

"The crew live on her, whether she's at sea or in port. Nobody's been aboard who didn't have a right to be there. Besides, both engines were in perfect order yesterday morning; they were tested."

We both reflected for some time. Hand's opinion was beginning to find favor with me. Perhaps a member of the party was at the bottom of the whole mystery. Someone, one of those people with whom I was going to live, might have slipped into the engine room and tampered with the motors just before we sailed. As I was reflecting thus, Henry King joined us.

"Hello!" he exclaimed. "Not interrupting a meeting of the diet, am I? Gave my hand to Flount. I inflicted my rotten luck on your wife long enough."

"No; come in and sit down," invited Garrison, looking up with a smile.

King, with the long, full-swinging stride of one accustomed to the open, crossed the saloon and threw himself into a chair. He gave the impression of being hemmed in by the narrow confines of the yacht. I would have given much to attain the physical shape that he kept himself in. It costs a lot besides money to live in the city.

Although his head was still swathed in a bandage, King had made a remarkable recovery from the blow he had suffered.

"You two looked so solemn, I was afraid I was intruding," he said.

"We were thinking about that motor," explained Garrison.

King sat up and grinned. "I suppose you'll think I'm an unsympathetic soul," he said, "but I'm rather fond of that motor—the one that's not working, I mean. It prolongs the sea voyage, you see. I was scared to death I'd be seasick; never been on the water before. But I'm keelhauled if I'm not as good a sailorman as ever trod a deck!"

"It's a relief that you are," said Garrison. "One's enough. Poor little Gladys; it's no fun to be seasick. It's this little ground swell that's come up that put her under. All in all, though, it's remarkably calm for this time of year."

"What's the matter with that motor, anyway?" asked King.

"I don't know," replied Garrison. "I'm not familiar with Diesel engines, but somebody tampered with it. The other one, too. But the engineer was able to fix that one. If he hadn't, we'd still be in New York."

"Hurrah for the engineer, then," said King. "But who tampered with them?"

"I wish I knew," replied Garrison, grimly. "Mr. Clark seems to suspect my crew, but I can answer for every one of them. The motors were all right, tested yesterday morning. Between then and the time we sailed, somebody got at them."

We had reached that point before. Now King helped us meditate upon it.

"Why don't you find out whether anyone was on the yacht before we sailed?" he asked at length. "Someone must have sneaked on here, or something like that.

"If anyone got aboard," said Garrison, "he wasn't seen."

"I suppose there was someone round the engines all the time," said King. "I mean, one of your own men."

"Not at all," corrected Garrison. "The chief engineer went ashore and didn't get back until about fifteen minutes before we shoved off. He asked my permission to go."

An alert expression, such as one sees on the face of a man who is about to unravel a dark mystery, came to Henry King's face. "Something funny here," he said, excitedly. "You say the engineer was not on the boat a half hour before we left. I say he was. I got on about that long before we left, and I met one of the boat's officers, right out on deck. I asked him if he was the captain, and he said he was the engineer!"

Garrison had been listening intently. Now he sat back with a grunt. "That was the assistant," he said. "No; there's nothing to that. Both the first and second engineers, the only ones who go into the engine room, had lunch before we sailed. Then the chief went ashore."

The conversation veered round to general subjects. At length I suggested that it was time we changed King's bandage. For some strange reason he had avoided letting Dr. Innes do that service for him. As he had learned that I knew something about bandaging, he had picked on me. I was only too glad to do it.

Garrison went to the bridge to speak to the captain. King and I went below to his room. As he closed the door, he turned to me. For a moment he seemed undecided. "That's a funny thing about those motors," he finally said. "What do you think about it?"

"I don't know," I replied. "Sit down here, and I'll get at that bandage."

I stood behind him and went to work on his head.

"You know," said King, "I don't like that dead-motor business. Since Garrison told us someone had tampered with them, I mean."

"Neither do I."

"I've been doing a lot of thinking about this whole deplorable business. I don't like to say anything, because, after all, I'm really an outsider. You are too; so I don't mind telling you what I think. It appears that no one was in the engine room when we came on the yacht. None of the crew, I mean."

"It seems that neither of the engineers was there," I agreed, wondering whether his train of thought was leading in the same direction as my own.

"I didn't like to say so to Garrison, but here's something you can't deny: one of his guests could have wrecked those motors!"

I gave a start. "You don't know whether one did?" I asked, quickly.

"No, I don't, unfortunately. But if one did, it was a man, don't you think?"

"Yes. At least, it seems logical."

"Well, there are only two. Disregarding ourselves, that is. One is Flount—"

"And the other is Dr. Innes," I breathed.

"Aha!" exclaimed King. "Do I detect that you are not so keen about that sullen young man either?"

"I shouldn't like to say."

"Well, neither should I, and, as I said before, you are the only person I feel able to talk to. I shouldn't think of expressing my opinions to any of the others. It would be unmitigated cheek if I did. But I've had a feeling all along that someone at that bridge party the night Miss Venora was shot could have told a lot about it!"

"Did your feeling, by any chance, have a leaning toward Flount or Innes?"

"I don't feel like suspecting Flount."

"Neither do I."

"Well, then, that leaves Innes. Mind you, I don't suspect him of anything. But just the same, this whole thing has given me the impression of having been engineered by someone on the inside, if you know what I mean."

"Precisely. I've had the same impression. If it's Innes, say, if you overhear anything that would seem to implicate him, let me know, will you?"

"Gladly. I'll keep my ears open. I had intended to, anyway. You see, I'm in just as awkward a position myself. I have an idea your friend Christopher Hand suspects the whole kit and caboodle of us."

I smiled. "You're pretty astute. Still, I don't think he suspects the whole kit and caboodle of you, as you say. He does think, just as you and I, that whoever is plaguing the Garrisons is a guest on this yacht."

"I'll bet he's on the right track! And so you are supposed to find out who it is, eh? Well, you can count on me to help you if I can. I think I'm in a better position to do it than any of the others, too."

"Thanks. There, I guess that bandage will do."

King admired my handiwork in the mirror. "That's a swell job, Doctor," he grinned. Then his expression became sober. "You see now why I didn't fancy Dr. Innes taking care of my head, don't you?" he asked.

"I wondered whether that was it when you refused his offer."

"It was. I don't think any sane man would want to do me in, but if Dr. Innes is the one who is after the Garrisons, in my estimation he's off his trolley. I've had one crack on the head, and that's enough. By the way, old man, I think I'll turn in for a little nap. I find that I'm liable to get a headache from this thing along about this time in the afternoon."

After I left King, I went out on deck. The *Dorothy* rolled lazily, taking the swell almost broadside. There was scarcely any breeze, and our slow progress made it very comfortable on deck. It was warm for October, a perfect day to be at sea.

Turning toward the stern, as I reached the after deck I came upon Dr. Innes. He was standing at the rail, gazing down into the wake. I stepped up beside him. "Bridge game all over?" I asked, with a smile.

He looked up, nodded curtly, and resumed his gazing at the tumbling waters. I wondered whether he was the one who had tried to prevent the propeller below him from churning the sea.

"We couldn't have a better day, could we?" I asked, determined, even at the cost of appearing too forward, to engage him in conversation.

"Nice enough day," admitted the young man, grudgingly, it seemed to me. There was a slight frown on his dark, handsome face. A fire seemed to be smoldering behind his black eyes as he gazed somberly down at the water.

"What's the matter," I asked, banteringly, "get cleaned up at bridge?"

Innes shifted his eyes to my face. He held them there, gazing coldly at me, for what seemed a year. "No," he said curtly, and then gazed at the ocean.

"Come, now," I said, a little nettled by this treatment, "why can't we be friends? We're going to have to put up with each other for quite a while, you know. Might as well make the best of it."

"I'm not in the habit of associating with policemen," he retorted, insolently.

Thank heaven I laughed. "Why, I've associated with lots of them," I cried, "and most of them were splendid chaps. As a strict matter of fact, though, I'm not one myself. I happen to be an honorary member of the New York police department, but that's all. You don't mind unbending to an honorary policeman, do you?"

Although he did not look up at me, Innes smiled. It took something unwholesome away from his face, a something that should not belong to a face so young. "You win," he said. "What shall I do, kiss you?"

"If you do, I'll pitch you right over the rail," I grinned. "But I still think you took a licking at bridge."

"No," he said, quite seriously, "we won four rubbers at a cent a point."

"Ye gods!" I exclaimed, "you should be out here dancing a hornpipe instead of moping over the rail like this. Don't you think so yourself?"

"Fact of the matter is," he said, seeming to stiffen, "I'm not so wild about this trip."

"Why not?"

Innes subjected me once more to that cold, disconcerting stare. "You know why not," he said.

"Why, my dear fellow, I can't imagine. I think it's lovely. Here we are, leaving the cares of the world behind us, all ready to have a delightful time. We have three charming young ladies in the party, a perfect host, and—"

"Oh, piffle!" cried Innes, disgustedly. "You know perfectly well what a delightful time we're due to have. We're being sent away like a bally lot of animals to perform. You're the trainer, but you're going to have a sweet time making us go through our tricks!"

I was resolved not to get angry with him. I let him sulk for a minute; then I approached him from another angle. "I hear one of the engineers is pretty sure he knows who monkeyed with his motor," I said, watching him narrowly.

Innes, once more looking over the stern, shrugged his shoulders indifferently. "I didn't know the motor was monkeyed with," he said, in a bored voice.

"But surely you knew only one was working."

"Oh, yes. One expects those things when everything is done with such a beastly rush. I suppose you are attaching a great deal of importance to it," he said, giving me a pitying smile. "See something sinister in it, I'll wager. Policemen are notoriously given to over-emphasis. That's the trouble with them. They go about in a pea-green fog of outlandish suspicion, mostly conjured up within their own suspicious, sluggish minds. No wonder they never see through anything. Too much of their time is watching innocent people."

I took this rebuff with a smile. "I suppose," I said, "that, not being handicapped by a suspicious, sluggish mind, you have solved this mystery all by yourself. It would be interesting to hear your version of it."

"Well, I'll tell you one thing," blurted young Innes, "whoever fired the shot that killed poor little Vera Venora was hired to do it!"

I was somewhat astonished. The view he had stated was precisely the view held by ourselves, but we had guarded it jealously.

"What on earth makes you think that?" I demanded, making an effort, a poor one I am afraid, to appear amused.

"I'll tell you more than that," offered Innes, smiling cynically. "The man who hired the assassin was right in the house, a guest, when the shot was fired."

This time I gasped openly. "Good Lord!" I exclaimed. Who do you think it was?"

"I have a very good idea who it was," declared Innes. "If you were half the detective you think you are, you'd have the same idea."

"But, my dear fellow, I'm not a detective at all. I happen to be very fond of Christopher Hand. He is a very singular, interesting person, and I find the cases on which he is engaged tremendously interesting. Not having anything in particular to do, I help out whenever I'm wanted, but purely from a standpoint of friendship. I don't pretend to

be even mildly discerning. But you, why, you're positively
penetrating. Whom do you suspect?"

"It is not my place to accuse anyone."

"I disagree with you; it is your duty! Your host and
hostess may be in deadly peril this very minute. You would
be devoid of all manhood if you didn't seek to save them
from harm when you felt you might."

Dr. Innes took his eyes off me and gazed far out to sea.
He knotted his brows and took his own time to ponder
the matter. Finally, still gazing absently out over the sea,
he spoke. "There is a man on this ship," he said, "who is
secretly in love; madly, desperately, and illicitly in love."

There was only one answer to that. "Mrs. Garrison?" I
asked.

Innes nodded. "Who else could he be illicitly in love
with?" he snapped.

"But who is it?" I insisted.

Suddenly Innes's face flushed angrily. "Find out for
yourself," he muttered, and, turning abruptly, he strode
rapidly away from me.

I remained at the rail, lost in thought. What was Innes
trying to do, anyway? King thought he was insane, and
I was beginning to believe so myself. Was Innes himself
the man who was shaken by a passionate love for Dorothy
Garrison? Was he so morose at the miscarriage of his desperate plot that he was paving the way for his own un-
doing? Clearly his implications included only three men:
himself, Henry King, and Archibald Flount.

Flount was out of the question. A woman-hater by in-
stinct, he was also quite incapable of the dastardly plot
against the Garrisons.

King? He had known the Garrisons but three brief days
before the tragedy. Love at first sight might seethe through
the blood of a youth, but King was nearly fifty or I missed

my guess. Also, he seemed a steady, well-balanced fellow. Another point in his favor was that, being a stranger to New York, he could hardly have arranged the elaborate plot.

The whole thing snapped back to implicate no one but Dr. Innes himself. But there were reasons, almost as strong as in the cases of the other two, that argued against this theory. At the time of the murder, at least, he was madly in love with Vera Venora. And then, unless he was a consummate actor, his reactions to Mrs. Garrison's presence were not those of a man passionately in love with her. So much I had seen for myself. To be sure, Dr. Innes quite possibly could have got possession of Mrs. Abbington's pistol, since he had been friendly with her. Flount too, for that matter, could have purloined it. King, on the other hand, could hardly have done so.

The only conclusion I came to was that Dr. Innes might have employed himself in dragging a red herring across the trail for my benefit. In doing so he had certainly hit upon one or two of our hypotheses.

At length, beginning to feel a little chilly, I left the deck. I found no one in the lounging-saloon. Determined to find someone to talk to, I made my way aft. The dinner table was being set for the evening meal as I passed through the dining-saloon.

I entered the reading-saloon and looked round. At first I thought my search for company was to end in failure. Then I saw a pair of legs protruding from a deep-seated chair. Moving round to see, I perceived that they belonged to Archibald Flount. My companion on the rescue of Mrs. Garrison was all hunched over, apparently in a brown study.

"Well, well," I said, cheerily, "what's got into everybody? Here it is a perfectly beautiful day, and there's just about as much gayety on this boat as there is in the headquarters of a defeated politician. What have you to say for yourself, Mr. Flount? Why aren't you filled with happiness?"

All I got for that was a sour look. Mr. Flount appeared to have liked his solitude and to be wishing for more. I refused to be discouraged.

"You should go out on deck," I admonished, dropping into a chair beside him. "Fill your lungs with the fresh salt air. Brace you right up."

Mr. Flount evidently could not find words to express himself on that point. All he did was to shudder. I made a third attempt.

"Don't tell me it was the bridge game that upset you. I hear you lost."

Mr. Flount sneered.

"Um-m," I mused, wondering what under the sun to say next. All at once I hit upon an idea. Feigning an accusatory air, I leveled a finger at him and said: "I know what's the matter, you are composing a love sonnet!"

The effect upon him was most startling. He shot out of his chair and stood trembling before me.

"I resent that!" he said, with such violence that his eyeglasses went tumbling to the end of their ribbon. "I will not be mocked, sir! You owe me an apology, and I demand it at once!"

I rose quickly to my feet. "Why—why, of course," I stammered. "I sincerely beg your pardon, sir. I was merely making a joke, I assure you. I usually put my foot in it when I do, and I guess I have again."

I saw immediately that I had only made matters worse.

"A joke!" shrilled Mr. Flount. "You think me a joke, then!"

"Not at all," I cried, in desperation. "Believe me, sir, I am sorry I brought this between us. I admire you. I admire your—er—your—your literary talents, and—well—your courage."

"You were trying to make fun of me!" spluttered Flount.

"But I insist that I wasn't! I was lonesome, that's all, and I sought your companionship. I enjoy your—er—your interesting intellectuality. I did not mean to give offense, but if unknowingly I have done so, I humbly beg your pardon. But," I said stiffly, "if I am not wanted, I shall go."

"Er—I think I was rather too strenuous," said Mr. Flount, loosing the dove. "It is my turn to apologize, sir. Please forget my warmth. You see, I was very deeply absorbed. I'm sorry, genuinely sorry."

"Oh, please think nothing of it, sir," I implored, getting back into my chair. "I had no business to intrude upon your meditations. I'm afraid I am not accustomed to the traits a profound thinker, such as yourself."

"Perhaps not," agreed Mr. Flount, thoroughly mollified. "I find it extremely difficult to bring my mind from the depths that it probes to the—what shall we say?—sunshine of sociability?"

"A very nicely turned phrase!" I cried. "By Jove, it takes you fellows with the intellect to put things cleverly."

Mr. Flount beamed. A sudden lurch of the ship sent him spinning back into his chair, but he adjusted himself, perched his glasses back on his nose, and beamed some more.

"It would be interesting," I said, "if I am not once more being too presumptuous, to know what you were pondering so deeply."

Flount seemed rather taken aback. He frowned, but this time meditatively. After adjusting his glasses, once more dislodged by the frown, he turned to me with an air of great profundity. "I was pondering the mystery," he confided, almost ominously.

"Ah!" I exclaimed, "I have waited for this moment. I knew your agile mind would not fail to seize upon so absorbing a subject, and one so intimate, too. I have not asked your opinion, because I knew when you were ready, you would speak."

Mr. Flount beamed again. "You have made a singularly accurate estimation of me, sir," he said. "I have gone into every detail of this thing. I can give it to you in a nutshell. On the whole, he added, airily, "it has been quite simple."

At least I was not going to be put to it to drag an opinion piecemeal from him. Words were trembling to be loosed from his lips. "You can't imagine how interested I should be to hear it," I said, breathlessly.

Mr. Flount leaned over confidentially to me. He punctuated his statement with a succession of light taps on my elbow. "The man you want is right on this boat!"

For the third time that afternoon my emotions careened through a somersault. "My word!" I breathed.

With a superior air, Flount smiled upon me. "I don't wonder that you are astonished," he said. "But, as I said before, it is all very simple. The way to solve crime is to take yourself into seclusion. Give yourself up entirely to cerebration. In the quiet of your study, where none of the jarring influences of the world can distract you, a clearer perspective can be obtained than by chasing about after clues. After all, there are so many irrelevant clues to be found that they merely muddle up the case."

"Um-m."

"You may not agree, you may not agree, sir, but I tell you, that is my method, and look what it has got me. You are still baffled, in the dark, and I have solved the mystery!"

"I don't suppose a man of your intelligence would think of keeping it a secret."

"Certainly not! You are welcome to my deductions. I might say, my astounding deductions. I don't expect to get any of the glory for them; neither do I want it. I am thoroughly magnanimous. After all, you make your living by solving crime.”

“On the contrary, I am merely helping a friend. If your solution is correct, I will not rest until you have received credit for it.”

“If it is correct, you say? There are no *ifs* about it!”

“I beg your pardon, of course not. I am all expectation.”

Flount once more tapped me significantly upon the elbow. “Your man,” he hissed, “is Henry King!”

“Good Lord!” I exclaimed. “Do you know what you’re doing? Accusing one of the Garrisons’ guests!”

Flount smiled pityingly. “Ah, that’s where you have all gone astray,” he said, with compassion. “You have concentrated all your attention on those two gunmen—who are they, Spatz and Spintz? Yes, that is where you took the bypath to failure. Those men were merely hired to abduct Mrs. Garrison.”

“What for? For what purpose?”

“Blackmail,” replied Archibald Flount, darkly.

“Blackmail,” I said, thunderstruck. “But surely Miss Venora was not murdered for blackmail.”

The expression of pity deepened in Mr. Flount’s eyes. “You see,” he said, deprecatingly. “The irrelevant clues. The unfortunate incident of that girl’s death was seized upon by the blackmailer to make his plot all the uglier. Resourceful of him.”

“Do you mean to say there is no real connection between the murder of Miss Venora and the abduction of Mrs. Garrison?”

“None whatever!”

The irrelevant clues pointed otherwise. I decided, however, not to mention them.

“And you think Henry King is the blackmailer?” I asked.

"He's the only logical person. He lives afar; has a ruthless personality, quite capable of such an undertaking; and he is thoroughly not to be trusted!"

"It is certainly a new train of thought," I mused.

Mr. Flount got to his feet and shook his head resignedly. "There is your case," he said, with a sigh. "I hardly expected much credence would be given to it. I fully expect you to go on chasing will-o'-the-wisps. Well, I have done my duty, and I will not be discouraged, either. And now, if you will pardon me, I shall get ready for dinner."

He left me before I could appease him. Hand, at least, was vindicated. I was getting evidence—too much of it.

15

ANOTHER ATTACK

At dinner that evening I paid particular attention to the
actions of King, Flount, and Dr. Innes. I observed nothing
of value. King was the same hale fellow as usual, Dr. Innes
was just as taciturn as ever, and Archibald Flount was his
customary pompous, pedantic self.

Perhaps Christopher Hand could have deduced something from what I had gleaned that afternoon. For my
part, I was thoroughly baffled by it. King had openly given
me to understand he suspected Dr. Innes. Dr. Innes, on
the other hand, had attempted to direct my suspicions
toward either King or Flount. Flount's odd reaction to my
jest concerning the love sonnet had seemed to link him
with the doctor's aspersion. And then Flount had openly accused King. There it was, a perfect vicious circle;
King suspecting Innes, Innes hinting darkly at Flount, and
Flount accusing King.

I could make nothing of it. None of the three had needed to tell me his views. Two of them, at least, were wrong,
and probably all three. It was impossible that they were in
league. Paradoxically, I was beginning to think that Hand
was wrong after all, and that the man behind the plot was
not on the boat.

As soon as I could detach myself, I went to my room.
I had decided, in the interests of forcefulness, to keep a

written record of events as they occurred. I intended, once arrived at the island, to get to the mainland as quickly as possible and mail it off to Hand.

When I had brought my record up to date, I locked it up in my bag and joined the others. I found them all, except Miss Dykeman, in the reading-saloon.

"Very few minds," Mr. Flount was saying, didactically, "are above the normal."

"I don't believe it's possible to set an average," declared Henry King. "How could you? No two minds are alike, you know. There's a chap out home who is uncanny at anything mathematical, but give him a good knotty business problem, a case where a quick decision is necessary, and he's all at sea. Minds develop along their natural penchants, and they're invariably lop-sided."

"Anything personal in that?" demanded Flount, stiffly.

"Nothing," grinned King, "except that you're included in the horde."

"I am included in no hordes!" corrected Flount, drawing himself up.

Dr. Innes took an unaccustomed part in the conversation. "Why argue about it?" he asked. "Connie is a mind-reader; she can tell you positively whether you are no better than the horde. She can tell whether you are worse, too."

"Tommy rot!" spluttered Flount. "No such things as mind-readers! Silly!"

"Maybe you think so," said Dr. Innes, with a shrug, "But I'll tell you right here, she can come pretty close to finding out what you are thinking. All she needs is a pack of cards."

Flount waxed suspicious. "What have the cards to do with it?" he asked.

"Oh, they have everything to do with it," cried Mrs. Abbington, running over to Flount and taking him by the lapels of his dinner coat. "Come, Archie, let me read your mind. It would be such a difficult mind to read, you know."

Flount colored painfully and made ineffectual efforts to get away. In spite of his evident embarrassment, he laughed as he protested against being made the victim of what he called a seeress.

"All right," pouted Mrs. Abbington. "If you have such thoughts in your head, Archie, that you are afraid of having a lady read them, I'll pick on somebody else. There's Mr. Clark, he's not afraid of having me read his thoughts, are you, Mr. Clark?"

"Well," I joked, "I'm afraid you'll find them quite terrible."

"That will be perfectly grand!" cried Mrs. Abbington, gleefully. "Get me the cards, Frank. In that drawer over there. Now, I'll sit right down here at this table, and you stand beside me, Mr. Clark."

I felt inwardly gratified at the attention I was receiving from the beautiful young woman. Mrs. Garrison, too, came over to stand beside me. As I made a great pretense at concentration, she regarded me with dancing eyes and laughed throatily. It appeared that I was to think furiously upon any subject that I chose. At the same time I was to keep a certain card in mind. I was not used to such mental gymnastics. Mr. Flount snickered at me. I think he was a little disgruntled at not having been coaxed more strenuously.

My part was as nothing compared to the gigantic task before Mrs. Abbington. The others all crowded about as she manipulated the cards. At length she had them all laid out, face upward on the table. She studied them intently for several minutes; then she calmly lighted a cigarette and looked up at me. There was a twinkle in her eye that made me a bit nervous.

"Your card is in the second horizontal row," she announced.

"That's right."

"And it is in the third vertical row; so it is the ace of hearts."

"Right again," I cried, leading the applause. "That's a clever trick. I haven't the faintest idea how it works, but I've seen it before. I thought, though, the idea was to read my mind."

'So it is," she affirmed, her smiling eyes on my face. "The card trick is only secondary, though it helps. You were wondering, Mr. Clark, whether Archibald Flount is in love with Dorothy Garrison."

I nearly swooned. The announcement was greeted with a burst of hilarity, but neither Flount nor I joined in it. Although Mrs. Abbington's guess was far wide of mark, I had been pondering that very question just before the trick was started.

How to get out of the distressing predicament was what I was hectically pondering just then. I should never have let myself in for it. To make matters worse, I turned about to find Robert Garrison's white, angry face at my shoulder. I decided to fall in with the others and consider the thing in the light of a joke.

"I swear this is the first time I have played the role of Cupid," I cried.

This also was lustily applauded. Even Flount and Garrison smiled stiffly. Finally the merriment subsided. I was unutterably relieved when Mrs. Abbington persuaded Henry King to be her next victim.

As the trick got started, I felt someone pluck at my coat sleeve. It was Garrison. With a motion of his head toward the door, he turned and entered the passageway. I was filled with an uncomfortable mixture of feelings as I followed him. Without a word he led me down the companionway to his cabin. When I had followed him in, he closed the door and locked it.

"I'm infernally sorry about that trick," I said, earnestly. "Of course I wasn't thinking anything of the sort. I didn't just know what—"

Garrison waved his hand impatiently "Never mind that," he said. "Connie is always getting someone into a pickle just for the fun of it. I want to talk to you about something quite different," he went on, grimly. "Mr. Clark, there has just been another attempt upon my life!"

"What!"

"But for the grace of God I'd be astern drowning at this very minute!"

"You mean—someone tried to throw you overboard?"

"That's it exactly."

"But I thought you were in the reading-saloon with the rest of us."

Garrison rolled back his cuff and bared his right wrist. It was swollen and discolored. "I didn't get that in the reading-saloon," he said. "No, I stepped out on deck to see what the weather was like, and someone pitched me over the rail. By the greatest luck I got my fingers in the wire netting of the rail and hung on. Sprained my wrist, I think."

"Good heaven! Surely you saw who it was."

"Surely I didn't! He was gone before I could climb back on deck."

"I didn't hear you shout."

"I didn't shout, because whoever it was took good care that I couldn't. He grabbed me first by the throat from behind. Then he gave me a shove. Strange as it may seem, when I found myself dangling from the rail, I was filled more with rage than with fear. I didn't shout even then. Instead I scrambled back on the deck as quickly as I could to get a look at my assailant."

Suddenly a significant fact became evident to me. "There is one thing positive," I said, "and that is that it was a member of the crew. Everyone else was in the reading-saloon at the time!"

Garrison smiled skeptically. "How do you know?" he asked. "You thought I was there."

I had to admit that he was right. "But if someone in the reading-saloon was the man," I objected, "it certainly had to be done in a hurry. Perhaps someone else saw him leave if I didn't."

"Perhaps someone did," agreed Garrison, fervently, "and I hope to heaven that is the case. And as for its having been done in a hurry, that's the only way it could have been done. It happened right outside the sliding door to the deck from the reading-saloon."

"Then your idea is that someone in the reading-saloon saw you on the deck through the glass panel in the door. He slipped through the door, pitched you over the rail, and bobbed back inside again. Did you go out on the deck through that door?"

"Yes, I did."

"And so did the other fellow, according to your theory. It's very funny that we didn't hear you."

"Not at all. The tracks those doors slide in are greased."

I thought the matter over for a moment. Then I looked searchingly at Garrison. "Whom do you suspect?" asked.

Garrison grunted angrily and paced the room. "I tell you I don't suspect a member of my crew!" he said, as if trying to convince himself that he was right.

"Bribery," I suggested.

"Impossible! I picked all those men very carefully. Not a one who hasn't been in my employ at least three years. Every man of this crew is faithful to me; I'd swear it! No, it was someone in that reading-saloon, I tell you!"

"Very well," I said quietly, "which one?"

Garrison stopped his pacing to and fro and halted before me. "The devilish part of this is," he growled, "that I
can't accuse a guest. How can I? I have my suspicions, yes;
but what can I do about it?"

"You don't need to accuse anyone openly," I pointed
out.

"No, and I can't, either. The only thing I know is this.
After I had scrambled over the rail, I peered down the
deck. Nobody was in sight. I just happened to glance into
the smoking-saloon. Everybody was grouped about the
table, but one man was outside the group near the door.
He was right behind you, and he was edging round to get
up to the table. That man was Henry King!"

"Henry King, eh?" I said slowly, thinking it over. "Has
he any reason that you know of for wishing you harm?"

Garrison banged his fist on the table, so hard that a
carafe and a tumbler nearly leaped to the floor. "No!" He
fumed. "Nobody has! That's the devilish part of all this.
What's the idea?"

"I seem to remember Inspector Gerrity voicing the
same question," I mused. "I can't answer it. The only thing
I can see in it is that it's the work of a lunatic. If it is, then
Dr. Innes is the most likely candidate. I don't like that
brooding manner of his. But let's get down to something
more concrete. It must have been a powerful man who
choked you and threw you over the rail at the same time.
Henry King has the best physical qualifications for that."

"Yes, but why should he wish me harm? I hardly know
the man."

"Archibald Flount could hardly have done it. He's elim-
inated."

"Oh, Archie could have done it, all right. I was leaning over the rail looking up at the sky, nearly off balance
as it was. But Archie, of course, is out of the question. It
wasn't he."

"Dr. Innes certainly could have, then. But here we are," I said, bitterly, "going round in circles again. The thing to do is to find out whether anyone was seen leaving the reading-saloon right after you did."

"But whom are we going to ask?"

"Everybody. We'll speak to them separately. You take your wife, Mr. Flount, and you might as well ask Mrs. Abbington, too. She and I had our backs to the door, but so did everybody else, for that matter. I'll take King and Dr. Innes. By Jove!" I suddenly exclaimed, "Miss Dykeman!"

Garrison laughed contemptuously.

"Well, I guess you're right," I admitted, feeling rather foolish for having for a moment suspected the girl. "Come on, let's get started. And, by the way," I added, "if you don't mind, I'll just keep you in sight from now on. Except when you go to your room, of course, but when you do, lock your door!"

Mrs. Abbington's mind-reading séance, we found, was over. One by one Garrison and I took each aside. We created a great deal of horror, but we got no help. Mrs. Garrison was virtually overcome. She was helped to her room by Mrs. Abbington, whose ashen face and shaking hands told the shock she also had received.

"I hope you gentlemen are not offended at the way we went about this," I said. "There was no sense of mincing matters. Someone on this ship is a potential murderer. Probably it is one of the crew. Nevertheless, a complete check-up of everyone on board was in order."

"Sure thing!" agreed Henry King.

"Quite so," said Dr. Innes. "But have you checked on the crew also?"

We had not, but we set about it at once. We were just as disappointed in that quarter. Every man, except two who had been in their bunks, was at his post, so far as we could find out.

The near tragedy had set a damper on our spirits. Garrison went off to look after his wife. The rest of us soon parted for the night. If one of the three gentlemen under suspicion were really guilty, he certainly carried off his deceit to perfection. I was no nearer the truth when sleep finally overcame me than I was when Garrison first told me of it.

16

FIRE AT SEA

I believe there is nothing that will strike terror to the human heart quicker than the cry of fire at sea. I awoke with that muffled, terrifying cry forcing itself in upon my slumber-fogged brain. I was fully awake at its first repetition.

In a frenzy of apprehension I fumbled for the light-switch. Thank heaven, the lights still worked. Hastily I thrust my bare feet into my shoes. I donned my overcoat over my pyjamas. Now the hoarse voices of men and the screams of women were joined with the high-pitched, tremulous voice that had spread the alarm.

Although there had been no sign of fire in my cabin when I opened the door a rolling cloud of smoke burst in upon me. My heart dropped. If the fire had gained so much headway, what would become of us?

At that moment the lights in the passageway came on. They glowed faintly through the smoke. My eyes smarted, and I was seized with a fit of choking. Blundering out of the room, I headed for the companionway.

"Man the hoses!" a voice boomed out above me. I made out the indistinct figure of the captain standing at the head of the stairs.

Another man lunged into me. I wiped the tears from my eyes and recognized Dr. Innes.

"Where's the ax?" he shouted. "Henry King's door is jammed! He can't get out of his room. Get me the fire-ax off the wall here; the smoke has blinded me!"

I was all but blind myself, but I did see the ax. Armed with it, Dr. Innes and I started back toward King's room. It was down the passageway beyond my door. Innes's room was across from it. Down that way the smoke seemed the thickest. Soon I was put to it to breathe at all.

As we approached the door, I heard King hammering powerful blows on it, evidently with a chair. Already he had broken out one of the panels.

"Stand back, King," I shouted. "I'm going to batter the door down."

The door, a stout affair, finally fell into splinters before my onslaught. King, trying to rush out of his room, was forced back into it by Dr. Innes and me. We had had quite enough of the passageway. Leaping across the room, we filled our lungs with the fresh air coming in through the port-hole. When we turned back to make our escape, King was gone.

As we regained the companionway, after dashing down the passage, we came upon two seamen with a hose.

"Where's the fire, sir?" one asked.

"It's aft somewhere," I choked. "Smoke seems to be coming from the stern."

Innes and I, choking and spluttering, made our way up to the lounging-saloon. To my relief, I saw that all the others were there. Only a few wisps of smoke were in the air here.

"Please let me go down with the boat," Miss Dykeman was moaning. She lay on a couch with Constance Abbington hovering over her.

"There you are!" cried King, as Innes and I stumbled up the stairs. "By thunder, you fellows saved my life! Where did you go, anyway? I was just going back for you; thought you'd passed out."

"Archie," said Robert Garrison, clutching the night-shirted Flount by the shoulders, "stay here with the women. If the captain gives the order, get them into a lifeboat. Come on, you other fellows, let's see what we can do. I think I know where to locate the fire."

He led us out on the deck. King and Garrison, like myself, had put on their overcoats. Innes, though, was wearing nothing but his pyjamas. I tried to get him to go back, but he refused.

Garrison ran up to a hatch on the after deck. He unfastened it and threw it back. A cloud of pent-up smoke burst forth and drove us back.

"It's down in that hold!" cried Garrison. "Quick! There's a hose in the passage to the dining-saloon."

We all made a dash for it. As Garrison was about to leave the deck, I pulled him back. "Keep away from rails," I cautioned him.

The reel was in the passage midway between reading- and dining-saloons. King got the nozzle. He started back through the reading-saloon, unwinding the hose as he went.

"You stay here, Doctor," ordered Garrison. "Mr. Clark, you stand on the deck just outside the door and give Dr. Innes the signal to turn on the water. I'll go aft with King."

Standing in the doorway to the reading-saloon, I helped unreel the hose as Garrison and King took it aft. Finally Garrison called for water. I passed the word along to Dr. Innes.

For what seemed an hour I stood there, staring at the flat hose, waiting for it to bulge with water. Nothing happened.

"Give us the water!" bellowed King.

Garrison ran up to me. "Maybe the pumps haven't been started," he cried. "I can't understand it; I heard Captain Arnold order them started."

As we entered the reading-saloon from the deck, Dr. Innes leaped into it from the passageway. He was soaking wet.

"We're finished," he said, quietly. "Somebody has cut the hoses."

"What do you mean?" gasped Garrison.

"Just what I said. I turned that hose on and got a fine bath. It's cut right near the valve. Had to turn it off. I heard one of the sailors down below shouting that a hose was cut."

At that moment Captain Arnold entered the smoking-saloon. The captain looked as if he could chew someone up. I fancy I could have helped him do it.

"There's a dirty rat aboard here, sir!" he said. "Every fire-hose on the yacht's been cut. This one too, I see."

"What can you do, Captain?" snapped Garrison.

"We're splicing the hoses. Can't do a thing until we do. Fire's in the after hold, and it looks to me like it was set!"

I glanced into the passage and saw a sailor at work on the hose. Captain Arnold left us to give him a hand. When I looked back, Henry King was storming into the saloon.

"What the devil's the matter?" he shouted.

"Fire-hoses have been cut," I explained. "We can't do anything until they fix them."

"Why can't we?" snapped King. "We can form a bucket brigade, can't we? Get some buckets; tie ropes to the handles; toss 'em overboard to fill 'em; and dump 'em down that trapdoor in the floor out there. The fire's down there; I can see it."

"Good idea!" cried Garrison. "Captain! Ho, Captain Arnold! Have you any buckets aboard?"

"You don't want any buckets," the captain roared. "Get somebody on that hose nozzle! We'll have it in commission in a minute."

King and I made a dash for the deck. The smoke billowing from the open hatch was now tinged with a ruddy glow. King snatched up the hose nozzle. Directing it at the hatch, he waited expectantly for the stream of water.

Suddenly a new sound, hissing up the hatchway with the crackle of the flames, sent a thrill of hope coursing through me.

"Water!" I cried. "They've got a line on it down below!"

A moment later the hose King was holding filled out stiffly and writhed in his grasp. Water gushed from the nozzle down into the hatchway. Garrison came out and joined us. King maneuvered round to the stern. From there, standing on the narrow strip of deck between the hatch and the stern, he was able to direct the water straight at the flames.

"Mr. Garrison!" came Captain Arnold's voice, thundering down the deck.

"Right here, Captain."

"We need men below. Smoke's so bad a man can't stay in it long. Got anybody for relief?"

Garrison turned quickly to King. "You can handle that hose alone, can't you?" he asked.

"Sure thing! You and Clark beat it down there to help those others. It must be fierce down in that corridor. If you like, I'll turn this nozzle over to one of you fellows and go down myself."

"No, you stay here, said Garrison. "Come on, Clark!"

To get below we had to go through the lounging-saloon. Here Archibald Flount and Mrs. Abbington were having a time of it with Mrs. Garrison. The lady was having hysterics. Even poor little Miss Dykeman had resumed sufficient interest in life to want to still cling to it. She was weeping weakly, but piteously. Flount looked frantic in his night-shirt and a pea-jacket, evidently supplied by one of the sailors.

Mrs. Abbington looked up as we entered. I think she never looked more striking than she did at that moment.

Her golden locks were all in disorder, her eyes were bright with mingled excitement and fear, and her soft lips were parted.

"Are—are you getting it out, Garry?" she panted.

"Darling!" cried Garrison, rushing over and taking his wife in his arms. She clung to him and cried wildly for him to save her.

"Come on, Flount," I said, taking him by the shoulder. "Leave Mr. Garrison here where he's needed. You and I will go below."

Garrison lifted his wife in his arms and turned to us. "No, you don't!" he said. "We'll all go below." Then he looked pleadingly down into his wife's terror-stricken face. "Sweetheart," he said, "you must calm yourself. We are getting the fire under control. We'll have it out in a few minutes. I'm going to leave you with Connie; she'll take care of you and Gladys until we get back. You can, can't you, Connie?"

"Yes; run along! Hurry!" cried Mrs. Abbington.

Garrison placed his wife in a chair. With an expression of mental agony on his face, he tore himself from her and dashed down the companionway. Flount and I were right after him. In the passageway the smoke was even worse than when I had left it. We groped our way down to the end. Ahead I could see the vague outlines of a group of men. As we approached them, I made out the figure of Captain Arnold.

"Good!" he choked, when he caught sight of us. "Can you relieve those fellows in there? I don't dare leave 'em there another minute! I sent three men through the engine room with a hose—got to see how they are."

"Are we making any headway?" demanded Garrison.

"We've checked 'er," replied the captain, his voice nothing but a wheeze. "If we can keep three lines on it—"

I lost his voice altogether as I stumbled into the room where the seamen were fighting the fire. It was a narrow room, extending the width of the ship, partially filled with baggage. A hole had been battered through the stern wall. Through it a sailor was playing a hose. Another was battering at the partition with an ax. The third fellow in the room was at the starboard port-hole filling his lungs with air.

"Give me the hose," I shouted into the ear of the man holding the nozzle. "Go outside and get some air."

The man, choking and gasping, willingly surrendered the hose to me. Glancing through the hole in the partition, I saw the angry red smoke, shot with vivid flames, that filled the compartment on the other side. At the center of the fiery mass I directed the hose.

Flount came up beside me with the ax. More at home with an umbrella in his hands, he attacked the partition without very great results. A moment later Garrison joined him with another ax.

The partition that the builders of the yacht had put there was a stout one. Perspiration poured from Garrison's face as he labored. Finally he had opened up another hole.

"Try the hose through that," he bellowed into my ear. "Looks bad, doesn't it?"

I nodded. The transfer of the hose from one hole to another I accomplished, but not without subjecting Flount to a drenching. He stopped his work long enough to glare indignantly at me; then he went back at the partition.

We kept pouring water through that partition until I thought surely the yacht would swamp. My lungs were bursting. My throat was so constricted that my breath fairly whistled through it. At length Garrison took hold of the nozzle.

"Go over to the port and get some air," he said. "I just did."

I wiped the tears from my eyes, located one of the port holes, and staggered over to it. Even there I had difficulty in getting any air. Flount seemed not to mind the smoke at all. He stood his ground, pecking at the partition with the ax. After a few minutes I regained my breath sufficiently to return to Garrison.

"We're winning, Clark!" he gasped. "Look, it's going out!"

He was right. Although the room was still densely filled with smoke, the terrifying red glow on the other side of the partition had subsided. Now I could see a stream of water descending into the compartment from above.

"There's Henry King!" I cried. "There must be another stream playing on the fire below us, too. By Jove, you'd think the compartment would be flooded by this time!"

"It must be nearly flooded," choked Garrison.

At that point the seamen whom we had relieved came back into the room. We were glad to let them take over our end of the fire-fighting. Blindly and gasping for breath, we staggered out into the passageway.

"Let's get up on deck," wheezed Garrison.

In the lounging-saloon we found a quieter scene than the one we had left. Mrs. Garrison was quite composed. Miss Dykeman had decided life was not worth living, after all.

"Garry!" cried Mrs. Garrison, rushing over to embrace her husband. "Oh! I'm so glad you're back! Your face is all smudged. You're not hurt!"

"No," replied Garrison, with difficulty. "Going out for air."

"Let them go, Dot," said Mrs. Abbington, guiding her friend over to a chair. "Captain Arnold told us the fire is nearly out. Is that right, Garry?"

"Yes," affirmed Garrison over his shoulder as he made for the deck.

We fairly bowled Captain Arnold over as we burst through the door. He was standing just outside the door, face upturned to the boat deck. He recovered his balance and once again, with a curious, puzzled expression on his face, looked intently up at the boat deck.

"What's the trouble?" I asked.

"Somebody using the wireless," he replied.

We listened for a moment. The whine of the wireless came to us quite plainly. The apparatus was located in a small house behind the bridge. As we listened, it stopped and was not resumed.

"Sending an S O S?" asked Garrison.

"Not by my orders," snapped the captain. "I sent an S O S when the fire was first discovered. The wireless-operator is below handling a hose, or he should be. He's the first mate, and I don't think he'd disobey my orders."

I was seized with a feeling of uneasiness about that wireless message. "By heaven," I cried, starting for the door, "I'm going to find out who sent that message!"

"This way, sir," called the captain. "There's a ladder up for'd here to the bridge. It's the quickest way up there."

We scrambled up to the boat deck. The wireless house was directly aft of us, but the entrance was on the other side. As I rounded the corner on the heels of Captain Arnold, I saw light streaming through the door.

We halted abruptly outside the door and looked in. A man in pyjamas was standing with his back to us, bending over the table, looking at some papers beside the wireless key. Suddenly he turned round. It was Dr. Innes!

"Well, sir!" exclaimed the captain, coldly, "what are you doing here?"

Innes regarded us blandly for a moment. "Where's your operator gone?" he asked.

"The operator is below handling a hose," blurted Garrison. "What were you doing at that wireless, Innes?"

"I beg your pardon!" said Dr. Innes, taking offense at Garrison's tone of voice. "What seems to be the trouble? I heard the wireless going and came up here to see what ships have been communicated with. When I got here, the place was empty. I've just been reading over the messages scribbled on the pad here."

Captain Arnold regarded the man narrowly. "I thought you were down on the engine-room hose," he said.

Innes's brow clouded still more. "I don't like being questioned in this fashion," he said, with an angry flash of his eyes. "I'm perfectly willing to admit I was down in the hold fighting the fire. Why shouldn't I be? I got my lungs jolly well full of smoke and came up for a breath of air."

"You say you didn't send that message?" I demanded.

Dr. Innes gave me an angry glance. "I suppose you are sleuthing now, Mr. Clark," he sneered. "Why, of course I didn't send the message. I don't know how to operate this bally thing, you know. Anything else you'd like to learn?"

"Let's get below," said the captain, impatiently. "That fire's not out yet. Every man is still needed."

The captain was wrong. The fire was out, or practically so. A good deal of smoke still filled the yacht, but the danger was over. The first mate, Mr. Yardson, came to report as much to the captain as we returned to the main deck.

"Have you been using the wireless, Mr. Yardson?" demanded the captain.

"Yes, sir," he replied. "I sent off the distress signal. There's a coast-guard cutter and a steam trawler coming."

"Were you using it just a moment ago?"

"No, sir. I've been below. I gave our position when I sent out the signal, right after you ordered it. We've been stationary since. I didn't think it was necessary to send any more signals."

I looked about for Innes. He had gone inside.

"All right, Mr. Yardson," said the captain, crisply. "How much damage is there below?"

"Less than I thought there'd be, sir; the fire didn't get by the bulkhead. Haven't thoroughly checked up yet, but I think we're all right."

"I'll come below and have a look at it. In the mean time, countermand that distress signal. Ask the cutter to continue to our assistance, though."

"Yes, sir. I was about to shut off that hose on the after deck."

"I'll attend to that," said Garrison. "Mr. Clark, run aft and tell Henry King not to pour any more water in that hatch. I'll close the valve."

King was still diligently directing the hose into the hatchway. I told him to play it overside. A moment the stream dwindled and died.

"Hurrah!" shouted King. "Fire's out, eh? Still a lot of smoke coming up, though."

"Yes," I said, "but I guess that's just what backed up down there. First mate says the fire's about out. They can handle it with the hose they have down there, I guess."

"'Tis well," said King, laying the nozzle on the deck. "I thought I'd sink the boat with all the water I poured down there. Some excitement, eh?"

As soon as I could, I got Garrison aside. "That wireless message bothers me," I said. "To be frank with you, I've been suspecting Innes, King, and Flount all along. Flount couldn't have sent the message, because he was with us. But King or Innes, either one, could have sent it."

"Why King?"

"Well, he was out on the after deck, all alone, for quite a while. I think we can settle the whole thing without much trouble. Come with me."

I took Garrison up to the wireless house. We waited several minutes before Yardson was through sending and receiving messages. Finally he pulled the switch and got to his feet.

"Cutter'll be here very shortly, sir," he said, touching his forehead.

"Look here, Mr. Yardson," I said, "someone sent a wireless message from this set just before we met you on the main deck. Have you any idea who it was?"

"None, sir. But I had an idea a message was sent—two of 'em."

"Would you mind telling us how you got such an idea?"

"No, sir. This is a particularly powerful apparatus for the size of the yacht. Mr. Garrison could tell you that," he said, with a glance at the owner of the yacht. "He had it installed because he wanted to be sure of keeping in touch with the stock-market wherever he went. When messages are sent, the drag on the current lowers the lights all over the yacht."

"And you saw the lights go down?"

"Twice. The first time was just after I went below, and the second time was just before I met you and the captain."

I thought that over for a minute. The affair was becoming more complicated. There was one question that needed clarifying before we could get much further. "Is there anyone else in the crew who can send messages besides yourself?" I asked.

"Only Snyder, the second engineer," he replied. "He wanted to learn, and the captain thought it was a good idea to have two operators aboard. I taught him."

"Was Snyder with you in the hold after you sent the S O S?"

"No; he was stationed at the pumps."

"Could he have got up here to send those messages without being missed?"

"Well, yes, I guess he could have, sir. All he had to do was hook the pumps into the engines and watch 'em."

"All right. Now, do you remember when Dr. Innes left the hold?"

"Yes sir. He was down in the hold with us. He said he got too much smoke, and I told him to go on deck."

"Did he leave before you saw the lights go down the second time?"

"Yes, sir; I think he did."

"Was he in the hold when you first went down there?"

"No, sir; he came down later."

"Then Dr. Innes was not in the hold at either time the lights went down."

"No, sir; he wasn't."

"Now, then, about that stream of water through the after hatch. Did it keep playing down into the hold all the time?"

"Yes, sir. A good piece of work it was, too. He could get at the fire better from up there than we could from the hold. Better than they could from the main deck, too."

I glanced significantly at Garrison. "All right, Mr. Yardson," I said.

"Very well, sir; I'll get below."

He quickly left us, and I turned to Garrison. "Well, there you are," I said, rather resignedly. "We can't pin anything on anybody. Without that infernal second engineer of yours we'd have made a clear case against Innes."

"What makes you suspect the second engineer?" demanded Garrison.

"Because I suspect he's going to deny sending those messages, principally. But he had the best chance to wreck that port motor, and he had as good a chance to send the messages as Innes. Besides, we know he can send wireless messages, and we don't know that Innes can. Seems unlikely."

Garrison grimaced impatiently. "What difference does it make, anyhow?" he asked, petulantly. "If Snyder did sneak up here to send messages, it was probably only because he wanted to make sure help was coming. Let's go see how much damage has been done. I want to look after the ladies, too."

I left Garrison, who went to see about the women, and went down to the hold. In the engine room I came upon Captain Arnold, who was on his way to report to Garrison.

"How does it look, Captain?" I asked.

"We got away lucky, sir," he replied. "Terrible mess in there, but not much damage to the gear. One steering cable I don't trust; they're replacing it. We should be able to get under way in an hour."

"Is your second engineer anywhere about?"

Captain Arnold turned about and placed his hand on the shoulder of a good-looking young chap beside him. "Here he is," he smiled.

"Snyder," I said, "that was quick work of yours, ducking up there to send those distress signals. We owe you a vote of thanks."

Snyder looked thoroughly puzzled. "Distress signals, sir?" he said, wonderingly. "That wasn't me, sir. Mr. Yardson's the one you want to congratulate. He sent 'em I suppose."

"Yes, I know it. But I thought you hadn't realized that and went up and sent some yourself. After he did, I mean."

Snyder laughed and shook his head. "Oh, I knew he sent 'em, all right, sir," he said. "I saw the drag on the current. But I was right here in the engine room all the time. We only had one motor to drive the pumps, and it would have been sad if anything happened to that!"

"Ouch! Don't think of it!" I exclaimed. "Well, you did a good job, anyhow, Snyder. The crew was wonderful, Captain. You have my heartfelt congratulations, I can tell you!"

We found the others in the lounging-saloon. Captain Arnold made his report. Then he said: "Who discovered the fire, sir? None of the crew did; that I've found out."

"I did," replied Archibald Flount, looking as pompous as possible in his strange costume. "I was on my way to the galley for a snack. I always have a snack at night. First I smelled smoke, and then I saw it. I woke everybody up."

Henry King snickered. "I'll say you did!" he agreed.

"Well! Well!—" sputtered Flount, sensing that he was being ridiculed.

"Never mind, Archie," said Mrs. Abbington, soothingly. "You were very brave, and we're all proud of you."

As soon as the smoke had cleared away, we were able to get back to our rooms. Daylight had broken. I got into my clothes and went up on deck again. A half-hour later coast-guard cutter pulled up alongside. Her skipper came over in a boat and boarded us.

"What's your condition, Captain?" he asked.

"We have a burned-out compartment," replied Captain Arnold. "Hull's sound, and so's the gear. Come into my cabin, and I'll give you the details."

When they left us, I turned to one of the officers who had come over from the cutter. "Did you get our wireless messages all right?" I asked.

"Yes," he replied, with a somewhat puzzled expression. "Who was doing the sending?"

"Why?"

"Well, we got your distress signals without any trouble—position and everything. Then there were two signals that must have come from your yacht. We couldn't make head or tail of them. Nothing but a lot of jumbled-up letters. It seemed to be code. Whoever was sending was able to do it; he sounded like an expert. He kept calling X Y, X Y. We didn't hear anyone answer him, but his call was followed by all that funny business."

"How many times did he call X Y?"

"Twice. We thought it must be the yacht, but maybe it wasn't."

"Maybe it wasn't," I agreed, but I knew that it was.

A half-hour later the *Dorothy* was once more under way. As we swung round to the north, we tooted a farewell to the cutter. I was sorry to see her dropping astern. The blue-jackets had brought with them a feeling of reassurance that was fast leaving me.

17

GHOST ISLAND

The nearer we drew to Ghost Island, the worse the weather became. A stiff wind was blowing, and against it the yacht made heavy progress. Mrs. Abbington and Flount had been added to the sick-list.

We passed Cape Elizabeth in close and headed into Casco Bay. The wind-lashed waves wet the deck down constantly. Now and then the flying spray would spat against the windows, and the yacht would lurch drunkenly.

I sat with Garrison and King in the lounging-saloon. Innes, although a good sailor, was below in his room, as was Mrs. Garrison in hers.

As we left the rugged tip of Cape Elizabeth astern, I turned to Garrison. "I suppose we'll get a look at Ghost Island any minute now," I said.

Garrison smiled. "Arrowhead Island, if you don't mind," he corrected.

"You don't mean to say you have two names for your island!" exclaimed King.

"Only one," replied Garrison. "The natives dubbed it Ghost Island after a shipwreck years ago. They still call it that. Arrowhead Island is correct."

"I suppose," smiled King, "the ghosts of the shipwrecked mariners still haunt it. That's quite picturesque; I rather like it."

"Oh, you'll like it, all right," said Garrison, enthusiastically.

He plunged into the glories of Maine, discoursing on his favorite subject until the island hove into view. Because of the stormy weather we were fairly close in before we could see the island clearly. All three of us crowded up to the forward windows. Picking up a pair of glasses, Garrison focused them on the island and handed them to me.

"It's larger than I thought it would be," I remarked, passing the glasses to King.

"It's a good-sized island," replied Garrison. "What seems to be one island from here, though, is actually a group of three. The nearest one is Thumbcap, just a little island. The one beyond mine is Barren Island. My island, of course, is by far the best. It's literally covered with large pines, except where the house stands. There, I believe you can make the house out now. Let's see the glasses. Yes, there you are, to the left. The cove is just in front of it. You can see where my island ends to the seaward by the waves breaking against the cliff. As we approach nearer, the three islands will fall away from each other. Can you imagine anything more ideal than that!"

"Certainly a wonderful setting," breathed King. "All these other islands over toward the land are grouped close together. But your island and those other two are right out in the ocean by themselves."

"There's Midway Light," cried Garrison, stretching his arm toward the open sea. "We see it very plainly from the island. Hear its fog-horn too, in thick weather. I'm rather glad we're having this storm, the waves dashing against the cliff are a beautiful sight."

"Robert," said a weak voice behind us, "I don't care for your wretched storm. When shall we arrive at the island?"

It was Flount, a harried look in his eyes and a pea-green complexion on his face. At another lurch of the yacht he closed his eyes, moaned softly, and sank into a chair.

"There's a fellow out in our town who's crossed the ocean a lot," said King, helpfully. "He says the best thing for seasickness is salt pork."

Flount gulped, turned a shade greener, and tottered toward the companionway. "If I die," he accused feebly, "you will have killed me."

He was replaced by Captain Arnold. "Shall we drop anchor in the cove as usual, sir?" asked the captain.

"Yes," replied Garrison. "Make the cove as soon as possible, Captain. Some of the ladies and gentlemen are not enjoying themselves."

As we swung round to the lee of the island, the yacht became steadier. We nosed into the cove, and the anchor let go with a rumble and a splash.

I had noticed Garrison, ever since we had entered the Cove, peering about the shore-line with a puzzled expression. As the yacht came to anchor, he stepped out on deck. I followed him.

"What seems to be the trouble?" I asked. "Something worrying you?"

Garrison shook his head dubiously. "Mapes, the man I sent up here, is supposed to be here," he said, "I don't see the motor boat, and there's no sign of Mapes. I don't understand that!"

"Maybe he's gone over to the mainland," I suggested.

"Perhaps," replied Garrison, with a shrug. "House looks all right."

I glanced up at it. The house, a large, rambling shingle building, stood at the top of a small hill rising from the west side of the cove. I could not agree that it looked all right. Some of the windows were boarded up; others stared blankly down at us. Two chimneys, at either end of the two wings, rose starkly against the lowering sky. From a third chimney, rising from the main portion of the house, a thin curl of smoke rose, to be whipped away by the wind.

The house had a curious appearance of being half in use and half closed up.

"Weren't you sending your servants on ahead by train?" I asked.

The man gave a start. "By Jove, that's right, the servants!" he exclaimed. "They should have arrived here yesterday."

"I think," I said, "the thing for us to do is to organize a landing party and investigate that house. The less delay about it, the better."

As we turned to leave the deck, we were arrested by a shout from the island. Garrison and I both whirled about. A man was running at top speed down the hill toward a large boat-house and dock. Either he had come from the house or run by it. The house stood at the base of a bare spit of land, which formed one side of the cove, on which he was running. As he ran, he waved his arms over his head and shouted again.

"It's Mapes!" cried Garrison. "What's the matter with him? Why wasn't he out here to meet us? And where's the motor boat?"

I glanced up at the house again. No one in sight there. A forest of pines rose behind the house and extended round to the other side of the cove. There was no one at its fringe. Mapes appeared to be alone on the island.

"Let's get ashore and ask him what's the matter," I suggested, as Mapes stopped at the end of the dock.

Garrison, stepping forward, called up to the bridge. "Lower the motor tender, Captain, we're going ashore at once."

The tender, carried on the stern, was swung out and lowered into the water. Henry King accompanied Garrison and me as we set out with two of the crew.

As we neared the dock, Garrison suddenly looked up at the house. "By Jove, there's Ridley!" he cried.

I followed his gaze. On the porch stood the Garrison butler, in the full panoply of his service.

"That's a relief," I said. "Maybe we were unnecessarily alarmed."

The boat came alongside the dock, helped to a landing by Mapes. The caretaker was a burly fellow with a stolid, good-natured face.

"Glad to see you, sir," he said, with considerable feeling. "This here's been quite an experience."

"What do you mean by that?" asked Garrison, leaping to the dock.

Mapes, shrugging his broad shoulders, appeared rather sheepish. "If you was to ask me about ghosts two weeks ago, Mr. Garrison," he said, "I'd of said: Stuff and nonsense! Yes, sir, stuff and nonsense. But now I ain't so sure."

"Oh," said Garrison, sarcastically, "the island's really haunted, eh?"

The uncertain smile disappeared from Mapes's lips. "I ain't sayin' it is, and I ain't sayin' it ain't," he retorted. "But they's some mighty queer things been goin on here, mighty queer. No answer for 'em."

"That so?" said Garrison, impatiently. "Servants get here all right?"

Mapes seemed embarrassed. "Yes, sir," he affirmed, "they got here all right. You better talk to Ridley about that. That ain't none of my business."

Garrison looked sharply at the man. "This isn't like you, Mapes," he said. "You're being mysterious. I don't like it!"

"I'll tell you about the island," said Mapes, defensively; "let Ridley tell you about the servants. None of my business what they did."

"Well, suppose you tell us about the island, then, while we go up to the house. I see Ridley up there; maybe he hasn't forgotten how to give information."

Mapes swung about to accompany us up the hill. "It's this way, sir," he said, in an injured tone. "I got down here a week and a half ago. There ain't nothin' you can do with them natives! They won't come out here, that's all. Just one, young lobsterman by the name of Fishy Headacher. He ain't afraid of ghosts, though one of 'em is supposed to be his grandfather."

"You mean the ghost of his grandfather is roaming the island, eh?"

"That's it. Er—I mean, that's what *they* think. Anyway, this here Fishy Headacher took me out here. I worked all day gettin' the motor boat out and moorin' her, and he helped me. Then he went back, after leavin' me my provisions. That night about ten o'clock, Mr. Garrison, I hope t' die, I heard 'em!"

"You heard the ghosts? Um-m, what did they do?"

"They hollered. Hollered somethin' fierce! A great big, low, hollow voice, it was. More like the mooin' of a cow than anythin' else. It come from over where the wreck lays. I ain't jokin', sir, I heard it!"

"You don't say so? Did they say anything in particular?"

Mapes stopped abruptly at the side of the path. The rest of the procession stopped with him. Placing his hands resolutely on his hips, he looked indignantly at his employer. "You can mock me all you like, Mr. Garrison," he said, spiritedly, "but I'm tellin' the truth! I been through a lot as it is!"

Garrison assumed a mollifying tone. "I'm sorry, Mapes," he said. "Of course you are telling the truth. Go on, I'm very much interested."

"Right. You asked me if they said anythin' in particular. Well, they did. They said: 'Keep away from them bones! Keep away from them bones!' And, comin' out of the darkness like that in that awful voice, it was somethin' fierce!"

"It must have been. What did you do?"

"Well, you may think I'm loony, but I sat up all night with my gat in my hand. They only hollered it about five times, once right after the other; then everythin' was as still as a graveyard all night. The next mornin', as soon as it was light, I went over to where I thought it come from. I walked clean across the island, and then I come upon the wreck."

"Oh, you found the wreck?"

"Yes, sir. You know where it lays over on the rocks in a sort of a little bay. She's pretty well rotted away, but it was low tide, and she was most out of water. I went on it, by gorry, and what I seen sent me back here in a hurry, let me tell you! Have you ever been on it?"

"No, I've never been on it. I didn't know you could get on it; thought it was all fallen to pieces. What did you see on it?"

Mapes glanced down at the cove. "It's low tide now, he said. "I'd rather you saw it for yourself."

"Oh, you can tell us, Mapes," said Garrison, impatiently.

"I think it would be a good idea if we did see it," I interrupted.

"Oh, all right, then," agreed Garrison, grudgingly. "What else has happened, Mapes?"

"The same thing happened the second night, and every night since. Just about ten o'clock. The third night I went over there and waited."

"Good boy! What did you see?"

"Nothin'! I was hidin' in the rocks, and all of a sudden they started to holler. Right in my ear, it was. Like t' split my ear-drums! I hopped up and flashed my light all over, but there wasn't a soul in sight! The wreck was right below me, half covered with water, lookin' black and deadlike. The voice sounded madder'n hops. Fierce! Terrible! 'Keep away from them bones!' it says. Finally it stopped. I got up and run all over, through the trees and round the rocks. Couldn't find nobody! I ain't ashamed to say, sir," added Mapes, self-righteously, "that I was scared! I was good and scared, and, praise be, I hope I never get that scared again!"

"I don't blame you," mused Garrison. "What did you do then?"

"I ain't ashamed to say, sir, that I made up my mind right then and there I wouldn't go near that spot again. And I made tracks through the woods to the house, scared to death that somethin' was goin' to hop on my back every minute! It's dark as pitch under them trees at night."

"And you haven't been back again?"

"Well, sir, after a fashion I did go back. About two nights later, after they'd got through hollerin' about the bones, I heard a clankin', sort of. Come from over by the wreck. Then I got an idea. I got in the motor boat and sailed round the island. But when I got round there, everythin' was quiet. I ran in as close to the shore as I dared and stopped. I was standin' there in the boat, lookin' all round, when off goes that voice again. 'Keep away from them bones!' it hollers, and if he was a ghost, he was a mad one. I couldn't see nothin'; so I went back to the cove. The next mornin' the motor boat was gone."

"Gone! Do you mean she sank, or what?"

"She didn't sink. I thought maybe she had, too, but she didn't. I rowed out there. It was low tide, and at low tide you can see the bottom of the cove. The moorin' was there, and the moorin' buoy was floatin' fine as silk. But the motor boat was gone! She's been gone ever since, and I ain't had no way to get off the island since. Not unless I wanted to row ashore, which I ain't got no use for, over that open sea."

"It wouldn't be safe. Anything else happen?"

"No. The voice hollers every night, and once since then I heard the clankin'. At least, that's all I know. You better ask Ridley about the rest."

"Oh, Ridley knows more, eh?" grunted Garrison. 'Well, let's go up."

I saw that we had made a mistake by allowing the two sailors to overhear Mapes's eerie tale. They were fidgety, glancing nervously round, and plainly frightened.

"When we reached the house, Ridley was half frozen. He had been standing, as stiff as a ramrod, just outside the front door ever since we had first seen him. Garrison, after greeting him, hurried him inside. The two sailors remained on the porch. The house, I was relieved to find, was quite warm.

Garrison turned resolutely to the butler. "Well, Ridley," he said, "it seems that you have something to tell me concerning the servants."

"Yes, sir," replied Ridley, bowing stiffly. "Shall I inform you right here, sir?"

"Yes, go ahead."

"Very good, sir. We arrived at the island yesterday, about noon, sir. The only person whom we could engage to bring us out went by the name of—I don't just remember, some kind of sea food, sir."

"Fishy," supplied Mapes, succinctly.

"Ah, yes," went on Ridley. "He was a most unruly, indecorous person, if I may say so, sir. Flirted most outrageously with the maids. Besides, he insisted upon—"

"Never mind Fishy!" exploded Garrison.

"Quite so, sir," acquiesced Ridley, with another stiff bow. "I only mentioned him to point out that not another soul on the mainland would consent to come out to this island."

"Yes, I've heard that before. What about the servants; where are they, anyhow?"

"The servants, sir, are on the mainland."

"What!"

"Yes, sir. You see, there have been some—ah—most unusual manifestations here, not to say weird manifestations."

Garrison threw himself into a chair. He frowned for a moment; then he looked up at Ridley. "Suppose you tell us all about it, from start to finish," he said.

"Quite so, sir. We arrived at the island, as I said before, about noon yesterday. I set the staff at work immediately to make the house habitable. At ten o'clock last night, sir, there came the most frightful howl from the wilderness on the other side of the island. A hollow, terrifying voice, crying: 'Keep away—'"

"—from them bones!'" finished Garrison, angrily.

Ridley's cheeks paled. This uncanny intuition of his employer nearly shattered the rigid mold in which he was cast. "Th-that's what it said, sir," he stammered.

"Very well, Ridley," said Garrison, more kindly. "What happened then?"

"The maids were badly frightened, sir, and so were Boynton and Mudge. About two in the morning there was a fearful screaming. It came from Heath and Frazer, the two upstairs girls, who were sleeping downstairs. They—they claimed, sir, to have seen a ghost at the window. A frightful apparition, they said. I was quieting them, telling them they must have been dreaming, when the cook, who was in the room at the rear, came scuttling out with the most outlandish screams and shrieks that one could imagine. She had or she claimed to have seen just such specter as the two upstairs girls. Whatever it was, sir, it had the power of stripping my last shreds of authority from me. I could do nothing with the household. They steadfastly refused to go back to their rooms. We spent the night huddled about the fireplace in this room. This morning, without the cook even waiting to make our breakfasts, the whole lot of them left. That Fishy person, with the encouragement of Heath, I am sure, had agreed to stay overnight to help us get settled. It was in his miserable, dirty little boat that they left! Mapes and I have been carrying on."

"Bully for you, Ridley," commended Garrison. "But why did they leave? They knew the yacht would be here any minute."

"They talked that over thoroughly during the night, sir. The yacht was due, you remember, last evening. They decided this abominable ghost had destroyed it at sea."

"What did they intend doing when they got to the mainland?"

"They intended being driven to the nearest railroad station and returning at once to New York, sir."

Garrison groaned. "More trouble!" he exclaimed, disgustedly. "Now we are here without any servants. Well, we'll just have to make the best of it, that's all. We have the cook from the yacht, and the stewards will work in very well. Ridley, you are in charge, as usual. You have acted very commendably, too; I'll not forget it. Mapes also. Well, Mr. Clark, what do you suggest now?"

"How about provisions?" I asked.

"We brought enough with us for a few days, sir," replied Ridley.

"That is taken care of, then," said Garrison. "We can send the yacht after more. How about the fire in this place, Mapes?"

"Not much to worry about, sir," replied the caretaker. "I ain't so bad with tools myself, and I've made all the necessary repairs in my spare time, which I had lots of. It was in the basement at the back."

"Good work!" commended Garrison. "Now then, Mr. Clark, we might as well get the others ashore, don't you think?"

"If you don't mind," I replied, "I think we should take a look at the wreck first. All this trouble seems to emanate from there. According to Mapes, low tide is the time to do it, and it's low tide now."

Garrison seemed curiously reluctant to visit the wreck. But after taking his time to consider it, he finally agreed with me. With Henry King and Mapes, who seemed to have forgotten his solemn decision never to go back, we set out.

The little hill that the house stood upon fell steeply away to the edge of the wood. Under the ancient trees a brown matting of pine needles lay inches thick. The wind whistled through the boughs over our heads, and the moan of the surf came to us on its wings. The occasional crackle of a dried twig as we trod on it was the only other sound.

Soon the glint of the sea was discernible through the trees. The surf by now was a turbulent roar.

We emerged from the trees to a strip of open ground. Across from us were rugged, brownish-gray rocks. Over them we looked out upon the angry rollers of the Atlantic, rushing on to hurl their might against the cliff.

At the edge of the cliff we looked down upon the surf. It was spending itself among seaweed-covered rocks extending from the base of the cliff, rocks that were submerged at high tide. Directly to our left a wide crevice broke the face of the cliff. It formed a basin at its bottom, protected from the surf by a rocky barrier circling out from either side. Even at high tide the water in it must have been quite calm.

Edging over to the side of the crevice, we peered down. The wreck lay cradled on jagged rocks, all but a foot of it clear of the water. She had evidently been a two-masted schooner. She had so gone to ruin even in her sheltered grave that it was hard to tell.

The hull lay heeled over, its planking moss-grown and waterlogged. The whole bottom of the craft along the keel was torn away, and the timbers up near the bow were crushed in. One of her shattered masts lay over her gunwale; the other had disappeared. Her rotted deck was full of holes, and the single hatch had fallen in.

"How on earth did she ever get in there?" I marvelled.

"Storm threw her in there," explained Garrison. "I've heard the story. Raked her over that ring of rocks out there. Her mainmast and rudder were gone; they couldn't manage her. Must have been a terrific storm, eh?"

"If you want to go aboard," said Mapes, 'you can do it from the other side without gettin' your feet wet. Here, I'll show you how to get down."

He led us back along the cliff, finally stopping at a spot where a shelf ran diagonally down to the base. We negotiated the perilous descent without mishap. Then we started off across the slippery rocks, slipping and sliding on the seaweed. Carefully feeling our way, we skirted the basin to the other side. Here we were able, by stepping from one rock to another, to get right up alongside the wreck. Mapes first, we scrambled up on the deck. What planking there was left looked thoroughly unsafe. I kept nervously near the rail.

"You have to go down the hatch to get below," explained Mapes. "I don't think this here deck'll hold the weight of the whole lot of us. Better go one at a time. I'll go first, but look here, you're gonna follow me, ain't you?"

"Go ahead, Mapes," grinned King, "I'm right behind you. Hunting for ghosts is my meat. If you see one, hold him until I get there."

Mapes crossed the insecure deck. He lowered himself cautiously into the hatchway and, with an anxious glance back at us, dropped from view. True to his word, Henry King followed. I was next, and Garrison came last.

The scene inside the cabin was one of desolation and decay. Seaweed grew on the slimy floor and half-way up

the sides. An indescribable litter was strewn on the lower
side of the deck. King reached down and from it extracted the rusted remains of a lantern. It was about the only
thing that retained any semblance of its original appearance. Although gloomy, enough light came through the
jagged openings in the deck above for us to see.

"Well, Mapes," asked Garrison, nervously, "where is
this terrible sight you were going to show us?"

Mapes slipped and slid across the deck toward the forward part of the vessel. Most of the bulkhead had fallen
away. We could see through into a black space. That, I
knew, was the forecastle. Mapes, as we reached his side,
got his electric torch out of his pocket.

In the half-light of the cabin I saw Mapes glance significantly at Garrison. Then he extended his arm and flashed
his light into the forecastle.

Each of us gasped as a gruesome spectacle flashed into
being. The deck of the forecastle was strewn with human
bones! I counted four grinning skulls lying about. The
action of the tide had mauled the bones apart. Not one
semblance of a complete skeleton remained, just a litter
of bones.

"It don't look so bad now with you all here," explained
Mapes; "but when I first seen it after hearin' that voice, I
got a jolt, let me tell you!"

"I don't hear the voice now," I pointed out. "If the departed spirits of these fellows are so anxious to have their ones
unmolested, why don't they do something about it now?"

Henry King turned to me. Although his face showed
whitely in the gloom, he grinned. "Daylight, he said.
"Ghosts only come out at night."

"Well, I've seen enough," growled Garrison. "Let's get back."

In silence we left the wreck. Garrison's opinion not-
withstanding, I thought Ghost Island a better name for
the place than the one he preferred.

18

CAP'N JOHNSON SPINS A YARN

The following morning the household was astir early. This phenomenon was due largely to the fact that many of us had not slept. We had heard the cry of the ghost. It came booming across the island, as hollow and terrifying a sound as I hope ever to hear again.

The yacht's cook, pressed into service at the house, did nobly. In spite of the early hour, a piping hot breakfast, served up by two of the sailors, was forthcoming in short order.

"Yum, that was good," said Mrs. Abbington, lighting a cigarette after she had finished the initial meal. "Now, then, you young ladies, one cigarette, and then we get after the beds. No loafing, now."

With a startled expression, Mrs. Garrison, her coffee-cup poised in mid-air, gazed across the table at the energetic Mrs. Abbington. "The beds!" she said, incredulously.

Mrs. Abbington blew a cloud of smoke into the air and smiled. "Just so, Hummingbird," she said. "You don't think I'm going to stand for a sailor making my bed, do You? He'd probably put a reef in the sheets, and I'd never be able to get into it. You and Gladys and I, my dear, are the staff of chambermaids."

Mrs. Garrison thoughtfully set her coffee-cup down. The thoughts that were passing through her pretty blond head were not hard to guess. From what Hand had told us of her early life, she had probably made many a bed. Also, she had probably made up her mind that she would never make another. Garrison was watching his wife expectantly.

Finally a smile curved her beautiful lips. She jumped to her feet, threw her napkin into the air, and clapped her hands. "Come on, then, Connie," she cried, "I can show you something about making beds. I've made more than either one of you have ever slept in. Tonight the beds in your house, Mr. Robert Garrison, will be made as they were never made before!"

We all applauded heartily. Mrs. Garrison put her arms about the other two young women and skipped out of the dining-room with them.

Garrison, looking aboundingly happy, took a sip of his coffee. "And here I am with a bunch of bachelors!" he exclaimed, setting the cup down. "You fellows don't know how wonderful it is to have a wife like that."

Covertly I glanced across at Flount. A far-away look a come into his eyes, and a pained expression to his face, looked quickly away.

"There's life aboard the yacht," I observed, glancing out the window toward the cove. In view of what had happened to the motor boat, we had left Captain Arnold and several of the crew aboard.

"She's shoving off presently," said Garrison. "Going to Sharpswell for some things the cook wants."

As we drifted away from the table, I took Garrison aside. "If you don't mind," I said, "I think I'll go over to the mainland with the yacht. I have a report to send off to Hand, and I trust it with nobody."

He promised me not to expose himself to danger, and I set off to my room to get the report. At the head of the stairs I passed a small second-floor reading-room. Through the tail of my eye I caught sight of a figure standing in

it over near the windows. Stopping, I perceived it was
Flount. I should have passed right by, but I was arrested
by the peculiar attitude in which he was standing.

Flount's back was to me. His head was thrown back,
and his hands were raised dramatically above his head.

"Oh, why should such a man come between us!" he
muttered, passionately. "Would that he were dead!"

I skipped down the hall to my room. I had detested suspecting Flount. Now there was no other course left open
to me.

Before I left the house I took Garrison aside again. "I
want to exact a promise from you," I said, "one that you
will think peculiar."

"What is it?"

"Don't allow yourself to be alone with Archibald Flount!"

Garrison looked at me in astonishment; then he laughed
harshly. "You're not suspecting Archie now, are you?" he
asked.

"I can't explain a thing," I replied. "But I want your
promise! Quick, I'll miss the yacht. Have I your word?"

Garrison shrugged his shoulders. "All right," he conceded, half angrily.

As soon as I had been rowed out to the yacht, we put
off. I went into the reading-saloon. There I supplemented
my report, bringing in the latest development concerning
Flount.

Sharpswell was a typical fishing-village on the coast of
Maine. The summer cottages, all boarded up, outnumbered
the natives' homes two to one. A rambling summer hotel,
drearily deserted, looked out over the sea from a knoll.

I walked into the general store. According to a sign,
the emporium also did for a post office. On the one hand
a woman was purchasing a pair of corsets and a cut of
beef, and on the other a man was acquiring a suit of
oilskins and a bottle of soda-water. Round a huge pot stove

in the center sat a group of fishermen. One, a patriarchal old fellow, in dignified possession of a chair. The others sat on overturned boxes. One of them, a sleepy-looking young fellow, reached back absently to delve into a box of prunes. He earned a scowling glance from the incredibly thin man who was cutting up the beef for the woman.

I thought the post-office department was not functioning, for a wooden shutter was in place behind the bars window. Nevertheless, I stepped hopefully up to it; whereupon the shutter flew up with startling violence. Quite the fiercest-looking woman I have ever seen glared at me from behind the bars. "Well?" she snapped.

"Huh?" I gulped. "Oh—er—a special-delivery stamp, if you please."

"Special delivery?" she repeated, as though I had asked the impossible. "Special delivery!"

She removed her hand from the shutter, which immediately slammed down again in my face. I was encouraged by sounds, coming to me from the other side of the amazing shutter, that seemed to indicate that the post-office department was being dismantled bit by bit.

"Frank!" at length came the raucous voice of the postmistress. "Special delivery?"

The vender of the oilskins and soda-water, without bothering to look round, raised his voice. "In the soap dish."

A moment later the shutter flew up again. My special-delivery stamp came spinning at me across the windowsill. After a series of wide, baffling loops, it made a landing on the floor at my feet. I retrieved it, stuck it to my envelope, and, with a sigh of relief, posted my letter.

As I turned to leave, I noticed the fishermen round the pot stove regarding me curiously. The old fellow's white beard parted somewhere beneath his nose. "Heh, heh," he cackled. "Thar's one o' them fools from Ghost Island."

I was inclined to be angry. Remembering Garrison's remark that one must stand in with the natives, I smiled benignly instead.

"Hello, Captain," I said, cheerily; "I hope you're not one of those who think we are going to be devoured by hobgoblins."

The crevice in the old fellow's beard snapped shut. His remarkably clear old eyes blazed. "Hobgoblins, say ye?" he cried, in his cracked, weather-beaten voice. "Callin' the sperits o' honest sailormen hobgoblins, be ye? My brother's sperit walks that island o' night!"

"Oh, I say, I'm sorry. I was merely joking."

"Ye may joke all ye mind, m'lad, but it ain't no joke! Not with Henry's sperit hoverin' over ye. Henry was a hard man in life, an' he's a harder un dead."

"I wonder," I said, stopping beside him, "whether you'd mind telling me about that shipwreck? I've heard only a vague account of it."

I had made a hit. The old fellow beamed upon me.

"Pull up a stool, Matey," he said. "I'll spin ye the yarn, an it'll make yer blood run cold!"

I glanced over to where the first mate of the *Dorothy* and two of her crew were making their purchases. They seemed in no hurry, and neither was I. A box was found for me, and I sat beside the old salt.

"I'm Cap'n Philip Johnson, I am," he began. "My brother Henry was ten year older'n me. 'Fore I was doin' more'n cut bait, Henry was cap'n o' the *Nancy Mary,* as smart a schooner as ever put t' sea. He was the youngest man aboard, too, but he could drive a nail into a water-keg with his fist, an' he could knock a man spinnin' acrorst the deck with a flip o' his elbow. Ah, he was a sailorman, was Henry. The last t' take a reef, an' the first t' head out into a nor'easter."

"And he was captain of that wreck over on Ghost Island?" I asked.

I saw immediately that I was not supposed to ask questions. After glaring me into complete submission, Cap'n Johnson continued.

"'Twas the fall o' '61 that the *Nancy* put t' sea fer the last time," he went on. "I was t' go the next trip, bein' then a skinner o' fifteen. A dirty nor'easter were blowin', but Henry laughed at it. He was not the man to lay in harbor, not him. Not his crew, neither. They put out, five on 'em, with their wives an' mothers an' sweethearts wailin' at 'em from the shore. They had her reefed, they did, but her gun'le was awash, an' I see her keel when they took the point. I was on the point, me an' the other young uns, with me daddy's spyglass. She was makin' heavy weather as she stood out atween Barren an' what used t' be Arrowhead. All the others was alow, but I could see Henry on her poop, spread-eagled, with his feet wide apart on the deck an' his arms athwart the wheel. Ah, he was a sailorman, was Henry!

"An' then her mainm'st carried! Snapped right off at the deck, it did. The wreckage hung overside, an' she come round an' jibbed the fores'l. The forem'st snapped then, half-way up, an' the only stitch o' canvas she had left was her jib. I see all hands come aloft an' commence clearin' the deck. Wan't no good; the seas had her, an' they couldn't bring her up into the wind. I see Henry, now an' then when the seas wan't pilin' over her, standin' on the poop with the wheel twistin' him most in two. Fin'ly the others went alow again.

"Wal, she drifted fast, right fer Arrowhead Island. Wan't nothin' we could do; nobody'd even put out a boat. She struck at last; I see her. A sea as big as a mountain picked her up an' threw her at the cliff. She jest disappeared, like she'd bin swallowed up. We thought she'd busted apart an' sunk."

"And instead she was in that crevice," I cried.

One of the fishermen laid a cautioning hand on my knee. Cap'n Johnson glared at me once more.

"It blew old Harry fer three days," went on the old man. "It didn't make no difference, nohow, acause we wouldn't think o' goin' after Henry's body."

This time I was supposed to speak. Cap'n Johnson paused, and gazed expectantly at me.

"Why not?" I dutifully asked.

"Ay, why not?" he repeated, significantly. "Thats the reason I said you was fools fer stayin' on Ghost Island. Henry Johnson was a hard sailorman, as I said afore. So was his crew. A pack o' young devils they were. Many's the time they said if they was drownded, they'd ha'nt the man what went after their bones. Lay in their ship where she went t' pieces, they would. No blubberin' foonerals fer them if the sea beat 'em.

"But jest the same, me an' me two cousins, John an' Rob, set out in a dory when the weather ca'med down. Ye could of strike us down when we see the *Nancy* layin' in the Devil's Cradle on Arrowhead Island! Peaceful, she were, all stove up, but holdin' together. We shouted, but nary a sound come back. We rowed in close. They wan't a sign o' nobody. We talked it over an' fin'ly decided t' board her. We didn't find no one till we got t' the fo'c'stle. There they were, four on 'em, all drownded! I lent over t' pick up Flem Dibber, his gran'daddy!" cried old Cap'n Johnson, pointing a withered finger at a man across the circle from him. "Jest as I got me fingers on Flem's wet shoulders, I heard Henry's voice! 'Keep away from them bones!' he yelled. I dropped Flem on the deck, an' he rolled off into a corner o' the fo'c'stle. Then Henry yelled again! It was his voice, that I knew, 'cept it were hollow an' dead-like!"

Again Cap'n Johnson paused. Again he glanced expectantly at me.

"What did you do?" I asked.

"Got!" said Cap'n Johnson, laconically. "Ef I'da had one fin, I'da swum t' England!"

He paused expectantly again, and a roar of laughter, which I judiciously joined in, rose dutifully from the circle.

"Well, Matey," resumed Cap'n Johnson, "you may think we was ahearin' things. That's what they thought back here at the point. But some o' the men went out t' bring the bodies back. They brought back nothin' but a set o' white faces! Henry ordered them away, too. Now there ye are. Ef ye want t' fool round with Henry Johnson's sperit, yer welcome to it. But Henry'll git ye, Matey, he'll git ye!"

"Well," I said, deprecatingly, "that was a long time ago—seventy years."

"Don't make no difference," said the man whose grandfather had been Flem Dibber. "I'm Mel Dibber, an' my gran'daddy's sperit's on that island, too. They're all there; we seen 'em!"

At this broad statement I gasped. "What?" I said, feebly.

"I ain't talkin' nothin' but the truth," said Mel, with much force. "We was out on Ghost Island, workin' on Mr. Garrison's house. It was foggy, an' all day long, or most of it, we heard a schooner's pump workin' over near the wreck. We fin'ly went over there, all of us. The wind was shiftin', an' the fog was clearin'. We stood atop the cliff, peerin' out to where we could hear the pump goin'. All on a sudden they was a rift in the fog. There she was, the *Nancy Mary,* hull down in the water an' dismasted! An' on her deck was her crew! Then the fog closed down on her. A couple o' minutes later the fog cleared away altogether, *an' the Nancy was gone!*"

"Maybe it was a motor boat that had pulled away into the fog," I suggested.

"Maybe nothin'!" exploded Mel. "The wind'd veered roun' t' the west'rd, an' the fog rose quick. Barren Island come into view, but the *Nancy* wasn't nowhere on the ocean! Besides that, before the *Nancy* disappeared, we heard Cap'n Henry Johnson shoutin' through the fog: 'Keep away from them bones!'"

I rose and thanked them for telling me their stories, trying to appear properly impressed by them. Calling good-by to them over my shoulder, I opened the door to the street and bumped squarely into someone. I found that it was a spruce young man. His force of impact was considerably augmented by a huge traveling-bag that he carried.

To my astonishment, he dropped the bag and grasped my hand. "Hello, there!" he cried. "I fancy you're surprised to see me, and I'm surprised to be here, too."

I remembered him vaguely, but I could not place him.

"I'm sorry," I began, "I don't seem to—"

Then it struck me. The young man was Wallace Hyatt Abbington! But he was well groomed and looked as fresh as the proverbial daisy, in contrast to the deplorable condition I had last seen him in.

"I say, is that the *Dorothy* I saw out there at the dock?" he demanded.

"Er—yes," I admitted. "Surely you're not going over to—"

I checked myself and flushed at what I had been about to say.

Abbington threw back his head and laughed merrily. "Going over to Arrowhead Island?" he asked, nudging me playfully in the ribs. "You bet I am! Behold, the return of the prodigal. Turned over a new leaf. Absolutely. My gosh, I'm cold. Drove down in an open flivver. Why don't you invite me aboard the yacht?"

He slipped his arm in mine, and together we set off for the dock. I tried to conceal my embarrassment. How did he get out of jail? Where did he get the effrontery to follow the Garrisons to Maine? And he must have known his wife was with them.

He seemed to divine thoughts. "Got you puzzled, what?" he laughed. "Well, I didn't execute any daring jail-break. I didn't come up here just to edge in, either. I was released from durance vile quite according to the best approved methods, and Bob Garrison sent me money and an invitation to come up here and visit him. Mighty decent chap, Bob. He's had more to do with my rejuvenation than anyone else. Now all I've got to do is convince my wife that I've washed myself whiter than snow. It won't be hard."

I had an uncomfortable trip back with him. Although he was in high spirits, and undoubtedly there was a spark about him that was winning, I reflected nervously upon what the effect of his arrival would be on the island.

It was worse than I feared. Abbington burst into the living-room, where all were assembled, and greeted everybody effusively. He certainly did not want for nerve.

Mrs. Abbington turned deathly pale. King, who did not know what it was all about, was the only one not painfully embarrassed.

Abbington clapped Garrison heartily on the shoulder. "Thank you a thousand times, old top," he cried. "Really the most wonderful thing you ever did for me. I was pretty low, but just by this simple act you've made a new man of me. Jove, I don't know how to thank you!"

"Quite all right, Wally," said Garrison, quietly. "Very glad to have you with us."

A miserable silence got started, but Abbington was equal to the occasion. He commenced giving a facetious account of his experience in jail, laughing heartily over the very idea that he could be accused of the murder.

"Connie, dear," said Mrs. Garrison, "we simply must finish the work upstairs. You know, Wally, our maids have all left us, and we've had to work our fingers to the very bone all day. You'll excuse us, won't you? Come on, Gladys, you can't get out of your share, you little imp."

I breathed a sigh of relief when Mrs. Abbington had been graciously spirited away by her hostess.

Abbington took a letter from his pocket and held it before Garrison. "I've never received anything more welcome than this!" he declared. "Bob, it was bully of you. You don't know how I appreciate it."

Abbington then turned his attention upon Flount, who openly resented him. Garrison took me aside.

"That's my writing on that envelope," he said, "but, by thunder, I didn't write it!"

I began to suspect that Christopher Hand had been utilizing his excellent powers at forgery. I dared not say so, however.

Flount was being bothered by Abbington, who was making fun of him. The little fellow seemed ready to lose control of himself. I stepped into the breach.

"I have just had," I said loudly, the unique experience of getting the story of our ghost first-hand from his brother."

"Sounds interesting," said King, helpfully. "Let's hear it."

As I was telling the story, Mapes entered the room with a basket of wood for the open fire. He set it down and remained to hear me out. When I had finished, he turned resolutely to Garrison.

"Mr. Garrison," he said, "I didn't like to say so at first, because I knew you'd only laugh at me, but those fellows told Mr. Clark the truth. I saw the same thing!"

"You did?" I cried.

"Yes, sir. The very first day I was on the island. Fishy had gone off, and I was monkeying with the motor boat, getting ready to launch it. I heard that there noise of a

schooner's pump you told about. I went out behind the
boat-house, where you can see down the west side of the
island. There was the schooner with her masts busted off
right off the seaward end of the island where it comes to a
point. And her crew was on her deck, too!

"That's right off where the wreck lies!" I exclaimed.
"That's where Mel and the others saw it, too. What did
you do then, Mapes?"

"I shouted and waved at 'em. Then I ran as fast as
could across the island. When I got to the cliff, the boat
was gone!"

"Perhaps it had gone off behind Barren or Thumbcap."

"Not a chance. There ain't a speed boat built even that
could of got to either one of them islands before I got to
the cliff."

"Maybe it went round the island where you couldn't
see it."

"Nothin' doin' there, either, Mr. Clark. You can see
down both sides of the island from the end of the point.
The only place on the whole ocean where it could of been
without me seein' it was in the cove. And it had no more
chance of gettin' to the cove before I got to the point than
it had of gettin' to Barren or Thumbcap. It vanished into
thin air, that's what!"

Garrison laughed harshly. "Are you trying to tell us,
that you saw a ghost boat?" he demanded.

"I ain't said it was no ghost boat," retorted Mapes,
defensively. "I said I saw a boat there, though, and it vanished. Maybe it sank."

"If we are to believe the natives," I said, "then two
boats sank in the same place."

"We aren't disposed to believe the natives," growled
Garrison. "I'll tell you what we're going to do, though!"
he cried, banging his fist on the table. "We're going to set

a watch for that infernal ghost tonight! If nobody else will go out with me, I'll go alone!"

One by one we pledged our support. Perhaps it was strange, but I felt the hair at the back of my neck rising.

19

GHOST HUNTS

"Garry, you are not going out to look for that ghost!"

Thus Mrs. Garrison put her foot down. Her husband remonstrated in vain. His case was lost when I joined forces with Mrs. Garrison. After all, I was supposed to see to it that no harm came to him.

Garrison glowered darkly at Wally Abbington. It had been the young man who gave our secret, carefully guarded from the ladies, away with a flippant remark about a ghost hunt. It was nine o'clock, too, nearly time for us to start our vigil. Archibald Flount, of all men, solved the problem.

"This ghost shall be captured anyway," said he. "I'm not going to have him terrifying the ladies any more. Robert, you are married; so you should be willing to look after your safety. Mr. Clark and Mapes and I will go out and catch him."

"Count me in on that," said Henry King.

"Me too," said Dr. Innes, shortly.

Abbington was the only one who had not spoken up. He looked appealingly over to his wife. Before he did it, I knew he was going to funk.

"Er—don't you think someone should help Bob look after the ladies?" he asked. "Not altogether right, leaving them unprotected, you know."

"I'm sure no harm can come to them if you look after them," sneered Flount.

"Well—but I mean, it isn't right," said Abbington,

I began to think that it would decidedly not be right if I left him alone with Garrison. "I think everything will be all right here without you," I said, not very civilly. "Mr. Garrison has three seamen, and he can get more if he wants them. Besides, he has Ridley as well."

"You run along, Wally," said Mrs. Garrison, sweetly. "Don't let us keep you from the pleasures of the hunt."

Garrison still sulked and said nothing. Abbington saw that there was no way out. He shrugged his shoulders and mustered a grin.

"How about guns?" I asked. "I have a pistol; what about you fellows?"

Innes had a pistol, and I knew that Mapes was armed. Flount, King, and Abbington were without weapons.

"There are some rifles on the yacht," said Garrison. "I have a pistol, but I think I'd better hang on to it. I'll send one of the men off to get the guns from the yacht."

He left the room. King walked over to the wood-basket beside the fireplace. He selected a good stout stick and flourished it menacingly.

"I've been noticing this all afternoon," he said. "I think I could put the quietus on any ghost with it. What do you say, Clark?"

"I shouldn't care to encounter you," I laughed.

Garrison returned, and we waited for the rifles from the yacht. I was leaning up against the table in the center of the room, busy with my own thoughts. Suddenly some-one clutched me by the arm. I turned quickly and looked into the white, strained face of Archibald Flount. He was peering, as if fascinated by some terrible agency, at one of the back windows. At that instant a piercing scream rang out.

My heart jumped, and I snapped my head round to look at the window. My breathing all but left me for good. Framed in the black square of window-pane was the most ghastly face ever seen in the wildest delirium!

It was a dead face, of that I felt certain. The high forehead was snow-white. The eyes were glassy and protruding. A fixed, leering, mirthless grin, showing the long upper teeth, was set on the mouth. Down one pale cheek dangled a spray of seaweed. The terrifying vision, viewed through the window, seemed to be floating on water.

"Keep away from them bones!" boomed the voice of the ghost hollowly. *"Keep away from them bones! Keep away from them bones!"*

The face at the window vanished. I looked about to see what devastation it had wrought. It was plentiful. Mrs. Garrison had fainted outright. Miss Dykeman was having hysterics, and Mrs. Abbington was little better.

"My—my bag," she gasped, tearfully.

I picked it up off the table. Opening it, I took out the ever useful smelling-salts and handed them to her. I frankly admit that my hand was none too steady when I did it.

Garrison picked up his wife and carried her up the stairs. I performed a like service for little Miss Dykeman. Flount fluttered round Mrs. Abbington.

"Help me upstairs, Archie," she cried.

I took Miss Dykeman into the same room into which Garrison had carried his wife. Mrs. Abbington, half supported by Flount and King, followed after us. Dr. Innes came bustling round, administering restoratives.

I left the room and rushed down the stairs. A seething rage coursed hotly through my veins. Almost before I realized what I meant to do, I had left the house and was rushing down the hill toward the wood.

Behind me I heard the front door slam. Someone called my name after me. I kept right on to the wood.

In the velvety blackness under the trees I began to repent the rashness of my act. My light I dared not use. I blundered through the island wilderness with outstretched arms, feeling my way among the trees.

At length I came to the shore. Certainly I was not at the point. My aim by that time was to ascertain whether anyone left the island. Somehow, the wreck seemed to draw me like a loadstone. I proceeded to follow the vague outline of the cliff to the point.

It was dangerous going. The cliff was by no means regular at the top, and a tumble over it meant almost certain death. I kept as far back from it as I could. But I had no desire to approach too close to the inkiness under the trees. A danger just as unwholesome seemed to be lurking there.

With a great deal of relief I arrived at the point. Although I could not see it, below me at the bottom of the dark cleft lay the wreck. Indeed, I could see little of any thing at all. I selected a spot among the rocks where I could gaze out to sea with the least chance of being attacked from the rear.

The regular flashes of Midway Light were in the distance. But the surface of the water so merged with the darkness that I despaired of seeing a boat even if one did put out. There I remained, straining my eyes over the black ocean, for a good half-hour.

Finally I heard a sound behind me. I peeped back over my rock, scarcely breathing. A light was moving among the trees.

"Ho, Clark, where are you?"

I recognized, with a long sigh of relief, the voice of Henry King. In order to guide him to me, I called out to him and flashed my light. As he approached, I saw Innes and Flount. Mapes was with him too.

"I was beginning to think the ghost had done you in," said King. "Did you see a boat?"

"I haven't seen a thing," I replied, disconsolately, "except the lighthouse and the surf below me."

"If you'll pardon my saying so," said Innes, "I think we're on a wild goose chase. A fool's errand, don't you now? I'll wager I could take three minutes to hide myself in that forest, and you'd never find me until daylight. As for a boat, fancy being able to see one out in that blackness."

We talked it over and decided he was right.

"Besides," said King, lightly, "you can't shoot a ghost even though you do see him."

We used our lights freely to guide us back through the trees. King had one that belonged to the yacht. With mine and Mapes's we had plenty of brilliance about us. King and Flount carried rifles from the yacht.

"Where's Abbington?" I suddenly asked.

"Couldn't find him," sneered Flount. "Probably ran away."

King laughed. "Swam away, you mean," he corrected. "We're on an island."

"I was aware of that!" snapped Flount.

Back at the house we found the women recovering from the shock. We also found Abbington recovering from it, in quite another way. He was drunk. Some men are not objectionable when in their cups. Abbington was not one of them. He seemed to have forgotten all his erstwhile gratitude. He was nasty to everybody. We put him to bed.

Garrison shook his head at learning our search was in vain. "I was sure you wouldn't find anything," he said. "I can't understand it. Most devilish thing! We leave the island in the morning!"

"I really think that's best," agreed King, becoming serious. "If we didn't have the women with us, it would be different. Another shock like that might very well wreck their nerves. I don't mind admitting I had a nasty turn tonight myself."

"Exactly," growled Garrison. "Now, then, I've arranged for them to spend as reassuring a night as possible. Ridley and I moved another bed into our room. All three of them are going to sleep there together. I've pulled the blinds over the windows, and I told them I'd stand guard outside their door all night."

Flount stepped up and took his friend earnestly by the hand. "That's fine, Robert," he said, "I'll keep you company."

Now, that was decidedly opposed to my ideas for Garrison's safety. I quickly sought to rectify it.

"I will accompany you both," I said.

Flount and Garrison both protested. In the end everybody had volunteered to stand guard outside the door.

"It's ridiculous for us all to stay up," I said. "Let's split the watches. Mr. Garrison and I will stand the first one of three hours, King and Dr. Innes can take the second, and Flount and Mapes the third."

My idea was finally accepted. The others went off to bed, leaving Garrison and me to guard the door. There we spent three uneventful hours. Relieved by Innes and King, we went off to bed.

I took off my shoes and threw myself on the bed. Sleep was not for me that night. Over and over again the strange business passed through my head from beginning to end. I could find no answer for it. I dreaded the trip back to New York on the yacht. We had come through by the narrowest margin on the way down. Surely some catastrophe would overwhelm us going back.

A gray dawn had broken before I heard Mapes and Flount going on duty. I hopped up to see how things had gone. King and Innes had had just as quiet a time as had we.

Before lying down again, I took a look out the window. The air was calm, but the sky was completely overcast. Through my window, at the back of the house, I could look out over the clearing to the wood. To the right lay the shore-line. Here the cliff narrowed down to a height of about ten feet. Thumbcap Island was just in my range of vision.

About to turn back from the window, my attention was suddenly rooted to the edge of the cliff. I had seen a man thrust his head up over the cliff and then hastily withdraw it!

I rushed from my room. Glancing down the hall, I saw Flount and Mapes at their posts outside the bedroom door. For an instant I cogitated my course of action. I held the advantage, since the man did not know I had seen him. If I raised the hue and cry, he would be warned. I quickly decided to take but one person with me, one whom felt I could trust.

Henry King's door was not locked. He was lying on the bed covered with a blanket, having removed his shoes and coat.

"What's the matter?" he demanded.

"I think I've seen our ghost," I hissed. "Will you come with me?"

For answer he got out of bed, hastily pulled on his shoes, and struggled into his coat. He picked up his rifle, resting against the bed, and turned to me. "Let's go," he said.

We ran swiftly across the clearing to a clump of bushes near the cliff.

"He stuck his head up right over there," I whispered. "He may still be hiding below the cliff."

"Well, let's go find out. The more time we waste, the better chance he has of getting away."

We stole cautiously over to the cliff and peered over. There was no one below us. Certainly there was no place to hide among the small bowlders on the narrow beach.

"He's gone," said King. "Where do you suppose he went?"

"Heaven knows! The only place that suggests itself to me is the wreck, and I don't know why."

King nodded, and without a word we set off. We quickly entered the wood.

"I hope you fellows will be careful of those fire-arms."

The voice that broke the stillness nearly caused me collapse. I whirled about. Behind us stood Christopher Hand!

20

SOME QUESTIONS ANSWERED

"By heaven," I cried, "now I'm sure I'm seeing ghosts!"

Hand smiled. "Nothing of the kind," he said. "You never saw anyone more alive than I. The air up here sends you back to the freshness of your boyhood."

Henry King was inclined to be wrathful. "See here," he demanded, "have you been playing these ghost tricks? You've frightened three beautiful young ladies half to death!"

"Not guilty, Mr. King," laughed Hand. "We'll let my activities go for the present. Clark, what have you discovered? I'm anxious to hear it."

"I mailed you a detailed report yesterday," I said. "I can remember it just about word for word, though."

Hand glanced round. "Let's hear it," he said. "We can't be seen here."

King showed more interest in my report than did Hand. That, however, was natural with my friend. He never shows his emotions, if he can help it.

"So right now," he said, when I had finished, "your strongest suspicions are directed at Archibald Flount, eh?"

"Oh, I say, you must be wrong there, objected King. "Flount hasn't much use for me, because I kid him. But I really like the little cuss."

"So do I," I cried. "But there's the evidence; what can you do?"

"How about Dr. Innes?" asked Hand.

I shook my head. "The only evidence I've been able to gather against him," I said, "is the possibility of his having sent those strange wireless messages from the yacht. But the second engineer might have done that, and that fellow could have put the engines out of commission, too."

"It occurs to me," said King, "that Mr. Wallace Hyatt Abbington may have had a hand in something. What about him?"

I turned accusingly to Hand. "Yes, what about him?" I demanded. "You forged that letter from Garrison and sent him up here. I should think you'd be ashamed of yourself."

Hand smiled wryly. "I've had to be ashamed of myself so many times that I'm used to it," he said. "Rather clever of you, Clark, figuring out that it was I who forged the letter. I should think the postmark would have indicated to you that I was in Maine. Your perception is not quite sharpened to the proper point yet, my boy. I wired Gerrity what I was up to, of course; so he didn't have to guess. In fact, he was my accomplice. I just thought it would be a good idea to round out the crowd. But I see they are becoming anxious up at the house. Evidently, your departure was not unobserved. Let's go up."

Garrison and Dr. Innes were out at the side of the house, peering about. As we emerged from the wood, Innes pointed excitedly at us. A few moments later Garrison recognized my friend.

"Mr. Hand!" he cried, truly as if he had seen a ghost. "How on earth did you get here?"

"Come inside and I'll tell you," replied Hand, grasping his client's extended hand.

The five of us trooped into the living-room. Hand waved us into chairs. Deliberately he tossed a log on the fire. Then, knitting his brows, he leaned against the mantel. Finally he glanced sharply over at his client. "I've discovered the motive for all this desperate business," he announced.

Garrison's face turned a shade paler. "Who is it?" he whispered.

"You have no enemy," said Hand, "and there is no one who directly wishes you harm. But there is a group of men who would have murdered you if they could to keep you off this island."

"But, see here," cried Garrison, "if it hadn't been for whoever is perpetrating this, I probably wouldn't be on the island at all!"

"If it hadn't been for me, you probably wouldn't be on the island at all," corrected Hand. "I sent you here, but I freely confess I did not know I was wrecking somebody's careful plans when I did it."

"Well, I'm hanged if I understand!" growled Garrison.

"Then I'll tell you. To begin with, the trouble started when it became known to this group that you intended to sojourn here this fall. They succeeded in frightening your workmen away by bogus supernatural manifestations. They based them on an old ghost story about the place. But the house was so nearly completed that it didn't do the trick. They had tried to set fire to it, but luckily that didn't work. Then Mapes arrived on the scene. Thereafter they didn't get another chance to destroy the house. Not without creating suspicion, that is. The faintest hint of foul play on this island would have ruined them. They couldn't frighten Mapes away; so they took his motor boat. They didn't want him sailing round the island in it.

"The next move was against yourself. In New York they had a free rein. Whatever happened there could hardly attract attention to Ghost Island. Nevertheless, their plans continued to miscarry. Miss Venora paid the penalty for

the attempt upon your own life. Instead of their preventing your trip to Maine, my fortunate suggestion that you
come right up here did just the opposite.

"The next move was to kidnap Mrs. Garrison. That
likewise failed. As a last, desperate measure, they attempted to murder you just before the yacht sailed. Again their
attempt was a failure, and one of them fell into our hands."

"Has Spitz confessed?" I asked, excitedly.

Hand smiled and shook his head. "Not Spitz," he said.
"He'll never confess, of that I'm sure. But to go on. An
attempt was made to put the yacht out of commission in
order to postpone the trip. Fortunately, one motor could
be repaired. A third attempt was made upon your life at
sea. Next an attempt was made to destroy the yacht by
fire. I gather from Clark that it was touch and go, but you
managed to save the yacht."

"See here," interrupted Garrison, "according to your
theory, a member of this band must have been on the
yacht!"

"There is no question about it," replied Hand, "a member of the band was on the yacht! There had to be! However, you reached the island. The last measures resorted
to were more fake spooks to drive you off the island. No
danger of violence here. That would bring the authorities
down upon their heads."

Garrison shifted in his chair. "I think you're right about
that—I mean the spooks," he said. "As a matter of fact,
they have driven us off the island. I can't keep these ladies
here with this going on. I'm positive, of course, that this
ghost stuff is a fake, but how are we going to prove it?"

"I've proved it already," replied Hand.

"How?" I cried.

"Perhaps I'd better tell you what I've been doing," he
said. "The morning after you left New York, I took an air-
plane for Portland, Maine. It had occurred to me, you see,

that perhaps the reason for your unwarranted persecution was that someone wanted to keep you off the island. At Portland I purchased some supplies and a tent. After dark I chartered a motor boat. Its skipper put me off at Thumbcap Island, left me a row-boat, and departed. I've been living there the past three days. Each night I rowed over to this island. Then I'd pull my boat up and hide it. I've seen some peculiar things. Last night," he said with a grin, "I saw your ghost—the one at the window. I was hiding out back. He was alive enough to trip and fall down as he ran away. He can swear, too, in German."

"But that face!" I cried.

"Yes, I fancy he'd put on a little make-up. I didn't see his face, but I rather thought he'd dressed it up a bit for your benefit. He wasn't the only ghost I've seen. There's another. He puts off in a skiff from a vessel that anchors off the spot where the wreck lies. He rows ashore, climbs the cliff, and bellows through a huge megaphone. He does it to keep people away from that part of the island. Because, you see, a diver goes down from the vessel anchored off the point."

We all sat up in astonishment.

"Did you say a diver?" asked Garrison, weakly.

"Precisely. A deep-sea diver."

"But what on earth is he diving for?" gasped Garrison. "Surely there's no treasure in that old wreck of a fishing schooner. Besides, we went on it with dry feet. You don't need a diver for that!"

"What he is diving for," said Hand, "I have no more idea than you. But a diver is going down nights from that vessel, of that I'm sure. I could vaguely make him out, and, besides that, I could hear the pumps that were supplying him with air."

"The schooner's pump!" I cried, banging the chair. "That's what Mapes and the natives heard. It was the air-pump of a diver!"

"Well, by thunder, I'd like to know what he's diving for," said Garrison.

Hand looked at his wrist watch. "I think you will before long," he said. "I rowed over to Thumbcap early this morning. About a half-hour ago I released three carrier pigeons. They each carried the same message. They should be at their aviary by this time. As a result, a coastguard cutter should be leaving for this island very shortly. If they comply with my request, she will carry a diver."

"Jove!" exclaimed Garrison, bringing his fist into the palm of his hand. "It's a shame we haven't a diver here. We have all the apparatus on the yacht."

"You have what?" cried Hand, delightedly.

"Why, yes. We used the *Dorothy* for diving purposes just a few weeks ago. We were looking for an old pirate vessel reported sunk off the Bahamas years ago. Thought I told you about it. I bought the diving outfit and hired a chap to use it. We had a lot of fun, but we didn't find the pirate galleon."

"What kind of shape is that diving gear in?" demanded Hand.

I was becoming nervous.

"Why, first-class shape, I should think," replied Garrison.

"Then we are all set!" declared Hand. "We have an expert diver right here."

He meant me. I had invented a control valve for diving helmets, and in perfecting it I had made many descents.

With the greatest glee Hand told them of my prowess in undersea work. I was roundly congratulated. All but one of us were overjoyed, and I was that one.

"Er—water's frightfully cold, don't you think?" I complained. "I shouldn't mind if it were summer. Besides, I've never done any practical diving."

"Clark is painfully modest," explained Hand. "This is your chance to be a hero, my boy, and none of us will stand in your way."

Nobody would have been doing me an injustice by standing in my way. I had felt of that water, and it was icy cold.

"You needn't worry about the cold," said Hand. "Remember that submarine they salvaged off the New England coast? That was done in mid-winter. Besides, you won't have to stay down long. Just see what it is they've been after, give the signal, and we'll yank you right up."

The question then developed as to who should go with us and who should remain at the house. Two of the sailors at the house were the ones familiar with the pump that was to supply me with air at the bottom of the sea. In the end it was decided to leave Flount and Innes with Mapes and Ridley to guard the house.

Before we left to board the yacht, Hand said he wanted to clear up one more thing. For this, he said, he needed the services of Dr. Innes.

"It will only take a minute," he promised. "I found something over on the other side of the cove. I think it will clear up the origin of the ghost business on this island."

We finally arrived at a dense growth of huge pines. Hand guided us into the center of it. There we came upon the skeleton of a man, bleached white, lying half covered by the carpet of pine needles.

Hand knelt beside it. "This," he said, pointing to a rust-encrusted knife, "I found lying beside the skeleton, almost buried in the pine needles. The handle is fairly well preserved. On it are carved the initials H. J. That would be Captain Henry Johnson's knife, don't you think so?"

"It must have been!" I cried. "And these are his bones!"

"Undoubtedly, "agreed Hand. "You notice, Doctor, the skull is cracked. It is my opinion that when the schooner struck, Captain Johnson, the only man on her deck, was pitched to the rocks. That crack in his head doesn't look as if it were enough to have killed him. Probably rendered him insane. What do you think, Doctor?"

Dr. Innes picked up the skull and examined it intently. "There's considerable depression there," he said. "No splinters that I can see. Yes, I should think there was enough pressure on the brain to cause insanity."

"But not enough to cause death?"

"No, I hardly think it would have caused death. Hard to say. Evidently it didn't."

"Then I believe this fellow was thrown ashore when the schooner struck," declared Hand. "He regained consciousness later, but from that moment on he was insane. It fits in with the natives' story of the shipwreck, doesn't it? He probably lurked up on the cliff and frightened his brother and the rest away from the wreck. Died of exposure, no doubt. When he came in here, these pines must have been small. They'd afford him a measure of protection from the wind, you see."

We left the skeleton where we had found it and silently walked away. Captain Henry Johnson's bones had not lain in his ship, after all.

21

THE GHOST BOAT

As we boarded the yacht, Captain Arnold came forward to meet us.

"Did Stevens and Garthwait tell you about the diving outfit, Captain?" asked Garrison.

"They did, sir," he replied. "They're below now, working on it. They say they'll have it in order in jig time."

"Good. Mr. Hand will show you where to anchor. At any rate, we want to go out to the east end of the island."

Being very much interested in the condition of the diving gear, I went below to inspect it. It was a first-class outfit that Garrison had. The pump was installed in the forward hold. The lines reached it through a small hatch in the deck above.

"Didn't want to spoil the deck by clampin her down up there, sir," explained Garthwait.

On the way over we started the pump. Everything seemed in good working order. Stevens gave me an old jumper and a pair of trousers, for which I exchanged my clothes. He also supplied me with a heavy sweater. As we carried the diving suit up on deck, the *Dorothy* was pulling slowly in toward the point of the island.

Hand and Captain Arnold were conferring over a chart on the fore-deck.

"But there's a reef dead ahead of us," the captain was protesting. "This one, right here," he said, placing his finger on the chart. "It's clear out of water at low tide, and the tide's ebbing now."

"I know the reef is there," said Hand. "It was low tide when I saw the vessel, and she was anchored just inside it at the southern end."

"If you'll notice the chart here," said Captain Arnold, "you'll see there's a ledge on the ocean floor, beginning at the south end of the reef. The water drops off to four hundred feet deep. Your vessel must have been anchored on the island side of that ledge, or she'd never have anchored at all."

"She was anchored right at the south end of the reef," insisted Hand. "She seemed right up close to it, too."

"We can get right up close; there's plenty of water," the captain assured him. "Both our engines are working now, too; so we can get a good position."

As the yacht was maneuvering to anchor, I drew Hand aside. "Something's bothering me," I said.

"What is it, old man?"

"You said there was a member of this sinister group on board the yacht when we came down from New York. Do you know who it is?"

"You're 'way late, Clark. The others asked me that long ago."

"Well, if he was on the yacht when we came down here, he must be on the yacht now! I don't care about descending to the bottom of the ocean with him monkeying round. He nearly pitched Garrison overboard, and he set fire to the yacht. He could just as easily cut my air-hose!"

Hand regarded me speculatively for a moment. "I told the others, Clark," he said, "that I didn't know who he was. I won't tell you that, though. I know who he is. I don't want him to know it, though. I want him to give himself away. If I tell you who he is, you'll let on. I know you of old; you can't conceal your emotions. But I have my eye on him, Clark. I know where he is. I promise you faithfully that he'll have no chance of cutting your air-hose. Come, you must get ready."

We had pulled up so close to the reef that we could see the seaweed waving below the surface of the water. We dropped bow and stern anchors, and the yacht held fast.

I climbed into the diving suit and sat on a bench, placed for me by Stevens. My helpers pulled on my shoes and affixed the weights. Hand, who had helped me on my other descents, adjusted the helmet and screwed it on. Once again I heard the roar of air whistling through a diving helmet.

Clumsily, with the aid of Garthwait and Hand, I moved over to the rail, where a section had been removed. I squatted on the gunwale. Then I slid overside, hanging the lifeline. They lowered away. As the water engulfed me, I felt the suit shrink in against my body. I shot swiftly down. My lungs labored for breath. A few twists on the control valve inflated my suit a little more, relieving the pressure against my chest. Then my feet struck bottom.

There was not much that I could see through my face plate. Great ribbons of kelp waved majestically in the dark green water on all sides. I started to move round. From the shelving rock I could tell which way the land lay. I walked away from the island. I felt my way carefully. If I stepped over the ledge, it might be disastrous.

Then I saw the reef rising to my left. Moving over toward it, I put out my hand to the rocks. My fingers encountered steel!

It was not the reef at all. I leaned back to look up. Silvery bubbles from the exhaust valve funneled upward and obscured my vision. The tide swept them away. Dimly I made out a low rail above me. I was standing beside a sunken ship!

Quickly I grasped the life-line and jerked the signal to rise. When on a level with the vessel's deck, I signaled to stop. I got my foot on the rail, clawed at the waving seaweed, and finally gained the deck, my weighted shoes ringing on it. Steadying myself, I glanced round.

Directly ahead of me a pole, extending out of the murky depths, pointed straight at my head. I advanced to it, touched it, and found that it likewise was of steel, passed along it, holding my head down to inspect it. At length I reached the end of it. My fingers fumbled at it. It was a gun. I was standing on a warship!

I passed along the deck. A large deck-house, or something of the sort, loomed before me. It was pointed, like the bow of a ship. Leaning back, I surveyed its height. Then I realized what it was—a conning tower! The vessel was a sunken submarine!

I passed round to the side of the barnacle-encrusted conning tower. Although my hands were nearly frozen, and I was shivering in my suit, I was too excited to give up then. I reached out and pulled the swaying seaweed aside. Placing my face plate close to the tower, I made out dirty white lettering on its side. A wide band extended downward, curved round and up again. The letter *U*. Then a single vertical stripe. Next I traced out a seven, and then another. *U-177!* This must have been one of the Kaiser's proud undersea craft! I remained standing there, grasping the seaweed in my outstretched hands, too amazed to move.

Finally the cold creeping into my body brought me back to my job. I proceeded on down the deck. From the shape of the conning tower, I then knew I was moving toward the stern. Here I encountered another deck gun. As I stood beside it, leaning against it, I felt a peculiar motion of the wreck. I could not have been mistaken, the stern sank ominously; then it lifted again.

I moved over to the rail. Bending over I peered down. Directly below me I could see the side of the submarine, below that black depths of water. I moved nearer the bow. Again I peered over the rail. Now I could see the bottom that the vessel rested upon.

My senses reeled. The submarine was balanced on the ledge, ready to slide into four hundred feet of water, and I was on it!

As quickly as possible I scrambled over the inshore rail and dropped. Fortunately, the life-line paid out slowly. I descended gently to the ocean floor. About to give four jerks on the life-line, the signal that I wished to come up, my hand was arrested. Before me a black hole gaped in the submarine's side. Moving over to it, I touched the edges with my fingers. The hole, about three feet in diameter, had been cut through the plates with a torch.

All at once I felt four tugs on my life-line. I stepped clear, returning the signal. Immediately I commenced to be hauled up. A silvery sheet glimmered over my head. The hull of the *Dorothy* loomed beside me. Then I burst out of the water and slid up the side of the yacht.

As my head protruded above the deck, I saw four men straining on the life-line. Hand and Garrison, standing ready, grasped me by the shoulders and hauled me inboard. I lay on the deck among the coils of the air-line.

Hand twisted off my helmet. To my surprise, I heard the anchor winches grinding. The *Dorothy* got swiftly under way and headed down the side of the island.

"What's the matter?" I gasped.

"Look!" cried Garrison, pointing astern.

I twisted my head and glanced aft. Bearing down upon us from Barren Island was a peculiar craft. As I watched, a puff of white smoke appeared on her deck. A second later I heard the report of a rifle-shot. Another puff of smoke, and a bullet whined overhead.

"Help me drag him into the cabin!" cried Hand, laying hold of my shoulder.

I was unceremoniously hauled along the deck and into the lounging-saloon. As we entered, a window on the starboard side smashed in, followed by the report of a third shot from the strange craft in pursuit.

"Keep below those windows!" ordered Hand.

My shoes and weights were stripped off. Hand pulled me out of my suit, spilling water all over the deck. By that time we had placed the island between ourselves and our pursuers.

Hand turned to Garrison. "When we get to the cove," he ordered, "have the yacht tied up to the dock. Then every man of us up to the house and barricade the doors. Those fellows mean business."

Anxiously we kept watch for a sight of the strange enemy. Just as we were entering the cove, she hove round the island. Now she was close by us.

"By thunder!" cried Hand. "A submarine! There's your mysterious ghost boat that disappears from the surface of the ocean!"

22

THE BATTLE

Only once have I run more swiftly than I did from the dock to the house. That was to get into a trench in France. Then I was younger, and it was not uphill.

We had gained the shelter of the house before the submarine entered the cove. The crew of the yacht, however, who had remained to make the vessel fast to the dock, were subjected to a fusillade. By good luck they reached the house without casualty. We slammed the door shut and locked it.

"How are we situated?" snapped Hand. "Enough fire-arms to go round?"

He was interrupted by Mrs. Garrison, who rushed down the stairs to embrace her husband. Garrison reassured his wife; then he turned to Hand. "We have three rifles from the yacht," he said. "I have a pistol, and Clark, Dr. Innes, Captain Arnold, and Mapes have each one. The rest are unarmed."

"I have a pistol; so that's six," counted Hand. "With the three rifles we have nine men armed. How about ammunition?"

"Plenty of ammunition for the rifles," replied Captain Arnold, quickly. "I only have what cartridges are in my pistol, though."

It developed that we were deficient in pistol ammunition. Hand ordered the pistol fire to be withheld until absolutely needed. He took one of the rifles, gave another to Garrison, who was an expert shot, and passed the third to me. We armed three of the sailors with our pistols.

"If we are attacked," said Hand, "it will probably be from the rear. There is less open ground for them to cover there. We will post the rifles back there. The rest will take positions along the front and sides of the house. Pick windows that will give you the best range."

"The sub's nosin' into the inlet across the cove," announced a sailor.

We crowded to the windows. Slowly, appearing to be swallowed up by the land, the submarine slid out of sight into a small bay. Their landing was made near the spot where Hand had found the skeleton of Captain Henry Johnson.

We posted ourselves and waited for eventualities. My station was in a small room in the opposite wing from the kitchen. Raising the window a trifle, I crouched before it, rifle in hand. Garrison, with the second rifle, was at the rear windows of the living-room. Hand, with the third, was in the kitchen. Those with the pistols were scattered about the front and sides. The rest of the men, armed with clubs, were guarding the women on the second floor. Thus we awaited the attack.

The charged stillness of the house was broken by a hoarse shout. The cry was followed by the sounds of a fierce struggle in the room adjoining mine. I glanced hastily out the window, saw that no one was in sight, and rushed out into the hall. There I met Garrison, his rifle at the ready.

"What is it?" he cried.

"In this room," I shouted, making for the door to it.

Reaching the threshold, I beheld two figures locked in combat. One was Christopher Hand. His back was to me, his opponent's face hidden behind his shoulder. The other man held a pistol, but Hand, by forcing his arm back, was preventing him from using it.

"Surrender or I'll shoot!" cried Hand.

As Garrison and I rushed into the room, the shattering discharge of a large-bore pistol smote our ears. Hand's adversary staggered back.

It was Henry King!

King, as we halted in consternation, clapped his hand to his chest. His lips, writhing in agony, he twisted into a smile. Swaying on his feet, he bowed to Hand.

"You win," he choked. "Congratu—"

He collapsed to the floor.

"King!" cried Garrison, leaping over to the fallen man.

Hand, his pistol held loosely, stood watching, breathing heavily. Garrison looked fearfully up at us.

"My God, he's dead!" he said, hoarsely.

"What did he do?" I cried.

"Saturated this room with kerosene," replied Hand. "I got to him just as he was about to throw a match into it. He sneaked down cellar by the stairs at the end of the wing, got the kerosene, and sneaked in here."

Garrison's white face turned whiter. "Who is he?" he asked, his voice unsteady. "What did—"

"Never mind that," snapped Hand. "You're supposed to be defending this house! Back to your posts, both of you!"

My mind a whirl, I turned from the room, leaving the body of Henry King sprawled on the floor. Garrison and Hand followed me.

"Where's your rifle?" I heard Garrison ask my friend.

"Gave it to Captain Arnold and posted him in the kitchen. I wanted to watch that fellow."

"Where did King get that pistol? I thought he was unarmed."

"Shoulder holster. We have another pistol in our defense now."

Almost before I had reached my window, Captain Arnold gave the alarm. "Here they come!" he shouted from the kitchen, his voice booming through the house.

His cry was followed by a rattle of shots. Immediately I realized the astute maneuver the enemy had executed. They had circled through the wood to the cliff. Dropping over it, they had, in complete safety under its cover, reached to within twenty feet of the kitchen door.

"All hands to the kitchen!" shouted Hand, from the living-room.

His order was well given. From where I was located the attack on the kitchen door was entirely out of my range. I sped through the living-room. As I passed through it, the windows shattered in at the rear. Plaster leap from the walls across the room, and the glass in a large picture-frame splintered.

The gun-fire was deafening as I entered the kitchen. I crowded up to a window. The pirates, if such they could be called, were swarming over the cliff. Some of them had gained the door. Others were covering their advance from the cliff-top.

A sailor lurched back from the window, lunged into me, and fell writhing to the floor. I took his place. A fellow outside the window aimed his pistol at Garrison, standing at my elbow. I fired, and he fell.

Above the firing I heard the kitchen door crash in, and a cry of warning from Hand. I turned from the window. The pirates were pouring into the narrow corridor inside the door!

We met them as they reached the end of it. Shots, cries, curses mingled with the thud of clubbed rifles and bare fists. Unable to get at the front of the fray, I leaped upon a table. Innes and a sailor followed my example. We fired over the heads of our friends, straight into the mass of humanity beyond them.

The effect of the maneuver was instantaneous. With howls of rage and pain, the pirates gave way. They bolted, leaving three of their number on the floor behind them.

"Quick, Clark!" cried Hand, grasping me by the arm. "Out to the front! I left a man there, but heaven knows what's happening!"

We rushed from the kitchen, leaving the scattered firing of our friends behind us. The first thing I noticed, upon running into the living-room, was that the front door was wide open. The living-room was deserted.

"Who opened that door?" cried Hand.

A feminine voice, half hysterical, answered from behind us. It was Mrs. Abbington, standing half-way down the stairs. "They've set fire to the house!" she cried. "Archie and Wally have gone to put it out. Oh, they'll be killed!"

We heard a burst of firing from the end of the house opposite the kitchen. Hand and I leaped through the doorway.

At the corner of the house knelt a sailor, firing his pistol in the direction of the shore. We came up abreast of him in time to see two men leap out of sight over the cliff. Abbington and Flount, round the corner, were kicking a pile of blazing driftwood away from the house. Hand and I jumped to help them.

A shot rang out from the cliff. Abbington spun about. He took a staggering step, and I caught him as he fell. As he looked up at me, his face lighted up with a smile.

"Guess I won't be able to reform, after all," he murmured.

His eyes slowly closed, but the smile remained on his lips. His body hung limp in my arms. He was dead.

Hand and the sailor were blazing away at the cliff. Flount had kicked the last burning embers away from the house. The paint was scorched, but the fire had done no other damage. Flount picked up my rifle from where I had dropped it. With no further ado we whisked round the corner of the house.

I carried the body of Abbington into the living-room, laying it reverently on a couch. As I straightened, I felt a light touch on my shoulder. I turned about to face Constance Abbington.

"Is—is he dead?" she asked.

I nodded and stepped back.

"He died like a gentleman and a hero," said Flount.

Mrs. Abbington wiped a tear from her eye. "You're all right, Archie?" she asked, anxiously.

Flount, whose forehead I then saw was creased by a rifle-ball, took Mrs. Abbington's hand impulsively in his. He looked far from the dapper little man that he usually was. His face was smeared with blood and soot, and his eyeglasses hung shattered at the end of their ribbon.

"Dear Constance!" he cried. "I know I should not speak at this time. But now I have the right, and I may be dead by tonight. I love you."

Mrs. Abbington, weeping softly, took the courageous little man to her bosom. With a blush of shame, I followed Hand into the kitchen. I no longer had any reason for suspecting Archibald Flount.

There was still intermittent firing at the back. The kitchen was a shambles. On the whole, however, we had come off rather well. Garrison had a flesh wound in his arm; one of the sailors was shot through the shoulder; a bullet had broken Mapes's leg; Dr. Innes had a bullet-hole in his coat; and Ridley looked very self-conscious with a broken nose.

"Smashed me right in the proboscis with the butt of his gun!" he was explaining to Mapes, as Dr. Innes put a splint on the unfortunate fellow's leg.

The enemy had left three of his dead behind him. I helped Hand carry them into the butler's pantry.

Two of the sailors were at the kitchen windows keeping up a desultory fire at the cliff. Three others had gone off with rifles to post themselves at other windows. We could hear them firing now and then. The wounded sailor, Stevens, my helper on the diving expedition, was gamely smoking a cigarette on the floor.

"The first victory is ours, sir!" said Captain Arnold, exultantly. "Three of them were killed, and I'm sure several were wounded. We captured three rifles, too. I think we've taught 'em to respect us!"

"And we have only two wounded," said Garrison, with satisfaction. "Mapes and Stevens are out of it. But there's plenty of fight left in me. Mine's just a scratch."

"We have one dead," I said, slowly. "They set fire to the outside of the house. Abbington died putting it out."

My announcement was greeted with silence. Garrison bowed his head.

"So he did make amends," he mused. "I knew there was something fine in him."

Across the waters there came to us a deep boom. We leaped to the windows. Bearing down on the island was a coast-guard cutter, the stars and stripes at her mast-head, and a smother of foam at her bow. Hanging in the air over her was a white cloud of smoke. The embattled kitchen rang with our cheers.

"Caught 'em red-handed, by thunder!" cried Garrison.

Just then there was a rattle of rifle-fire at the other end of the house.

"They're trying to escape!" shouted Hand. "The cutter's a long way off yet. Come on, let's try to head them off!"

There was, we found, no chance of doing that. We learned from one of the sailors that the crew of the submarine had leaped over the cliff and gained the wood.

Forgetting our caution, we ran outside. Anxiously we watched the approach of the cutter. The submarine at length backed out of the inlet. It swung round, stern first, to the center of the cove. Then its propellers churned it forward. We held our fire, as there was not a soul on her deck.

"That's a small sub," remarked Captain Arnold. "What's that on her foredeck?"

"She'll not submerge yet," growled Captain Arnold. "There isn't water enough until she's well out from the cove."

Not until the submarine had cleared the mouth of the cove did the cutter spy her. They were scarcely three hundred yards apart, both going full speed. The cutter's gun belched at the submarine. A white geyser of water flew up at her bow. The submarine plowed on.

"They won't surrender," said Hand, tensely.

Again the cutter sent a shot across the submarine's bows. Again the weird craft paid no attention to it. Evidently the cutter was loath to sink her. She continued the chase. Out into deep water they raced, the submarine steadily drawing away.

"She's submerging!" cried Garrison, in an agony of suspense. "She's going to escape!"

The skipper of the cutter had other ideas. Again the gun on the deck of the pursuer belched flame and smoke, against the submarine's side. The undersea craft seemed to shudder in agony. Her bow came up, and she rolled half over on her beams. Her bow rose higher into the air, she half rolled round, and then she dived, stern first. The water leaped high into the air where she went down. A sickening, gurgling sound came to us across the sea. I glanced round at my companions. Their faces were white and set.

23

THE LAST MAN

We stood in a group, fascinated, at the front of the house. The cutter nosed round, looking vainly for survivors of the submarine sinking. Suddenly Hand struck an attitude of listening.

"Did you hear a moan?" he asked.

A moment later we all heard it. It came from the direction of the cliff. With one accord we broke into a run. Opposite the kitchen door we halted at the cliff-top. Below us lay a man, on his face, groaning dismally.

We leaped down beside him. Hand knelt and turned him over. I gave a start. The wounded man was Spawn!

Hand peered intently at the senseless face of Spawn. On his own was a curious expression. Slowly he placed his hand into his inside coat pocket. From it he took a small photograph. He gazed back and forth, first at the photograph and then at Spawn. I leaned over and looked at the picture. It was a snapshot of Spawn, taken as he stood beside an automobile.

"Where's Dr. Innes?" snapped Hand.

"He's taking care of Stevens," replied Garrison.

"Go ask him to come out here," ordered Hand.

Garrison and I went after the doctor. We found him leaning over Stevens, who was lying on a divan in living-room. Mrs. Garrison was holding a bowl of water for him.

Garrison walked up to his wife. For a while they looked into each other's eyes. They leaned toward each other, and their lips met. Then they smiled at each other.

Garrison reached down and patted Stevens affectionately on the knee.

"Mr. Clark," he said, his voice shaking with emotion, "didn't I tell you every member of my crew was loyal to me?"

Dr. Innes accompanied us out to where Spawn lay. He dropped down beside the wounded man and examined him. Finally he looked up. "It's all over with him," he said. "Riddled with bullets."

"Can you bring him round for a minute?" asked Hand.

Dr. Innes shrugged his shoulders. "I'll try," he said, as he opened his medicine-case.

Hand, taking me by the arm, led me aside. Garrison and Captain Arnold came with us. Archibald Flount, looking unutterably happy, skipped down beside us.

"First chance I've had to ask you, Clark, said Hand. Did you find anything on the ocean floor out there by the reef?"

"I should say I did!" I cried. "Just about the most amazing thing possible. There's a sunken German submarine there, the *U-177!*"

Hand clucked in astonishment. Suddenly he gave a start. The *U-177?*" he demanded. "Are you sure it was the *U-177?*"

"Positive! I read the numerals on the conning tower."

"By Jove! That's it, then!

"What's it then?" demanded Flount.

"The *U-177,*" replied Hand, speaking deliberately, "was sent over to this side of the Atlantic in September 1918. She was not only an undersea destroyer, she was a treasure ship as well. She carried in her five million dollars for the use of the German espionage system in the United States. She never returned, and now we know why."

"A German submarine on this side of the Atlantic!" scoffed Flount. "Impossible!

"Not impossible at all," retorted Hand. "A good many of them came over in the spring and summer of 1918. As a matter of fact, they sank more than one hundred and fifty of our merchant vessels right off our coast. I happen to have been in the U. S. Army intelligence service at the time, and I know! And by the same token I knew of the *U-177.*"

Dr. Innes came up and touched Hand on the elbow. "He's conscious now," he said. "I don't dare move him. If you want to ask him anything, you'd better be quick about it."

Hand lost no time in reaching Spawn's side. He dropped down beside him.

"How are you, Mr. King?" he inquired, to my astonishment.

"W-what's happened?" said Spawn, feebly.

Dr. Innes quickly placed a flask to Spawn's lips and poured some whisky down his throat. The man's eyes seemed to brighten. His cheeks flushed slightly.

"I—I remember, now," he gasped. "Where's the submarine?"

"Sunk," said Hand, grimly. "The man who was using your name is dead. You are the last man."

"Has Kli—has Spitz been captured?"

"Spitz is dead," lied Hand. "Killed when you escaped in New York."

"Then—then I'm the last man!"

"You are the last man."

Spawn closed his eyes. After a moment he reopened them and looked up at Hand. "I suppose," he said, weakly, "that you want me to tell you what we've been up to. Am I going, Doctor?"

Dr. Innes slowly nodded his head.

"Then I'll tell you," said Spawn, wildly. "Perhaps it will clear my conscience."

"Don't waste your strength," cautioned Hand. "Let me ask you questions. You wanted to keep Mr. Garrison and his party from coming here so that you could salvage the treasure on the *U-177* in secret. Is that right?"

Spawn's feverish eyes regarded Hand intently. "Yes. If you want to salvage it, you'll have to work quickly. She's sliding into deep water. We had to work swiftly, she's almost ready to go. The tide is dragging her."

"Who is the man who used your identity? The one we knew as Henry King."

"His name was Felix Schmidt. He was an agent of the Imperial German Government, operating in the United States during the war. So was I. Heinrich König is my right name. Schmidt was arrested. Armistice saved him from death penalty. Deported."

"Was he the one who knew about the *U-177?*"

"Yes. He saw her wrecked on that reef. He was to get the money and take it to Portland in his motor boat for distribution from our headquarters there. All hands were lost on the *U-177*. Schmidt kept it a secret."

"Why didn't he attempt to salvage it before this?"

"He went to England. Attempted to rob a bank to get money for the salvage operations. He was arrested. Got out of jail a year ago."

"Am I right in this, then? Schmidt didn't dare salvage the treasure openly for fear the United States Government would intervene and claim it."

"Yes."

Spawn suddenly gasped and lay still. Dr. Innes immediately went to work over him. He poured more whisky down his throat, and the man opened his eyes. After a moment he spoke weakly to Hand.

"How did you know I was the real Henry King?" he asked.

"The police of your town, at my request, sent me your picture," replied Hand, quickly. "The first time we met, you had a beard; the second my eyes were full of tears. I didn't recognize you until just now."

Spawn smiled wanly. "Clever," he murmured.

"Did Spitz shoot that girl at the Garrison home in New York?" asked Hand.

"Yes. But he meant to kill Garrison."

"Then Schmidt was the one who planted Mrs. Abbington's pistol in Garrison's library?"

With a weak nod Spawn acknowledged that Hand was correct.

"Schmidt was the one who put the yacht's motors out of commission and set fire to her, wasn't he?"

"He was going to try. He wirelessed us that he'd started the fire. A little later he wirelessed us he'd failed."

"Where did you get that submarine?"

Spawn chuckled faintly. "Good, wasn't it? It was one of the Kaiser's subs. Her commander, Oberleutnant Franz Kopf was at sea when Armistice. Refused surrender her. Hid her away little bay Greenland. Beached her. Built screen over her. King got money secretly recondition her. Enlisted select crew. I secretly stocked base Barren Island. They made—wonderful trip—over. Secret—"

Spawn's voice trailed off. His body twitched, and he lay still. Dr. Innes clapped a stethoscope to his chest. At length the doctor straightened.

"It's all over," he said.

Garrison broke the silence. "Good heaven, this is amazing!" he exclaimed. "So Henry King wasn't Henry King at all! Wait till I see Lessington, he introduced him!"

"Lessington was just used," said Hand. "He never knew Henry King. His father was the only one who ever dealt with him. Too bad I didn't get this snapshot before you left for Maine. We might have cleared this up in New York if I had."

"But," objected Garrison, "I can't understand how King could have been operating against us. Think of that blow he got on the head in New York. And then, how could he have set fire to the yacht when his door had jammed and locked him in his room? He couldn't have sent those wireless messages, either, because he was playing a hose on the fire all the time."

Hand grinned. "Not hard to explain all that," he said. "That bump on the head was either self-inflicted or he got one of his comrades to do it for him. Rather heroic, but worth it. Think how far it went to divert suspicion from him. As for his door being jammed on the yacht, doesn't it occur to you that he just locked it on the inside? The bolt is bent. He had plenty of time to send the wireless messages, Mr. Garrison. It's no trick to wedge a hose into something so that it will play into an open hatchway all by itself."

Garrison shook his head resignedly. "It's simple enough when you explain it," he said. "But see here, why did you leave us here to the tender mercies of that villain when you knew what he was up to?"

"Paradoxically," replied Hand, "you were perfectly safe after you arrived at the island. To have committed an atrocity up here would have invited an investigation that would have utterly ruined their plans. You see, they were in a desperate hurry. They were further embarrassed by the fact that divers can work only in calm weather. Such days are rare at this time of year, and they couldn't work in the summer without being detected. It was now or never, with them."

"If they were so chary of us after we got on the island," asked Garrison, "why the deuce did they try to annihilate us today?"

"We can only guess at that," replied Hand. "Sheer viciousness, I suppose. Perhaps they thought they could wipe us out and then make one last stab at the *U-177*. Think what their emotions must have been when they saw us sending a diver down to that sub. All the dangers they had faced, all the money they had spent, were going for nothing. I must say those fellows were intrepid. It's a shame the real Henry King didn't live a little longer. The trip of that submarine from Greenland to North America would have made an interesting tale. Just imagine those fellows—"

He was interrupted by an excited cry from Captain Arnold. "The *U-177!*" he shouted. "Look, she's rising!"

We whirled about and out to the point of the island. Like some huge denizen of the deep, the bow of the *U-177*, all mottled brown and gray, was breaking the surface of the sea. Slowly, majestically it rose into the air, until fully a third of the submarine was exposed.

"The tide is dragging her over the edge," I said in an awed voice.

The *U-177* balanced for a moment, rising almost vertically from the sea. Then, quickly and gracefully, it slid from view forever.

The Bolt

P. R. Shore

A CHRISTOPHER HAND MYSTERY

THE RESURRECTION MURDER CASE

STANLEY HART PAGE

A CHRISTOPHER HAND MYSTERY

FOOL'S GOLD

STANLEY HART PAGE

A CHRISTOPHER HAND MYSTERY

TRAGIC CURTAIN

STANLEY HART PAGE

COACHWHIP PUBLICATIONS

COACHWHIPBOOKS.COM

FEAR OF FEAR

FLORENCE RYERSON
COLIN CLEMENTS

MURDER IN THE FAMILY

NICE PEOPLE MURDER

Mary Hastings Bradley

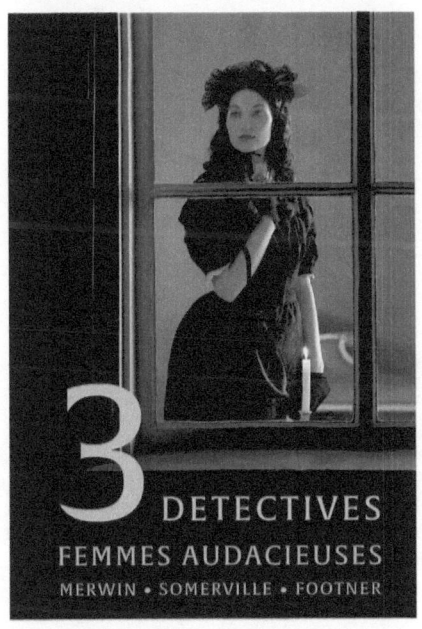

3 DETECTIVES
FEMMES AUDACIEUSES
MERWIN • SOMERVILLE • FOOTNER

DEATH DOWN EAST

Eleanor Blake

COACHWHIP PUBLICATIONS

COACHWHIPBOOKS.COM

THE
MYSTERY
OF THE
FOLDED
PAPER

HULBERT
FOOTNER

The
Hollow Tree
Mystery

MADELON ST. DENIS

VIRGINIA RATH

FERRYMAN,
TAKE HIM ACROSS!

NO FACE TO
MURDER
EDITH HOWIE

COACHWHIP PUBLICATIONS
COACHWHIPBOOKS.COM

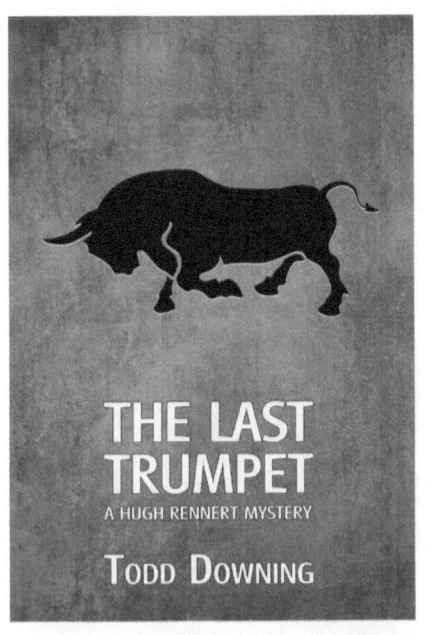

THE LAST
TRUMPET

A HUGH RENNERT MYSTERY

TODD DOWNING

THE MAY DAY MYSTERY

OCTAVUS ROY COHEN

MURDER'S COMING

GRAVE WITHOUT GRASS

BY
DONALD CLOUGH CAMERON

MURDER IN
MALAYA

FATAL SHADOWS

DEATH OVER
HER SHOULDER

DOROTHY
COLE
MEADE

COACHWHIP PUBLICATIONS

COACHWHIPBOOKS.COM

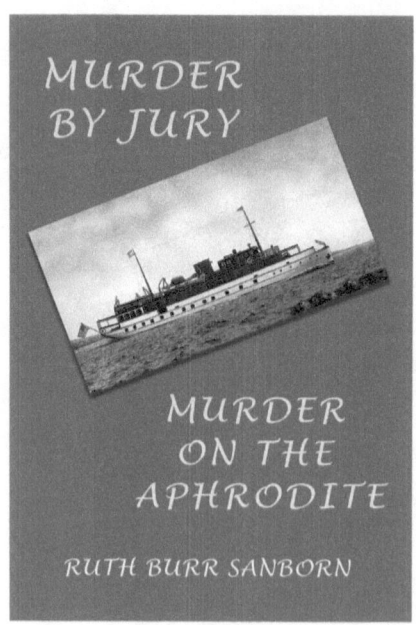

COACHWHIP PUBLICATIONS

COACHWHIPBOOKS.COM

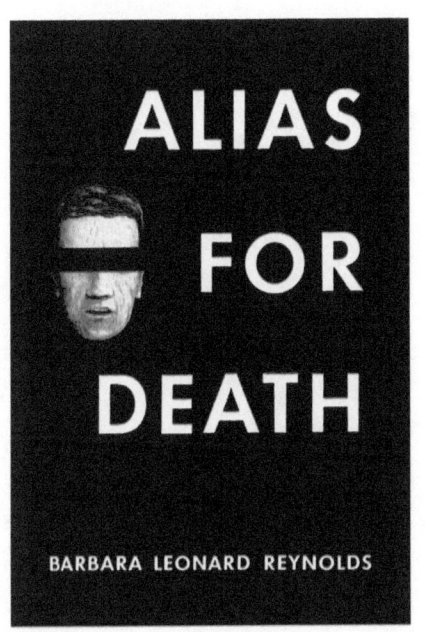

ALIAS FOR DEATH

BARBARA LEONARD REYNOLDS

THERE IS NO RETURN

THE ADELAIDE ADAMS MYSTERIES

ANITA BLACKMON

Jack Dolph

MURDER MAKES THE MARE GO

FEAR CAME FIRST

VERA KELSEY

COACHWHIP PUBLICATIONS

COACHWHIPBOOKS.COM

MURDER AT DRAKE'S ANCHORAGE

E. LEE WADDELL

MURDER AT THE KENTUCKY DERBY

CHARLES PARMER

MURDER ENDS THE SONG

ALFRED MEYERS

3 DETECTIVES

MURDER ON THE RAILS

WHITECHURCH • THORNE • TORGERSON

COACHWHIP PUBLICATIONS

COACHWHIPBOOKS.COM

THOMAS KINDON

MURDER
IN THE
MOOR

DRESSED
TO KILL

Emma Lou Jetta

GRIM
DEATH

THE
GROUSE
MOOR
MURDER

JOHN FERGUSON

COACHWHIP PUBLICATIONS

COACHWHIPBOOKS.COM

www.ingramcontent.com/pod-product-compliance
Lightning Source LLC
Chambersburg PA
CBHW032207030726
47494CB00020B/657